A R E V I V E D

M O D E R N

C L A S S I C

ELEPHANT'S NEST IN A RHUBARB TREE

ALSO BY H.E. BATES

A MONTH BY THE LAKE & OTHER STORIES

With an introduction by Anthony Burgess

A PARTY FOR THE GIRLS: SIX STORIES

H.E. BATES

ELEPHANT'S NEST IN A RHUBARB TREE & OTHER STORIES

A NEW DIRECTIONS BOOK

Manufactured in the United States of America
First published clothbound and as New Directions Paperbook 669 in 1989
New Directions Books are printed on acid-free paper

Library of Congress Cataloging-in-Publication Data

Bates. H. E. (Herbert Ernest). 1905-1974.
   Elephants nest in a rhubarb tree & other stories/H.E. Bates.
      p.   cm.
   ISBN 0-8112-1087-1.   —   ISBN 0-8112-1088-X (pbk.)
   I. Title.
PR6003.A965E45   1989
823'.912—dc19   88-38040
                                                                              CIP

New Directions Books are published for James Laughlin
by New Directions Publishing Corporation
80 Eighth Avenue, New York 10011

CONTENTS

ELEPHANT'S NEST IN A RHUBARB TREE

ELEPHANT'S NEST IN A RHUBARB TREE

The summer I had the scarlet fever the only boy I could play with, during and after the scarlet fever, was Arty Whitehead. Arty had some buttons off and he lived with his uncle. His uncle had an elephant's nest in a rhubarb tree.

It was very hot that summer. As I leaned from the bedroom window and looked down on the street of new brick houses and waited for Arty to come and play with me the window-sill would scorch my elbows like hot sand-paper. On the wall of our house my father had planted a Virginia creeper. That summer, under the heat, it went mad. It pressed new shoots forward every day and they ran over the house and the house next door, and then the house on the corner, like bright green and wine-red lizards with tiny hands. One of the games I played was to watch how far the creeper grew in a week, sometimes how far it grew in a day. After three or four weeks it grew round the corner of the street and I could no longer see the new little lizards glueing their hands on the wall. So I would send Arty round the corner to look instead. "How far's it grown now, Arty?" Arty would stand by the green railings of our house and look up. He had simple, tender eyes and his hair grew down on his neck and over his ears and he always talked with a smile, loosely. "Growed right up to mother Kingsley's! Yeh, yeh! Growed up to the shop," he'd say. Mother Kingsley's was a hundred yards up the next street. But I was only six, I couldn't see round the corner, and either I had to believe in Arty or believe in nobody. And gradually, as the summer went on, I got into the way of believing in Arty.

Arty came to play with me every day. Another game I played was blowing soap bubbles with a clay pipe. They floated down from the open window and Arty ran about the street, trying to catch them with his hands. One day I blew a bubble as big as a melon, the biggest bubble I'd ever seen, the biggest bubble that anyone would ever have seen if there'd been anyone in this street to see it. But there was no one but Arty. The great melon bubble floated slowly down in the hot sunshine and then along the scorched empty street. The funny thing about it was that it wouldn't burst. It floated beautifully away like a glass balloon polished by the sun, keeping about as high as the windows of the houses. When it got to the street-corner a puff of wind caught it and it turned the corner and disappeared. I called to Arty to run after it and he ran like mad after it with his cap in his hand. It was then about two o'clock in the afternoon but Arty didn't come back until six that evening.

When he came back again his lips were tired and looser than ever and I could see that he'd been a long way. "Where you been?" I said.

"After the balloon."

"All this time? Didn't it bust?" I said.

"No," he said, "it never busted. Just kept like that. Just went on. Never busted."

"Where?" I said. "How far?"

"Went right up past the school and over Collins's pond and over the fields. Right out to Newton. Past our farm."

"Whose farm?"

"Our farm. Went right over. Never busted."

"I never knew you had a farm," I said.

"Yeh, yeh," Arty said. "My uncle gotta farm. Big farm."

"Where?"

"Out there," Arty said. "Just out there. Great big farm. Catch foxes. Catch wild animals."

"What wild animals?"

"Foxes. All sorts," Arty said. "All sorts. Elephants."

"Not elephants," I said.

"Yeh, yeh," Arty said. "Yeh! Catch elephants. My uncle found elephant's nest one day." His eyes were pale and excited. "Yeh! Elephant's nest in a rhubarb tree."

That was the first I ever heard about it. In the beginning I had to believe Arty about the Virginia creeper, then I had to take his word for the bubble, which no one but Arty and I had ever seen. Then I did something else. Perhaps it was the after effects of the fever, the result of being shut up for nearly eight weeks in a bedroom which was almost like a boiler-house in the late afternoons; perhaps it was because I had temporarily forgotten what the world of reality, school and fields and sweetshops and trains, was like. Perhaps it was having Arty to talk to, and only Arty to play with. But gradually, from that day, I began to take his word too for the elephant's nest in a rhubarb tree.

After that, I began to ask him to tell me what it was like, but he never gave me the same description twice. "Yeh," he would say. "It's big. Ever so big. Big rhubarb." And then another day it was different. "It's jus' a little squatty tree. Nest like a sparrow's. That's all. Little squatty tree." Finally I was not sure what to believe in: whether the rhubarb tree was like a chestnut or an oak, with a nest of elephants like a haystack in the branches, or whether it was just rhubarb, just ordinary rhubarb, the rhubarb you eat, and it was a nest like a sparrow's, with little elephants, little shiny black elephants, like the ebony elephants that stood on my grandmother's piano. I was sure of only one thing: I wanted to go with Arty and see it for myself as soon as I got better.

It was early August when I came downstairs again and about the middle of August before I could walk any distance. When I went out into the street everything seemed strange. I had not walked on the earth for eight weeks. Now, when I walked on it, it seemed to bounce under my feet. The things I had thought were ordinary seemed suddenly odd. The streets I had not seen for eight weeks seemed far stranger than the thought of the elephant's nest in a rhubarb tree.

One of the first things I did when I got downstairs was to go and see how far the Virginia creeper had gone. When I got round the street-corner I saw that someone had cut that part of it down. The little wine and green lizards had been slashed with a knife; they were withered by sun and the tendril-fingers were dead and fixed to the wall. As I looked at it I was not only hurt but I also knew that there was no longer any means of believing whether Arty had been right about it or wrong. I had to take his word again.

Then about three weeks later Arty and I set off one morning to find the elephant's nest in a rhubarb tree on his uncle's farm. Arty was about twelve years old, with big sloppy legs and thick golden hair all over his face, so that he looked almost, to me, like a grown man. All the time I had a feeling of being sorry for him, of knowing that he was simple, and yet of trusting him. I wanted too to make a discovery that I felt my father and mother and sister and perhaps other people had never made. I wanted to go home with a story of something impossible made possible.

It was very hot as we walked through the bare wheatfields out of the town. Heat danced like water on the distant edges of the white stubbles. We walked about a mile and then I asked Arty how much farther it was.

"Ain't much farther. Little way. Two, three more fields. Little way, that's
all."

I saw a farm in the near distance, against the woods. "Is that your uncle's
farm?"

"Yeh," Arty said. "That's it. That's it."

"Where's the nest?" I said. "This side the farm or the other?"

"Other side," he said. "Just other side. Just little way other side, that's
all."

We walked on for another half-hour and then when we reached the farm
Arty said he'd made a mistake. His uncle's farm was the next farm. We
walked on again and when we reached the next farm he said the same thing.
Then the same thing again; then again. Finally I knew that it was time to
turn back, that we were never going to see the thing we had come to see.
As we walked back across the fields the heat of midday struck down on us
as though it came through glass. Clear and direct and sickening on the sun-
baked stubbles, it seemed to take away my strength and turn the tears of disappointment sour inside me.

When I got home I felt pale and weak and my feet were blistered and I
felt like crying. Then when my mother asked me where I had been and I
said, "With Arty Whitehead, to find an elephant's nest in a rhubarb tree,"
they all burst out laughing. "Why, Arty isn't all there! That's all it is," they
said, and I knew that they were right, and because I knew that they were
right, and that what I had hoped to see never existed, I began crying at last.

Since that day, twenty-five years ago, a good deal has happened to me,
but nothing at all has happened to Arty Whitehead. I no longer live in the
same town; I have been across the world and I have grown up. But Arty still
lives in the same town; he has never been anywhere and he has never grown
up. And now he never will grow up. He is now a man of nearly forty but
he is still the boy who ran after the bubble as big as a melon.

For the last twenty years Arty has worked for a baker. All he does is sit
in the cart and hold the reins and tell the horse to stop and go. He does
something that a boy of six could do. At the end of the week the baker gives
him a shilling or two and every night he gives him a loaf of bread. Arty
understands that. He understands the most fundamental thing about living:
a loaf of bread. He understands perhaps all that anyone needs to understand.

Sometimes when I go back home I go to have my hair cut. Occasionally,
as I sit in the barber's shop, Arty come in. "Arty," the men say as they greet
him, and I say "Arty," too, but Arty does not recognize me. I have grown

up, whereas Arty's face is still the face of a boy. His eyes are still simple and remote and tender and as the men in the barber's shop talk Arty does not listen. He does not need to listen. They talk about Hitler, war in China, Mussolini, the cup-ties, the newspapers, women. Arty does not know who Hitler is; he does not know where China is or what is happening to China; he does not know anything about women. He understands that he wants his hair cut. He understands a loaf of bread.

And there is also one other thing he understands. I sometimes see him walking out of the town. His glassy simple eyes are fixed on and perhaps beyond the distance. He does not walk very fast but he looks very happy. And because I know where he is going there is no doubt in my mind that he is very happy. He understands the most fundamental thing about living, a loaf of bread, and he also understands the most wonderful.

It seems to me that Arty understands what perhaps the rest of the world is trying to get at. He understands the elephant's nest in a rhubarb tree.

THE CAPTAIN

When the Captain and the woman first took the cottage, they looked out for a boy. "Just a kid to mow the grass and tidy up a bit," the woman said. At the end of a week they found him. His name was Albert. He was sixteen, one of a large family. He had little black arrogant eyes and a cool way with him and some unconscious habit of looking not quite straight. He was talkative, always on the spot, and the woman liked him from the first. She was amused by his sauce, and he liked to talk to her, bring her little things. He told her of otters one day, five cubs in the river-bank, at the foot of the field beyond the garden, among the meadowsweet. He could bring one. The Captain was listening. "You ever seen what a dog can do to an otter?" he said.

The Captain himself had a dog, a greyhound, the colour of a field-mouse. It was a sharp, dainty sensitive creature, and the Captain liked to lie under the apple trees, in the grass, and roll with it and muzzle its mouth with his two hands and tease it into a pretence of anger. He liked the dog, the boy thought, almost more than the woman. The Captain was a heavy dark stiff browed man, about forty, with a way of answering people as though shaken out of an ugly dream. "Huh! Eh? What? What? Huh?" The woman was rather common, with her fair loose hair drooping about and her flopping poppy-coloured pajamas, but she was human, warm, with a sugary red-lipped little grin for the boy whenever she met him. At first the boy did not understand them, did not get the relationship. Then once he called her Mrs. Rolfe. "Mrs. Rolfe! Ha! That's good. Oh, boy! Mrs. Rolfe. No, I'm just Miss Sydney. That's all. Plain Miss Sydney."

All the week, from Monday to Friday, the boy would be alone, working in the garden, with only the dog for company, and the house locked up. All he had to do was to cut the lawn, trim the quick hedge flanking the lane, sweep the paths, weed the flowers, feed the dog. At first he could not get used to it, with the cottage lying at the dead end of the lane and no one coming, the summer days hot and empty, the warm flowery stillness of the little garden almost deathly. He had been used to company. There was not enough to do. And sometimes, in the heat of the day, work finished, he went down in the rough grass among the hazels and beat about for snakes or the young rabbits that scratched under the wire netting from the field. Bored with that, he would lie half in the potatoes, half in the shade of the empty hen-run, and go to sleep for a bit.

Then when the weekend came again he was excited. He was like a dog himself, joyful, eager to please. He nosed into the house, could not stop talking, followed the Captain and the woman about everywhere, like some little cocky terrier.

He brought the woman a snake. It was a little viper. He had it in a seed-box, with gauze stretched over it, and the snake kept darting up, striking, flicking the gauze. He brought it to the woman as she sat lounging in a deck-chair on the lawn, in her red pajamas, by herself.

"Look," he said. "I got him for you. Look. I caught him."

The woman saw the small darting head and shrieked. The Captain came running out of the house, hands clenched.

"What's up?" Then he saw the snake. "Christ almighty, take that damn thing away! Take it away, damn you! Take it away!"

Afraid, the boy stood still, held the box tight, did not know what to do. Suddenly the Captain tore the box from his hands in a rush of passion and flung it away across the grass. The boy saw with small slantwise eyes the snake slithering out over the grass.

A sudden flat-handed blow stunned him for a moment. He could not see. The garden went black, surged to crimson and then went black again. On his right wrist the Captain wore a leather strap, with double buckles. It seemed as if the buckles had made hot prints of pain on the boy's cheekbone. He stood dumb.

"I'll teach you to scare people. D'ye hear? You hear me? Look. You see that?"

The Captain wore a leather belt round his waist. It was heavy buckled. He took it off. He held it loose, like a flat whip.

"You see that? Well! Do you see it or don't you?"

"Yes, sir."

"You see it. Good. Next time you'll not only see it but feel it. You understand that? You understand?"

"Leave him alone, George," the woman said. "That's enough. He knows. It's all right."

"Leave him alone be damned. Bringing snakes. What next? What the hell?"

"All right. But let him go. He understands. You understand, don't you?"

"Yes, miss."

"I just don't like snakes. They scare me."

"Yes, miss."

"And what goes for snakes goes for anything else," the Captain said. "See that?" He still held the belt. The boy had his eyes half on it and on the thick black-haired wrist. "And now make yourself damn scarce! Quick!"

The boy went, humble, half watching.

"There's something about that damn kid I don't like," the Captain said.

"You shouldn't have got the belt," the woman said.

"Huh! Eh? What? What? Why not?"

"He's only a kid."

"Kid be damned. Isn't he old enough to know?"

After that the boy was glad to be alone. It was a comfort, the empty week, the hot stillness, and nobody but himself and the dog among the sunflowers and hollyhocks. He liked the small drowsy world, the feeling of being shut off, of having no fear. He felt boxed-up but secure, like the creatures he caught. It had become quite a habit now, since he had so little else to do, to catch something and box it up, half for companionship, half to satisfy in himself some small demon of joy. So at one time he had another snake in a box gauzed over, two fragile lizards in another, a bank vole, reddish-tinted like a fox. He would lie and watch them at the bottom of the garden, in the shade behind the hen coop, out of the hot white edge of sunlight, teasing the snake with straws to make it strike, holding the little vole under his hand, half letting it go, then catching it again, like a cat. All the time he wanted an otter cub, but fear held him back: fear of the Captain, of what the dog might do. In consolation he caught a small rabbit; he fell on it in the grass and then kept it in the hen-coop, in the full blaze of sunlight, until it scratched a way out of the soft cake-floor of hen-muck.

Then the weekend came, and he let his creatures go. He was miserable. He watched the Captain, sheered away when he saw him coming. He scarcely spoke to the woman. She gave him her little sugary grins, but he no longer brought her anything.

She saw what was the matter with him. She caught him alone and said, kindly: "How are your little otters? Do they grow much? Can they see yet?"

"They're all right," he said.

"Funny, are they? Nice? You said you'd bring me one." She gave him a little petulant smile.

He brightened. "So I will," he said. "I will. I will. I'll get one. I can get one."

He came with it the next day. It was Sunday, his day off. He had the little otter in a birdcage. It lay in one corner, dead frightened, eyes like slate. It never moved. He came in by the back of the house. When he knocked at the door there was no answer. He waited, set the otter and cage down on the path by the fringes of catmint, and listened. Then he heard voices: the Captain's, the woman's, giggling.

The boy went across the lawn towards them, cage in hand. His mind was on one thing: the otter. He had to give it to the woman. She wanted it. She'd asked for it. He had to give it to her.

He got to within the shade of the tree before anything happened. Then the woman suddenly stopped laughing. "Shut up, you fool. Shut up. There's someone here. It's the kid. Let me go, let me go."

The Captain sat up, swivelling round on his heavy buttocks. "Huh! Eh? What? What? Huh?"

Then he saw the boy. He leapt up in a passion, stopped.

"What the blazes you got in that damned cage? Eh?"

"I got the otter, sir."

"You got what? Didn't I tell you not to bring your damn pets here? Didn't I tell you?"

"It's all right, George, it—"

"You know what I've a good mind to do to you, eh?" He took a step forward towards the boy, his two hands in his belt. "Coming here, with your damn pets, disturbing people, Sunday afternoon. What the blazes you mean by it?"

The boy dropped the cage, stood frigid, paralysed.

"It's all right, George. I asked him. I—"

"Then you ought to know better. That damned thing can't live. It's a water animal. Don't you understand? You can't keep it. It'll die, in misery."

"Well, I—" She stood a little embarrassed, folding her arms, unfolding them, smoothing her white shoulder-straps over her white skin.

"Look at the damn thing," the Captain said. He kicked the cage round, so that the woman could see the little otter, cringing, terrorized, almost dead, in the corner of the bird-splashed cage. "Expect that to live? How can it? It's nearly dead already. It wants killing out of its misery. It—-"

Suddenly he had an idea. He whistled, called once or twice "Here! Here! Here!" and then whistled again. In a moment the dog came bounding out from the porch, in great leaps over the flowerbeds. He stood quivering by the Captain, in delicate agitation, waiting for a command.

"Down, Bounder, down. Down!" the Captain said. He turned to the boy. "You've never seen what a dog can do to an otter, have you? Down, Bounder! Down! Eh? Have you?"

"No, sir."

"All right."

Suddenly the Captain bent down and unfastened the cage and took out the little otter and let it run across the grass. "No, Bounder! No! Down, down!" The otter ran a little way, cramped, crouching. It ran and limped four or five yards. It was small and helpless. The dog stood quivering, watching, waiting for the word, his mouth trembling, in pain. Then the Captain shouted. The dog took an instant great leap and was on the otter and it was all over. The otter hung from the dog's mouth like a piece of sodden flannel, and then the dog began to tear it to pieces, throwing it about, ripping it in lust, until it was like a blood-soaked swab.

"Now you know what a dog does to an otter, eh? Don't you? No mistake about that, was there?"

The boy could not speak.

"George, let him go home," the woman said. "You go home now," she said to the boy. "You go—"

The boy turned to go, white-faced, his eyes half on the woman, half on the dog playing with the bloody rag of the dead otter.

"Wait a minute," the Captain said. "You understand this, once and for all? You stop bringing things here. Stop it. We don't want it. And now get out! And when we come next week don't come here on Sunday afternoons, nosing. Behave your damn self!"

The boy turned to go. In a rush of rage the Captain kicked out at him, catching him on the flank of the buttocks. The boy ran, hearing the Captain protest to the woman: "It had got to die, I tell you. How could it live? It's a water animal, the little fool."

In the morning the boy was back again early. The Captain and the woman had gone. The garden was still, hot already, the dew drying off.

The boy had a fixed idea. He had worked it out. Nothing could stop it. In the mornings, when he arrived, his first job was to feed the dog. That morning he did not feed it. He let the dog out of the wash-house, where it slept, and the dog bounded about the lawn, sniffing, cocking its leg, coming back to be fed at last.

The boy did nothing. The dog watched him. When he moved the dog followed him. Then, about nine o'clock, he took the dog down to the hencoop. Already the sun was hot, with a fierce July brassiness, the sky without cloud or wind. The boy opened the hen-coop and put his hand on the floor of hen-muck. It was hot. He looked up at the sky. The hen-coop was full in the sun. For the whole day it would be in the sun.

Then the boy called the dog. "Bounder, Bounder! Rabbits! Look! Fetch'em, Bounder! Fetch'em, fetch'em!"

In an instant the dog tore into the hen-coop. The boy slammed the door. The dog tore round and round for a moment and then stood still. The boy bolted the coop door and went up the path.

When he came back, half an hour later, the dog was scratching frenziedly. The boy had not thought of that. So he rushed back to the toolhouse and came back with a hammer and a small axe. He began to cut short stakes out of bean-poles and hammer them into the ground all round the foot of the coop. The dog stopped scratching and watched him.

Then when the boy had finished, it began its frenzy of scratching again, clouding up grey dust, already terrorized. The boy watched for a moment. Then he got bricks and laid them in a single row alongside the stakes. He was quite calm. His mouth was set. He was sweating.

But he was still not satisfied. He went up to the toolhouse and came back with a spade. Then he chopped out heavy sods of rough grass and piled them over the bricks, hammering them firm down with the back of the spade, until he had built at last a kind of earthwork, heavy and tight, all round the foot of the wire.

Then he stood and looked at the dog. Every time he looked at the dog he hated it. Each time he remembered the otter, saw the bloody piece of flannel being ripped and slapped to bits. His hatred was double-edged. He hated the dog because of the Captain; he hated the Captain because of the dog.

All that day, at intervals of about an hour, he went and looked at the dog. At first it scratched madly. Then it tired. In the afternoon it did nothing. It lay huddled up, as the otter had done, in the corner of the coop. Then, towards the end of the day, it got back its strength. It stood up and howled, barking in fury. Whenever the boy went near it hurled itself about in a great bounding frenzy of rage and anguish.

All the time the boy did nothing. The next day he did nothing. In the morning, first thing, he was frightened that something had happened, that the dog might have escaped, might be waiting for him. But the dog was still there. He set up a howling when the boy approached. The boy looked at the sods and bricks and then went away.

All that day he did nothing. All morning the dog scratched and leapt about in a kind of india rubber agony. Then in the heat of the afternoon he quietened again. He lay motionless, abject, tongue out. The boy looked at the tongue. He had an idea that it ought to turn black. He wanted it to turn black.

He wanted the dog to die, but also he wanted it to die slowly. By Wednesday the dog was sick. Heat had parched it, withered it, made an inexorable impression of misery on it. Lean always, it now had the look of a dog skeleton, with the grey skin drum-tight over its ribs. It held its tongue out for long intervals, panting deeply, right up from the heart, in agony. Then the tongue would go back, and the eyes would shine out with dark mournfulness, strangely sick. Then the panting would begin again.

The boy was satisfied. On Thursday he did not go too near the coop. He had some idea that, in time, before death, the dog would go mad. On Thursday he thought he saw the beginning of madness. The dog began to slobber a great deal, a sour yellow cream of saliva that dribbled down its lower lip and dried, in time, in the hot sun, into a flaky scab. By the end of that day the dog had lost all fight. It lay in supreme dejection. It no longer howled. When its tongue fell out, for brief, slow stabs of breath, the boy could see a curious rough muskiness on it, as though the dog had been eating the sun-dried dust of hen-muck. All the time his hatred never relaxed at all: hatred of the dog because of the Captain, of the Captain because of the dog, and all during Thursday he watched for the dog to show its first signs of madness and dying.

He wanted the dog to die on Friday: on Friday because it would leave him clear, free. He could drag the dog out and bury it and then go and not come back. To his way of thinking, it seemed simple. The Captain would be back on Saturday.

On Friday morning he hoped to find the dog dead. It was not dead. It still lay there, against the wire, eyes sick and open, waiting for him. The boy had a spasm of new hatred, really fear, because of the dog's toughness. Then suddenly he saw the tongue come out, slowly, in great pain. It was swollen, almost black. He jumped about, glad. It was black; it was mad. He knew, then, that it was almost the end.

Friday was not so hot. White clouds ballooned over and gave the dog a little rest from heat in the afternoon. By afternoon the boy was afraid. The dog still lay there, strangely still, the deep mad eyes almost closed, the mouth sour-flaked, the tongue terribly swollen. But it was alive, and he could do nothing. Once he got a goose-necked hoe and opened the coop door, holding it half open with his feet. He fixed the dog with his eye. If he could hit it once it would die. Then the dog stirred. And in a second he slammed the door shut with terror.

Then he had another idea. He made a loop with a piece of binder string and let the string down through the mesh of the coop-wire. He let it down slowly, until the loop was level with the dog's head. But the dog, mouth against the floor of the coop, would not stir, so that he could not slip the knot. He called it once, and for the first time, by its name, "Bounder, Bounder!" but it would not move.

Then he was frightened. He'd got to kill it. He'd got to finish it. Then he though of something. He could give it food and poison the food. He could give it bread and rat poison, with water.

He ran up the path. Then he thought he heard something. He stopped and listened. He could hear the noise of a car, braking on the gravel and stopping. He stood paralysed, for about a minute, listening. Then he heard the woman's voice. He could not believe it. Then he heard it again. There was no mistaking it. She was laughing and he heard also, in a moment, the Captain's voice in answer.

The Captain. He could not move. After what seemed a great time he heard a shout. It was for him. It was the Captain, bellowing his name.

"Boy! Albert! Boy! Where the devil are you? Where are you? Boy!"

The voice moved him. He began to walk up the path, slowly, in terror, without intention. The dog, hearing the new voice, was making strange whimpering sounds in the coop behind. The boy half ran.

At the crest of the path he slowed down. He could hear footsteps. They were coming towards him. He raised his eyes, so that when the Captain came round the corner his eyes were fixed on him.

In the coop the dog was crying bitterly. And hearing it, the boy stood still.

ITALIAN HAIRCUT

I was in a great hurry. I went up the steps to the barber's saloon two at a time. The stairs were iron-tipped and had blue lettered tin plates on every rise: haircutting, shaving, shampoo, saloon, haircutting, and so on, the letters chipped by countless shoe-toes.

"A haircut," I said.

From the moment I got upstairs I didn't like the place. The saloon was small, boxed-in, cheap. It smelt fiercely of old men and brilliantine. There were bottles all over it cupboards and shelves and wash-basins, pink, lavender, vitriol, green, jaundiced colours, all a little sinister. The whole place was dirty. I didn't like the barber either. He was dirty. It was not his fault: he was sallow, greasy-haired, thick-lipped, a sort of dago.

"You like it long?" he said, "or short?"

"Medium."

"Ver' good"

He was Italian. I didn't like him at all. He didn't seem to like me either. He wrapped the sheet round my neck like a shroud, ramming it into my collar, tight. We might have been enemies. We were alone in the place. And what with the stink of old men, and the dirt, and the odd-looking bottles and his own surly down-look eyes I didn't like it at all. I wanted to get out.

"Just as quick as you can," I said. "I've an appointment."

He didn't say anything. He began working the scissors, without hurrying. He pressed my head forward, suddenly, very hard: so that I was like a man with his head on an invisible chopping block. And with my head down I could see a razor on the rim of the wash-basin. It was open.

Then all at once he stopped clipping. I lifted my head, and we looked at each other in the glass. He was catching hold of my hair, running his fingers through it, making it stand up. He was a big man. He could have lifted me clean out of the chair. I have very light hair and when it stands up I look silly. With his derisive yellow fingers he made it stand straight up, like a comedian's.

"Look at your hair," he said.

"What about it?"

"My dear sir, only look at it. It's going white. You're losing it."

"It's a little dry," I said. "Certainly."

"Dry?" You use anythink on it?"

"No."

"It's coming out. You're losing it. Look here, see." Almost tender now, his derisiveness gone, he wafted my hair about again. "'Fore long you be bald. How old are you? Thirty-three? Thirty-four?"

"Thirty."

"Oh, dear! Oh, my God!" He took his hand off my head and put it on his own. It was a good gesture, Italian, overdramatic. "Thirty? Look at me. Look at my hair. Seexty-five. That's what I am. Seexty-five. And as black as—but you can see it. You can see for yourself."

"Yes."

"And you, look at you. A young man. And such nice hair. Such lovely hair. Don't you care about it?"

"It's worry," I said.

"Worry? Who said so? It's not worry. It's nerves. Starvation. You live on your nerves and your hair comes out."

"I work hard," I said.

"Work? What work? Pardon, but what work do you do?"

I told him. He changed at once.

"Books? That so? Interesting. Books? My daughter write books."

"Yes?"

"Yes! She writes books all her life. She write her first book when she was twelve. It was a beautiful book, a sensation. She got seventy-five pounds for it."

"Good."

"Everybody wanted her to write for them. Everybody. She was the craze. She wrote an essay for the gas company. A beautiful essay. The most beautiful essay a child ever wrote. For the gas company."

"Good."

"Success everywhere. She could of been famous. And you—what about you? You published anythink?"

"Some books."

"Oh! Thass encouraging? Encourage you to go on? You make a name for yourself?"

"I may do."

"You make a name for yourself," he said, "and then have hair like this? It's awful shame. Dreadful. Now if you was interested—perhaps you don' care, I don' know—if you was interested I could make your hair look different before you left this shop."

"You could? How?"

"Wid my treatment."

I didn't say anything. He clopped my hair a bit, ruffled it, pushed my head about, made a great show of indifference.

"Maybe you ain't interested?"

"What sort of treatment is it?"

"Special. A secret."

He clipped.

"Of course if you ain't interested."

"Tell me what you do," I said.

"Maybe you ain't interested," he said. "I don' know. It make no difference. I'm only here to oblige. I ain't the boss. I don't get nothing out of it. In the summer I work in Brighton. Twenty pound a week. I don't get nothing out of the treatment. I ain't the boss."

He took up the razor.

"Maybe you ain't interested?"

"I want to know what you're going to do." Just then I wanted to know very much what he was going to do.

He flickered the razor. I didn't like it at all.

"It's electric. Electric must pass through my body. And then I massage wid ointment. Wid special stuff."

"And how much?"

"Maybe you ain't interested. I don' know. Five an' six. You don' want to be bald, do you?"

"And how long does it take?"

All the time he was flashing the razor.

"Five minute."

"You're sure?"

"Sure. Five minute. A young man like you, going white. At thirty. You don' want to be white do you?"

"I've got an appointment," I said.

"It won't take five minute. Sure. You won't regret it. You don' want to be bald, do you?"

"All right," I said. "I'll have it."

"Good. Thass fine." He went dashing round the screen, out of sight. I heard him tramping about. He came back with great alacrity, carrying a box. It had long lines of flex running out of it, and switches on it, like some antique wireless set. He plugged it in. The box was black, a little sinister. I didn't like it at all.

"Jus' take your feet off the iron," he said. I took my feet off the footrest. "Jus' in case," he said. He had become extraordinarily cheerful. "You don't want to be contacted? Just hold that." It was a kind of handle, of ebonite. I held it under the sheet, with the wires connected.

"Does it hurt?" I said.

"Hurt? No. A little. Not much. A bit of tickling. Thass all."

"It's safe, isn't it?"

"Oh! It's O.K. If anybody's going to be electrocuted it's me. Oh! You won't regret it. You don't want to be bald, do you?"

He suddenly switched on and attacked me. His fingers danced on my head like springs. My scalp jumped with pins and needles. He attacked me until the sweat stood like grease on his face.

"Yes, my daughter write books. Wonderful. After she write for the gas company she could do anything. It don't hurt? You're all right? You won't regret it. And then I made her give it up. Altogether. She could of written for anybody. She write wonderful stuff. Stories, essays. Anything. She got genius."

"Why did you make her give it up?"

"You know what they done? It don't hurt? Them editors? You know what they done? What I find out?"

"What?"

"The lousy —— they sent her scarves. Bits of ribbon. Anythink. Trinkets. I ain't a fool. The child was sitting up all night—writing that beautiful stuff. And all they sent her was scarves. I would of been a fool, wouldn' I, to of let her go on?"

He was still massaging, the electricity dancing on my head like springs.

"You know I'm right, ain't I? Ain't that what they do? Send scarves. There ain't no money in it. Kipling perhaps people like that—it's all right. But for people like you and my daughter it's different. Thass right? You know it is, don' you?"

"My hands have gone dead," I told him.

"Gone dead? You don't feel well?" He rushed to the switch and cut it off.

"It's all right. How much longer?"

"Five minutes."

He rushed about. My hair now stood up, as in a caricature of fear. I looked like a wild man. He came back with a hot towel, wrapped it round my head, and I sat like a potentate with white turban.

"You feel all right? One day you'll come back and thank me. You'll have beautiful hair one day."

"Just after this?"

"Oh! no, no, no. You gotta persevere. I make you up some ointment, and some spirit. My own recipe. You put that on."

"How much is that?"

"Ointment. Thass five an' six."

He took off the towel. My head felt beautiful: fresh and yet on fire. He rushed away with the towel and came back with a bright blue bottle. He was shaking it.

"How much longer?" I said.

"Five minute. I just put this on."

The bottle had "chloroform" on it. I didn't like it at all. Suddenly he poured it on my head, and it was as though my hair had gone up in flame. The effect was terrific, a hot pain driving right down to the roots of my hair.

"You take a bottle of this," he said. "And the ointment. And persevere."

"By God, how much is that?" I said.

"The spirit? Thass forty-two an' six."

"I'll take the ointment."

"You want both. I'll charge you ten shilling for the spirit."

"No. I'll leave it."

He became suddenly very nice, beaming, the real Italian, his voice sweet.

"Is it a question of cash?"

"Oh! no."

"If it's a question of cash, don't let it worry you."

"No, I won't take it."

"I tell you what. I won't charge you for the ointment. You take the spirit and the ointment and you come in some other time."

"No."

"I tell you what. I won't charge you for the spirit. Only the ointment. Because I'm interested in you. You can't afford it, can you? I know. I don't care. I know, because of my daughter. The lousy —— sending her scarves!

For that beautiful work. You needn't wonder I wouldn't let her go on? You see, I understand."

"No. How much does it come to?"

"You mean?—you take the spirit?"

"No."

"Take it if you like. I trust you. I ain't the boss. I don't care."

'Only the ointment.'

"O.K. Thass twelve an' eightpence. Wid the haircut."

I gave him thirteen shillings. He brushed my coat. "One day you'll come back and thank me. You will. I ain't like one of them editors. Don't give nothing in return. Your hair looks better already. Beautiful. It'll be so thick and beautiful.'

"What time is it?" I said. "How long have you been?"

"Five minutes."

I rushed out.

It's no use. Somehow my hair is as bad as ever.

THE LITTLE JEWELLER

[I]

Mr. Elisha Peacock woke suddenly at four o'clock in the morning, in the dead of darkness, feeling very ill. For some moments immediately before waking he was aware of a strange sound of tinkling glass, of his whole body fighting a violent constriction in his chest. When he woke at last it was some time before he realized that the sound was that of the night wind shaking the coloured glass chandelier above his head, that the conflict in his body was in reality a wire of pain boring down into his heart.

It was then that he realized he was very ill. In the moment of realization he suddenly heard too the striking of ten or a dozen clocks downstairs in the small jeweller's shop he had kept for thirty-five years. The sounds, not quite simultaneous, at first clear and then discordantly confused, rolled over and over his half-wakened mind in waves of metallic tumult. He managed at last to struggle up on one elbow. The pain, as if a hot gimlet were being turned slowly down into his chest, had now slightly lessened. The clocks had ceased. In the night silence he could hear no sound except the small renewed clash of the glass hangings above his head, and there was only one thought in his mind. It was the strange, painful thought that he, Elisha Peacock, after sixty-eight years of tranquil living, had reached the point where he must die in the night, alone, frightened like a child by the silence and the darkness, before anyone could reach him or he could get downstairs to the telephone.

With this thought in his mind he managed to get slowly out of bed and put his feet into his slippers. The pain in his heart had now ceased to have direction or motion, and lay there only like a dull embedded bullet. He felt that he wanted to press it away and so held both hands locked across his chest, staggering a little as he walked. He felt very weak as he walked downstairs, slowly, not troubling to put on the lights, feeling his way by the cold walls of the staircase, and he was troubled by a remote but fierce idea that he did not want to die. By the time he reached the passage which led from the stairs to the glass door of the shop this thought had replaced all others: had become not merely a wish but a determination. He at last put on the lights of the shop, where the telephone was, and then stood still: a small, grey, perplexed little figure, his pain-washed eyes blinking in the white reflected light that sprang at him from the cabinets and shelves of glass and silver with which the shop was full.

For one moment he looked at the telephone, thought better of it, and then went into the room behind the shop, switching on the light. By the fireplace, in which the fire was quite dead, there was a cupboard. He stood with his hand on the brass knob of it, intending to get himself a glass of brandy. But for a long time he could not move. The upward motion of his arm had brought on the pain in his heart again. Suddenly he shut his eyes and felt that he was falling.

It was some moments later that he came to himself, knowing that he must have fainted. He pulled himself up to the cupboard and found the bottle of brandy and a glass. He poured out a little brandy and drank it. It smoothed away the harsh edges of his weakness and pain and for a second or two he looked vaguely about him, slowly coming back to his senses before going back upstairs, still carrying the bottle and the glass, still half-stupefied, so that he forgot to switch off the lights.

From that moment until eight o'clock he lay in bed, thinking. The pain in his heart had ceased, there remained in its place a huge, accumulative fear. He felt that he had been down to the edge of life, had looked over into a vast space of unknown darkness, and had only just managed to come back. This fear was sometimes so strong that he held himself immobile, not daring to move. He lay looking at the grey winter morning light distribute itself reluctantly on the tiny pieces of rose and emerald glass of the chandelier, which still shook and tinkled in the moving air. After sixty-eight years something almost catastrophic had happened to him, and now fear of its recurrence drove his thoughts back into the past. He recalled his life in the shop. He was not married. Outside, in permanent gilt lettering, he had had put up a quarter of a century ago a large notice: "Peacock for Presents. Pence to Pounds," and on this simple motto he had built up a secure, comfortable business. He had tried during all that time not to harm anyone; he felt he could recall honestly that he had never cheated a single person out of a single penny. He was not afraid of the opinion of any man. He had tried to be decent, upright, considerate, and he felt that perhaps he had succeeded. No, he was not afraid of that.

It was only the conscious realization of his fear of death that disturbed him. He knew suddenly, as he lay looking at the pieces of glass quivering above his head in the increasing light, that he had been afraid of it for years. The desire never to give pain to others had made him sensitive to the thought of any pain to himself. In one sense it had made him an ultra-careful man—he remembered how in the days of gas-lighting he would never go to bed without turning off the main for fear of being blown up or asphyxiated in the night—in another, quite careless. What had happened that morning had brought to his mind another result of his fear. Somehow he had shrunk from making a will.

But now he would rectify that. Yes, now he must see to it. When Edward came at eight o'clock he would explain what had happened; they would call in a solicitor. Edward would understand; you could talk to Edward. Edward was his assistant: a thoughtful, conscientious young man remarkable for resource and promptitude. He was not only a shop-assistant, but he came in every morning an hour earlier than opening time in order to cook break-fast. When he thought of Edward the little jeweller felt his mind instantly strengthened and tranquillized.

At eight o'clock the clocks downstairs began striking the hour and they had no sooner finished than he heard the sound of Edward unlocking and opening the back door. He lay still for a few moments, listening, and then called.

"Edward!" he called. "Edward!"

He was surprised at the weakness of his own voice. It dissolved against the walls of the room, unheard. He tried to raise himself slightly on his elbow, but it seemed as if his body were made of wax that dissolved too under its own slight motion. He could only lie back on the pillows, weakly repeating Edward's name.

A few moments later he heard the young man mounting the stairs; then his voice:

"Mr. Peacock! Are you there, Mr. Peacock? Was that you calling? Mr. Peacock!"

"In here, Edward," was all he could say. "In here."

Edward came hurriedly into the bedroom, a bespectacled young man with brown, alarmed eyes.

"Oh! there you are, Mr. Peacock. All the lights were on downstairs, Mr. Peacock, and I couldn't make it out. Whatever's the matter?"

"Nasty turn, Edward," he said. "In the night. About four o'clock." He

tried to smile. "An awful pain in my heart, Edward. Nasty." He tried again
to struggle up in bed.

"I wouldn't try to get up if I were you, Mr. Peacock," Edward said.

"No good lying here, Edward."

"That's all very well, Mr. Peacock," Edward said, "but if you're not well,
I ought to ring up the doctor. Shall I?"

"I don't know, Edward. I don't know what to say. I've never been like
this before, Edward. I don't know—"

He tried again to get up. For the second time his body melted like wax
on the pillows. He shut his eyes for a moment, weak and tired, and when
he opened them again Edward had gone out of the room, and he called after
him:

"Edward! Edward!"

It was only after he had called six or seven times that he realized once
more how weak his voice was, that it had no more strength than the gentle,
insistent sound of the chandelier trembling above his head, that it was now
very like the voice of a child, crying in trouble and getting no answer.

[II]

He lay in the bedroom all that day, irritated and tired, yet restless.
Frequently he found himself troubled by the motions and the sound of the
chandelier. It was a very strange thing that he had never noticed it before.
Yet now it troubled him. Once or twice he settled back on the pillows, trying to sleep, but the tinkling of the little pieces of glass, stirring in the wind
blowing in at the open window, made a tiny maddening curtain between
himself and oblivion. At other times he lay thinking: about the shop, then
Edward, about the chrysanthemums in his little greenhouse behind the
shop, about the doctor. When the doctor had been and departed he turned
over in his mind what he had said. He tried to read into his reticent words
at first more and then less than they seemed to mean. "The heart has had
a nasty bump, Mr. Peacock, that's the trouble. A nasty little bump. It needs
rest and quiet, that's all, Mr. Peacock. If I were you I should get someone
in to look after you." In time these words began to have on him the same
effect of irritation as the sound of the chandelier. They told him nothing.
Very clever to say the heart had had a nasty bump; wonderful to advise getting someone in. The trouble was that he had nobody: except a sister who

lived at the far end of the town, married to a third-rate insurance-agent who rolled his own miserable ragged cigarettes for the sake of economy. He did not like either his sister or her husband; he did not think they liked him. It annoyed him that he should be forced even to think of them now.

He was glad when, about twelve o'clock, Edward came upstairs to say that his solicitor had arrived. Yet once again his feelings instantly took the form of fresh irritation.

"All right, all right, all right!" he said. "Show him up! What's the sense in tramping upstairs twenty times when once will do?"

"Yes, Mr. Peacock, yes." Edward hurriedly left the room.

"Wasting shoe leather!"

He lay back on the pillows, ashamed. His heart was beating very rapidly. He had not intended to speak like that. Far from it. No. He did not know at all what was coming over him. A few minutes later his solicitor came in, a tall narrow-jawed man who enjoyed a little shooting two or three days a week and who now entered the room with great heartiness, smiling. Suddenly the little jeweller, who had lived for so many years without contention or malice, felt that he hated him. He felt illogically that the solicitor and the idea of the will were the causes and not the result of his pain. His mouth set itself coldly against the bed-sheet, his eyes levelly transfixed.

"Sorry to see you like this, Mr. Peacock. Awfully sorry. Understand you wanted to see me?"

"No!" the little jeweller said. "No!"

"Well, Mr. Peacock—"

"I don't want to see you! I don't want to see anybody!"

"All right, Mr. Peacock, all right, all right. As you like, Mr. Peacock. As you like. Perhaps I might come in again to-morrow?"

"No!" the little jeweller shouted. "No!"

For some moments after the solicitor had gone he was still speaking, repeating that angry monosyllable in a voice that was foreign to him. When he had finished he was again ashamed. He lay silent, his hands pressing his nightshirt against his heart. Closing his eyes, he tried to search for the causes of his strange behavior. He then discovered that he was lonely. He felt suddenly a great need for companionship, for some objective event or circumstance that would make him forget his fear.

Lying there, he recalled the chrysanthemums in his little greenhouse behind the shop, and it seemed to him that he had found a solution. He felt a great hunger for the sight of the flowers. He called Edward, and then when

Edward came upstairs he began to explain what he wanted: how Edward was to go downstairs to the greenhouse and cut the chrysanthemums. The young man stood listening reticently, with an expression of grave concern, asking at last how many chrysanthemums he was to bring? Something about the young man's earnest gravity suddenly seemed very funny to the little jeweller and he began laughing.

"Cut them all," he said. "Cut them all, Edward. Bring them up here so that I can look at them. All of them, Edward, all of them! Go on! Go on!"

"You don't mean it, Mr. Peacock?"

"Bless me, mean it? Of course I mean it. Why should I say it if I didn't mean it?"

"What shall I do for vases, Mr. Peacock?"

The little jeweller suddenly began laughing again, telling the young man that he was to get the vases out of the shop. The assistant looked very troubled but said, "Yes, Mr. Peacock," and left the room. Ten minutes later he began to bring up the first of the flowers, great stalks of bronze and yellow and amber and pink, which he held at arm's length, like torches. He laid them first on the bed, where the little jeweller could reach out and touch them with the tips of his fingers, and then began to arrange them in bowls and vases brought up from the living-room and the shop. The little jeweller watched him with bright, alert eyes, the chandelier and the solicitor and the pain in his heart momentarily forgotten. It seemed to him now that the room was alight. For the first time that day he lay untroubled by fear. He let the lids of his eyes relax and from his prostrate position on the bed he watched the great curled chrysanthemums swim about the room like constellations that brightened and soothed his mind. He asked at last how many flowers there were. The young assistant said he did not know, and the little jeweller said, "Count them, Edward, there must be fifty or sixty."

"Yes, Mr. Peacock," the young man said and began to move his hands, counting the flowers, turning his head at last to say, "Sixty, Mr. Peacock. Exactly sixty. Funny how you guessed."

"Guessed?" The little jeweller began laughing in a strange way again. "No, Edward, no. I counted them! Counted them." He laughed at the young man's grave disturbed face. "Caught you that time, Edward, eh? Caught you?"

"Yes, Mr. Peacock," Edward said.

"Caught you nicely, eh, Edward?" He continued for some moments to laugh with bright eyes. He ceased only to turn again to the young man and speak.

"Like having sixty moons shining in the room together," he said. "Eh, Edward, eh?"

[III]

Later that afternoon he fell asleep, awaking with fear in his heart about half-past three, momentarily disturbed by the November twilight and the sound of the chandelier. Earlier, before sleeping, he had been along to the bathroom. The catch of the bedroom door had not fastened properly, and the door now stood partially open. In this way he could hear voices. He lay listening intently for some moments, and then it came to him that they were the voices of his sister and her husband, talking to Edward at the foot of the stairs.

For some time he could not hear what they were saying. He caught only the tone of their voices. They seemed almost to be arguing. He heard Edward make a sudden exclamation, as if in protest. He heard the aggressively pitched note of his sister's voice, surprised, resentful, dominating Edward. He did not know why he concluded that his brother-in-law was there: except perhaps because he was completely silent.

Soon the voices came nearer. He heard the sound of feet on the stairs, and caught a sentence of his sister's: "Well, then I think we'll go up and see what just *is* the matter."

He lay gripping his hands under the sheet. He did not know why he should feel suddenly so antagonistic towards his sister, towards everyone. He had never liked his sister, but his attitude had been one of remote indifference. But now pain had ripped away the neat edge of his nerves, and he was angry because his sister had somehow been able to discover that he was ill.

He had withdrawn himself almost entirely under the sheets by the time his sister, preceding Edward and her husband, came into the room: a small, juiceless, volatile woman, with crinkled skin, her hands grasping a large patent leather handbag.

"Well?" she said. "Well! What have you been doing to yourself?"

He muttered sounds of denial and protest that had on her the effect of a challenge.

"Well, of course, if you're going to be like that after we've traipsed all the way up from North End!"

"Like what?" he murmured. "Like what?"

"Jumping down folks' throats! Muttering!" she said. "Muttering!"

He did not say anything. The slight exertion of protest had made him feel once again old and tired. In a moment the tranquillizing effect of sleep and flowers had been lost. He turned with slight weariness in the bed.

At that moment he saw that his sister had seen the flowers. Her eyes were behaving like lights of warning in their wrinkled sockets. Her mouth, falling open, revealed a colourless dark gap between the plate of her false teeth and the roof of her mouth; but a single word of speech was enough to bring the plate into place again with a click of acid astonishment.

"Well!" she said. "I wonder what next, I wonder what next!"

The little jeweller clenched his hands even harder under the sheets. As he did so his brother-in-law spoke for the first time.

"Been bringing the greenhouse indoors, eh?" He spoke with false robustness, as if trying to be funny. His words became as it were knotted in his moustache, which his habit of smoking loose cheap cigarettes had turned a gingery yellow.

"And what if I have?" the little jeweller said. "What if I have? What exactly is it to do with you?"

"Mr. Peacock," Edward said. "Mr. Peacock. The doctor said you were on no account to get excited."

"Excited?" the woman said. "Excited. It looks as if that's the trouble. Over-excitement about something. Bringing a greenhouseful of flowers into the house."

"Can't I do what I like with them?" he said, trying to raise his voice. "They're my flowers! Without you interfering?"

"Mr. Peacock," Edward began.

"Be quiet, Edward!" he said. "Get downstairs! Get down to the shop. What do you suppose customers will be doing? Get down to the shop!"

As the young assistant went reluctantly out of the room the little jeweller's sister began speaking again, in protest, but he suddenly cut her off with an attack of angry words, at the same time throwing up his hands and bringing them down on the sheets.

"And you get out too! Both of you. Before I lose my temper. How can I get rest if you come up here arguing? How can I? How can I?"

"All right!" his sister said. "All right! But it looks to me as if you want someone to look after you!"

"I don't want anything except a little peace and quiet!" he shouted. "Get out!"

Rather hurriedly his brother-in-law went out of the room, his sister following, her lips strangely set. Suddenly he shouted after them that they could leave the door open. He wanted a little fresh air in there, a little fresh air!

The door was left slightly open. Exhausted, astonished at himself, feeling slightly ashamed, he lay back on the pillows. It took him some moments to get his breath. Then in the silence he lay listening, hearing again the voices from downstairs.

It was only after three or four minutes, after his anger was really passed and had become in recollection something foreign and meaningless to him, that he got out of bed, put on his slippers, and went to his bedroom door. As he opened it, he took his grey woollen dressing-gown off the door-peg and slipped it over his shoulders. Then he went slowly along the landing. The voices had already become clearer, yet not distinct. It was already late in the afternoon and as he went cautiously down the first few steps of the stairs he could see the chinks of electric light splintering sharply the darkness between stairs and shop. Half-way down the stairs he sat down, looking very small, slightly perplexed with his head to one side, and very solitary. He could hear the voices quite clearly now.

They came from the living-room: mainly the voices of his sister, catechizing, and of Edward, answering. His sister seemed to be immensely concerned about the flowers.

"Didn't it strike you as very funny," she said to Edward, "that he should ask you to cut *all* the flowers?"

"Well, it did rather. Yes."

"Fifty of them if there's one," she said.

"There's just sixty," Edward said. "Mr. Peacock counted them. He said it was like having sixty moons shining together in the bedroom."

"What?" she said. "*What?*"

The little jeweller heard Edward repeat what he had said.

"Well!" she said. "Well! Well, that settles it, that settles it. I'm stopping here until things are straightened out a bit. First he acts funny with the solicitor, then with us. Then he talks about seeing moons shining in the room. I think it's a good job we found out about it when we did."

The little jeweller made his way slowly back upstairs while she was still speaking, catching now and then some more strident passage in what she was saying. In the bedroom the colour of the many flowers had died, but the room was full of a strong odour of chrysanthemums that hung pleasantly

on the damp November air. Tired now, he lay down in bed. As he began
to try to think, turning over in his mind what he had just heard, the chandelier stirred and began to drop down on him its small tinkling irritant bits
of sound. It was this repetitive maddening sound, he thought suddenly, that
throughout the day had goaded him into brief fits of anger. Why was it? He
did not want to be angry. He felt recurrently ashamed of himself, miserable.
Yet underneath the shame he was aware of a strange, dormant anxiety. It
seemed to him that unless he took a terribly firm hold on himself he must
sooner or later leap up in bed and seize the chandelier and smash it to pieces.

He was struggling with the perplexity brought about by this desire when
his sister came upstairs and into the darkening room. Though he did not see
it, she had taken off her hat and coat. It was in explanation of this that she
addressed him in a challenging voice:

"Well, I've decided to stay for a night or two and look after you, Elisha,
whether you like it or not. I've sent Fred home for the things. I hope you
hear what I say?"

He did not answer. In a momentary flash of cunning he decided to lie still
and silent, in a pretence of sleep.

[IV]

When he woke again it was late in the evening; the room was dark and still,
and he was no longer tired. He did not know what time it was, but soon
he caught from the street outside the broken echoes of passing voices and
traffic and then, raising himself on his elbow, he looked out of the uncur-
tained window and saw lights in the street below. He felt briefly reassured,
and then turned to look at the bedroom. He could see better now, and suddenly he realized that something strange had happened.

The flowers had gone. He sat up in bed and switched on the light. An accidental breath of wind stirred the hanging glasses of the chandelier, and in this
moment he felt all the violence of the day's anger renew itself with tremendous strength. It was beyond mere irritation now. It no longer sprang from
within him. It was an external force which seemed to take hold of him
bodily and jerk him out of bed.

For a few moments he stood in the centre of the room, in his nightshirt,
staring before him. Yes: the flowers had gone. They had gone and he knew
that only one person could have taken them away. His anger at these simple

facts beat him into violent movement. He put out the light and began to dress. Anger directed his hands to things he did not consciously know were there: trousers, coat, a loose black beret which he often wore in the shop, his boots, which he did not lace up. It seemed to take hold of him and lead him downstairs: the same immense external anger aroused simply by the fact that his flowers had gone. Outside on the landing he almost stumbled over the vases of flowers lined up against the railings of the stairs, but his anger did not cease. It drove him from the stairs into the passage that ran between stairs and living-room, shining through the glass door of which he could see a light.

This light made him stop. Through the lighted glass door he could see his sister and her husband. They had taken possession. They were having supper at a table directly under the electric light. Beating straight down, the light threw their faces into shadow, depressing them. Bottles of stout stood on the table. He saw his sister, mouth full, reach out her hand and grasp the glass of stout and drink rapidly, her face excited by food and drink and some expounded intention he could not hear.

He turned away and went back along the passage. He unlocked the side door at the foot of the stairs and went out into the street. It seemed again as if anger had driven him there. The night air was not cold, and he was still not tired. He began to walk rapidly, knowing in a strange way that he was not fully responsible for his movements.

But soon, as he walked along the street, his anger underwent a change. It became an idea. It was the idea that his sister and her husband had installed themselves at the house for the sole purpose of taking away his money. He moved under the street lights with an oblivious swaying movement, looking at the ground. From the nucleus of his single idea sprang others. He began to walk more quickly, impelled by the idea of escape. He became aware of the idea that he was being persecuted. They had taken away his flowers, they had come to take away his money. In time, if he did not escape, they would take away him.

He struggled along to the next corner, and then he had another idea. Out of the darkness there came a taxi, driven slowly, going home perhaps after meeting the last important train at the station. He put up his hand and shouted. The taxi pulled up and he told the driver to go straight to Mr. Archibald Foster's house, forty-five Edward Street.

"What street?" the driver said.

"Edward Street."

"Edward Street?" the driver said. "Never heard of it. Edward Street?"
The little jeweller stood slightly swaying by the side of the taxi, trying to
think. Edward Street? No, that was not right. It couldn't be right. He was
thinking of Edward. It occurred to him suddenly that he needed Edward.
What street did Edward live in? Foster Street? Archibald Street? He ran his
hand vaguely across his face. No, he thought, no, what was he thinking
about? Archibald was the name of his solicitor, who lived in Foster Street.
It was his solicitor he needed, Mr. Archibald. He needed to make his will.
Then he remembered that Mr. Archibald was dead, that the firm was carried
on by somebody of another name. Mr. Foster? No: he recalled abruptly that
Foster was his sister's married name. He stood swaying on his feet, his mind
for the space of several seconds quite blank. Where did he want to go? What
was he trying to remember?

The voice of the taxi-driver aroused him at last. "Thought of it yet?"

"No," the little jeweller said, "I haven't thought of it." He now suddenly
felt weak and cold from standing. "Let me get in. You can drive on and I'll
tell you when I remember. I shall remember it in a minute."

What was it? he thought. What was it? As he lay back on the cushions
of the taxi he tried desperately to beat his mind into a coherent effort of
memory. What in God's name was it? He shut his eyes, pressing his hands
against his forehead. The taxi swung from side to side, turning a corner,
swinging him as if he were suspended by a rope. He knew again that he was
very ill. His mind had ceased in its reactions. The knowledge of his illness
was part of the darkness, the street lights swinging giddily past, the strange
droning noise of the taxi boring with infinite melancholy down into his
brain. Once the driver turned and spoke to him, but he did not reply. He
was seized by the idea that he was being forcibly carried away into the darkness of a strange place. He had long since ceased his effort of memory. He
felt now that he was fighting to escape. He felt very frightened by the dark
confinement of the taxi and suddenly began to shout like a child.

"Let me get out!" he shouted. "Let me get out!" He wiped his hand across
his face and found his forehead cold with the sweat of great anguish. "Let
me out! Stop it! Stop it! Stop it! Stop it!" he shouted. "Please stop it now!"

[V]

When he came to himself again he did not recognize his own skinny white hands lying on the dark grey blanket of the bed. In the same way, when he lifted one of his hands and drew it unsteadily across his face, he could not recall who he was. The strange details of the face, a growth of beard, the fleshless cheekbones, the deep-sunken eyes, might have been those of some other person. He knew that the bed, too, was strange. He fixed in his mind the reality of its black iron shape, the grey blanket, the grey light falling on it from a distant window. Then he realized that it was one of many others.

Where was he? His eyes cast themselves with slow weariness from side to side. They alighted and dwelt upon a double row of grey beds. In these beds, all exactly resembling his own, other men were lying, one or two asleep. He tried to understand his relationship to them. He looked at the walls of the room, the ceiling. The whitewash had begun in places to peel away. He considered again the grey winter light falling through the high narrow windows, trying to determine what time of day it was.

Gradually his mind began to clear. Wakefulness itself had broken a tiny hole of light in his troubled consciousness. It now began to widen, and as the distribution of light quickened he gripped his hands tightly on the blanket, remembering. Fixing his eyes on the ceiling he remembered the chandelier, his bedroom, the flowers, his sister. But between these things and the present moment he was aware of a great blank. Then slowly he realized that this blankness was the key to where he was.

He looked again at the faces of the men about him. Some were staring at the ceiling, some straight before them, out of the windows; a few were asleep. With an abrupt calmness of pity he saw them as the faces of men not responsible for themselves: the faces of the partially insane. For a moment or two this realization did not trouble him. He saw calmly, with detachment, that it did not affect him. He himself was not one of those silent staring creatures; he had no part in their strange immobility. He understood and was sorry for them, his heart no longer calm but crying unspeakably with pity.

Suddenly it was as if he had stepped on a revolving trap. He seemed to take a step forward and was flung violently out of calmness into a pit of terror. He had a sensation of being hit on the head. He struggled to save himself, and all at once was completely calm again. This new calmness remained for a moment unbroken. Then it was shattered by his own voice, shouting at him in his own brain. "You are one of them!" it shouted at him. "You are one of them! You are! *You are!*"

As the voice died, he lay very still. A voice calling in his mind? In answer he felt fear slowly begin to creep back to him: not merely his former, shadowy fear of death, but the very cold, terrible fear of truth.

He lay for a long time trying to reason things out. He found memory very difficult, but finally he had an idea. As it came to him he looked slowly around the room. The figures of the men, staring and wooden, had not moved. Cautiously he moved his legs under the blanket, bending his knees. At either end of the room were double glass doors, beyond which he could see a corridor. He watched this corridor during some moments for a sign of life, but nothing happened. He was thinking with peculiar clearness now.

Suddenly he leapt out of bed, flung himself bodily at the swing doors at the nearer end of the room, and rushed down the corridor. He heard behind him an abrupt murmur of voices, which the closing of the swing doors cut off again. For a short space he was alone in the corridor, running along the grey stone floors in his bare feet. Then he heard other feet running behind him. They were feet with heavy boots on them. They ran fast, catching up with him. He turned to look, involuntarily holding up his hands. The feet with boots belonged to a man in a brown uniform. The man rushed at him and locked his arms behind his back. The little jeweller began to struggle. He felt himself possessed suddenly by a colossal strength. He began shouting. The attendant put one of his hands over his mouth, bruising his lips. The little jeweller swung one arm free and then the attendant began to hit him, striking him again on the face and the body. He continued to fight violently and the attendant continued to hit him, until at last he gave up the struggle.

"Come on," the attendant said. "Back you go. They all try this trick once, but you'll learn better. Come on. Back again."

It was almost two hours later when he opened his eyes to see two figures, a doctor and a nurse, standing over him.

"Where am I?" he said. "Where is this?"

The doctor did not answer the question. "You're all right now?" he said. "Better?"

"I want to go home, please."

"In time."

"I want to know who brought me here? Please who brought me here? A lady?"

"Your sister."

"I want to see my doctor," he said. "My own doctor. You know him—

Doctor—Doctor—" he tried to make a great effort of memory, "Doctor—"

"It's all right. I'm your doctor."

"I want Edward," he said. He suddenly felt an intense revulsion of feeling against his sister. "Why did she do this?" he said, raising his voice. "Why did she do it? She'd no right! I never did anyone any harm! I never did anything." He clenched his hands. "Damn her! Damn her!"

"Please," the doctor said.

"She wants my money!" he shouted. "Damn her!"

"Listen," the doctor said. "Quietly. Your sister is paying to keep you here. She is struggling to pay as best she can. Don't misjudge her. How can she have your money if it's safe in the bank?" The doctor spoke with heavy kindness, as if in reality the little jeweller had no money and was under an immense delusion. "Now how can she?"

"She gets it if I die!" he said. "There's no one else. She gets it if I die!"

"I know," the doctor said. "But you're not going to die." He held clean light fingers on the little jeweller's pulse. "You've been getting excited. You mustn't do that. If you want us to help you, you must help us. Couldn't you manage some sleep again?"

"I want to go home," the little jeweller said. "Please, I want to go home."

The doctor walked away, passing like a white ghost out of the swing doors. Seeing him go, the little jeweller lay back on his pillows, determined for one moment to be quite calm. The nurse remained about his bed, tucking in his blankets. He looked at her face, quite young, alive and soft, and it seemed to him suddenly the most human thing he had seen since waking in the grey, impersonal room.

"Nurse," he said. He held himself rigid under the blankets, more than ever determined to be quite calm.

"Yes," she said, "yes?"

"Nurse," he said, "Nurse." He was speaking with great earnestness, in a whisper, unaware that his eyes were glancing rapidly to and fro about the room, for fear of listeners. "Nurse, I've got money," he said. "Plenty of money. Two or three thousand. See? Plenty." He spoke in a whisper of desperation. "If you'll help me get away I'll see that you get something. A cheque for fifty pounds. More than that." He stared at her with terrible earnestness, almost wildly. "You can come to my shop and pick yourself a little jewellery. Anything. You see? You see?"

For a moment there no response in her face except a remote smile. Then she spoke. "Jewellery. Well, that's nice," she said. "Jewellery?"

He wanted to speak again, but he could not. He looked instead at her eyes, which contained no hint of understanding. They were regarding him instead with a kind of impersonal pity.

He knew then what she was thinking. He lay back and closed his eyes in order to shut her out, and when he opened them again she was gone. On the walls and the blanket and on the scarred ceiling the grey light was growing greyer now with the dying of the afternoon.

When the nurse came back past the bed again she saw the little jeweller lying with closed eyes and the palms of his small, shrunken hands upturned across the bed. His lips were moving very slightly, but with her casual glance she did not notice them.

Nor could she hear what he was saying now. "Take me away. Take me away, please. O Lord! take me away."

CHATEAU BOUGAINVILLAEA

The headland was like a dry purple island scorched by the flat heat of afternoon, cut off from the mainland by a sand-coloured tributary of road which went down past the estaminet and then, half a mile beyond, to the one-line, one-eyed railway station. Down below, on a small plateau between upper headland and sea, peasants were mowing white rectangles of corn. The tide was fully out, leaving many bare black rocks and then a great sun-phosphorescent pavement of sand, with the white teeth of small breakers slowly nibbling in. Far out, the Atlantic was waveless, a shade darker than the sky, which was the fierce blue seen on unbelievable posters. Farther out still, making a faint mist, sun and sea had completely washed out the line of sky.

From time to time a puff of white steam, followed by a peeped whistle, struck comically at the dead silence inland. It was the small one-line train, half-tram, making one way or the other its hourly journey between town-terminus and coast. By means of it the engaged couple measured out the afternoon.

"There goes the little train," he would say.

"Yes," she would say, "there goes the little train."

Each time she resolved not to say this stupid thing and then, dulled with sleepiness and the heat of earth and sky and the heather in which they lay, she forgot herself and said it, automatically. Her faint annoyance with herself at these times had gradually begun to make itself felt, as the expression of some much deeper discontent.

"Je parle Français un tout petit peu, m'sieu." In a voice which seemed somehow like velvet rubbed the wrong way, the man was talking. "I was all right as far as that. Then I said, 'Mais, dites-moi, m'sieu, pourquoi are all the knives put left-handed dans ce restaurant?' By God it must have been awfully funny. And then he said—"

"He said 'Because, m'sieu, the people who use them are all left-handed.'"

36

"And that's really what he said? It wasn't a mistake? All the people in that place were left-handed?"

"Apparently," she said, "they were all left-handed."

"It's the funniest thing I ever heard," he said. "I can't believe it."

Yes, she thought, perhaps it was a funny thing. Many left-handed people staying at one restaurant. A family, perhaps. But then there were many left-handed people in the world, and perhaps, for all you knew, their left was really right, and it was we, the right, who were wrong.

She took her mind back to the restaurant down in the town. There was another restaurant there, set in a sort of alley-way under two fig trees, where artisans filled most of the tables between noon and two o'clock, and where a fat white-smocked woman served all the dishes and still found time to try her three words of English on the engaged couple. From here they could see the lace-crowned Breton women clacking in the shade of the street trees and the small one-eyed train starting or ending its journey between the sea and the terminus that was simply the middle of the street. They liked this restaurant, but that day, wanting a change, they had climbed the steps into the upper town, to the level of the viaduct, and had found this small family restaurant where, at one table, all the knives were laid left-handed. For some reason she now sought to define, this left-handedness did not seem funny to her. Arthur had also eaten too many olives, picking them up with his fingers and gnawing them as she herself, as a child, would have gnawed an uncooked prune, and this did not seem very funny either. Somewhere between olives and left-handedness lay the source of her curious discontent. Perhaps she was left-handed herself? Left-handed people were, she had read somewhere, right-brained. Perhaps Arthur was left-handed?

She turned over in the heather, small brown-eyed face to the sun. "Don't you do anything left-handed?"

"Good gracious, no." He turned over too and lay face upwards, dark with sun, his mouth small-lipped under the stiff moustache she had not wanted him to grow. "You don't either?"

For the first time in her life she considered it. How many people, she thought, ever considered it? Thinking, she seemed to roll down a great slope, semi-swooning in the heat, before coming up again. Surprisingly, she had thought of several things.

"Now I come to think of it, I comb my hair left-handed. I always pick flowers left-handed. And I wear my watch on my left wrist."

He lifted steady, mocking eyes. "You sure you don't kiss left-handed?"

"That's not very funny!" she flashed.

It seemed to her that the moment of temper flashed up sky high, like a rocket, and fell far out to sea, soundless, dead by then, in the heat of the unruffled afternoon. She at once regretted it. For five days now they had lived on the Breton coast, and they now had five days more. Every morning, for five days, he had questioned her: "All right? Happy?" and every morning she had responded with automatic affirmations, believing it at first, then aware of doubt, then bewildered. Happiness, she wanted to say, was not something you could fetch out every morning after breakfast, like a clean handkerchief, or more still like a rabbit conjured out of the hat of everyday circumstances.

The hot, crushed-down sense of security she had felt all afternoon began suddenly to evaporate, burnt away from her by the first explosion of discontent and then by small restless flames of inward anger. She felt the growing sense of insecurity physically, feeling that at any moment she might slip off the solid headland into the sea. She suddenly felt a tremendous urge, impelled for some reason by fear, to walk as far back inland as she could go. The thought of the Atlantic far below, passive and yet magnetic, filled her with a sudden cold breath of vertigo.

"Let's walk," she said.

"Oh! no, it's too hot."

She turned her face into the dark sun-brittled heather. She caught the ticking of small insects, like infinitesimal watches. Far off, inland, the little train cut off, with its comic shriek, another section of afternoon.

In England he was a draper's assistant: chief assistant, sure to become manager. In imagination she saw the shop, sun-blinds down, August remnant sale now on, the dead little town now so foreign and far off and yet so intensely real to her, shown up by the disenchantment of distance. They had been engaged six months. She had been very thrilled about it at first, showing the ring all round, standing on a small pinnacle of joy, ready to leap into the tremendous spaces of marriage. Now she had suddenly the feeling that she was about to be sewn up in a blanket.

"Isn't there a castle," she said, "somewhere up the road past the estaminet?"

"Big house. Not castle."

"I thought I saw a notice," she said, "to the château."

"Big house," he said. "Did you see that film, 'The Big House'? All about men in prison."

What about women in prison? she wanted to say. In England she was a school-teacher, and there had been times when she felt that the pale green walls of the class-room had imprisoned her and that marriage, as it always did, would mean escape. Now left-handedness and olives and blankets and the stabbing heat of the Atlantic afternoon had succeeded, together, in inducing some queer stupor of semi-crazy melancholy that was far worse than this. Perhaps it was the wine, the sour red stuff of the *vin compris* notice down at the left-handed café? Perhaps, after all, it was only some large dose of self-pity induced by sun and the emptiness of the day?

She got to her feet. "Come on, m'sieu. We're going to the castle." She made a great effort to wrench herself up to the normal plane. "Castle, my beautiful. Two francs. All the way up to the castle, two francs." She held out her hand to pull him to his feet.

"I'll come," he said, "if we can stop at the estaminet and have a drink."

"We'll stop when we come down," she said.

"Now."

"When we come down."

"Now. I'm so thirsty. It was the olives."

Not speaking, she held out her hand. Instinctively, he put out his left.

"You see," she said, "you don't know what's what or which's which or anything. You don't know when you're left-handed or right."

He laughed. She felt suddenly like laughing too, and they began to walk down the hill. The fierce heat seemed itself to force them down the slope, and she felt driven by it past the blistered white tables of the estaminet with the fowls asleep underneath them, and then up the hill on the far side, into the sparse shade of small wind-levelled oaks and, at one place, a group of fruitless fig trees. It was some place like this, she thought, just about as hot and arid, where the Gadarene swine had stampeded down. What made her think of that? Her mind had some urge towards inconsequence, some inexplicable desire towards irresponsibility that she could not restrain or control, and she was glad to see the château at last, shining with sea-blue jalousies through a break in the mass of metallic summer-hard leaves of acacia and bay that surrounded it. She felt it to be something concrete, a barrier against which all the crazy irresponsibilities of the mind could hurl themselves and split.

At the corner, a hundred yards before the entrance gates, a notice, of which one end had been cracked off by a passing lorry, pointed upwards like a tilted telescope. They read the word "château," the rest of the name gone.

"You see," she said, "château."

"What château?"

"Just château."

"You think we'll have to pay to go in?"

"I'll pay," she said.

She walked on in silence, far away from him. The little insistences on money had become, in five days, like the action of many iron files on the soft tissues of her mind: first small and fine, then larger, then still larger, now large and coarse, brutal as stone. He kept a small note-book and in it, with painful system, entered up the expenditure of every centime.

At the entrance gates stood a lodge, very much dilapidated, the paintwork of the walls grey and sea-eroded like the sides of a derelict battleship. A small notice was nailed to the fence by the gate, and the girl stopped to read it.

"What does it say?" he said. "Do we pay to go in?"

"Just says it's an eighteenth-century château," she said. "Admission a franc. Shall we go in?"

"A franc?"

"One franc," she said. "Each."

"You go," he said. "I don't know that I'm keen. I'll stop outside."

She did not answer, but went to the gate and pulled the porter's bell. From the lodge door a woman without a blouse on put her head out, there was a smell of onions, and the woman turned on the machine of her French like a high pressure steam-pipe, scrawny neck dilating.

The girl pushed open the gate and paid the woman the two francs admission fee, holding a brief conversation with her. The high pressure pipe finally cut itself off and withdrew, and the girl came back to the gates and said: "She's supposed to show us round but she's just washing. She says nobody else ever comes up at this hour of the afternoon, and we must show ourselves round."

They walked up the gravel road between sea-stunted trees towards the château. In the sun, against the blue sky above the Atlantic, the stone and slate of it was burning.

"Well," she said, "what do you think of it?"

"Looks a bit like the bank at home," he said. "The one opposite our shop."

Château and sky and trees spun in the sunlight, whirling down to a momentary black vortex in which the girl found herself powerless to utter a word. She walked blindly on in silence. It was not until they stood under the château walls, and she looked up to see a great grape vine mapped out all across the south side, that she recovered herself and could speak. "It's just like the châteaux you see on wine bottles," she said. "I like it." "It doesn't look much to me," he said. "Where do we get in?" "Let's look round the outside first."

As they walked round the walls on the sun-bleached grass she could not speak or gather her impressions, but was struck only by the barren solitude of it all, the arid, typically French surroundings, with an air of fly-blownness and sun-weariness. To her amazement the place had no grandeur, and there were no flowers.

"There ought to be at least a bougainvillaea," she said.

"What's a bougainvillaea?"

Questioned, she found she did not know. She felt only that there ought to be a bougainvillaea. The word stood in her mind for the exotic, the south, white afternoons, the sea as seen from the top of just such châteaux as this. How this came to be she could not explain. The conscious part of herself stretched out arms and reached back, into time, and linked itself with some former incarnation of her present self, Louise Bowen, school-teacher, certificated, Standard V girls, engaged to Arthur Keller, chief assistant Moore's Drapery, sure to become manager, pin-stripe trousers, remnants madam, the voice like ruffled velvet, seventy-three pounds fifteen standing to credit at the post office, and in reaching back so far she felt suddenly that she could cry for the lost self, for the enviable incarnation so extraordinarily real and yet impossible, and for the yet not impossible existence, far back, in eternal bougainvillaea afternoons.

"Let's go inside," she said.

"How they make it pay," he said, "God only knows."

"It has long since," she said mysteriously, "paid for itself."

They found the main door and went in, stepping into the under-sea coldness of a large entrance hall. Now think that out, now think that out, now think that out. Her mind bubbling with bitterness, she looked up the great staircase, and all of a sudden the foreignness of her conscious self as against the familiarity of the self that had been was asserted again, but now with the sharp contrast of shadow and light. She put her hand on the staircase, the iron cool and familiar, and then began to walk up it, slowly but lightly, her hand drawn up easily, as though from some invisible iron pulley, far above her. She kept her eyes on the ceiling, feeling, without effort of thought, that she did not like and never had liked its mournful collection of cherubim painted in the gold wheel about the chandelier. For the first time that day, as she mounted the staircase and then went on beyond into the upstairs corridor, and into the panelled music-room with its air of having been imported as a complete back-cloth from some pink-and-gold theatre of the 'seventies, her body moved with its natural quietness, accustomed, infinitely light, and with a sense of the purest happiness. All this she could not explain and, as they went from music-room to other rooms, ceased to attempt to explain. Her bitterness evaporated in the confined coolness just as her security, outside on the hot headland, had evaporated in the blaze of afternoon. Now she seemed incontestably sure of herself, content in what she knew, without fuss—an unrepeatable moment of time.

She did not like the music-room but, as she expected, Arthur did. This pre-awareness of hers saved her from fresh bitterness. As part of her contentment, making it complete, she thought of him with momentary tenderness, quietly regretting what she had said and done, ready now to make up for it.

"Shall we go up higher," she said, "or down to the ground-floor again?"

"Let's do the climb first," he said.

To her, it did not matter, and climbing a second staircase they came, eventually, to a small turret room, unfurnished, with two jalousied windows looking across to the two worlds of France and the Atlantic.

She stood at the window overlooking the sea and looked out, as from a lighthouse, down on to the intense expanse of sea-light. Her mind had the profound placidity of the sea itself, a beautiful vacancy, milkily restful.

"Funny," Arthur said. "No ships. The Atlantic, and not a ship in sight."

"You wouldn't expect to see ships," she said, and knew that she was right.

Looking down from the other window they saw the headland, the brown-lilac expanse of heather, the minute peasants scribbled on the yellow rectangle of corn, the estaminet, the one-eyed station. And suddenly also, there was the white pop of steam inland, and the small comic shriek, now more than ever toylike, pricking the dead silence of afternoon.

"Look," he said, "there's the little train."

"Yes," she said, "there's the little train."

Her mind had the pure loftiness of the tower itself, above all irritation. She felt, as not before in her life, that she was herself. The knowledge of this re-incarnation was something she could not communicate, and half afraid that time or a word would break it up, she suggested suddenly that they should go down.

Arthur remained at the window a moment longer, admiring points of distance. "You'd never think," he said, "you could see so far."

"Yes you would," she called back.

Now think that out, now think that out, now think that out. Her mind, as she went downstairs, sprang contrarily upwards, on a scale of otherwise inexpressible delight. Arthur engaged her in conversation as they went downstairs, she on one flight, he on one above, calling down: "It may be all right, but the rates must be colossal. Besides, you'd burn a ton of coal a day in winter, trying to keep warm. A six-roomed house is bad enough, but think of this," but nothing could break, suppress or even touch her mood.

Downstairs she went straight into the great reception hall, and stood dumb. At that moment she suddenly felt that she had come as far as she must. Time had brought her to this split second of itself simply in order to pin her down. She stood like an insect transfixed.

Arthur came in: "What are you looking at?"

"The yellow cloth. Don't do anything. Just look at it. It's wonderful."

"I don't see anything very wonderful," he said.

At the end of the room, thrown over a chair, a large length of brocade, the colour of a half-ripe lemon, was like spilled honey against the grey French-coldness of walls and furniture. Instantaneously the girl saw it with eyes of familiarity, feeling it somehow to be the expression of herself, mood, past and future. She stood occupied with the entrancement of the moment, her eyes excluding the room, the day, Arthur and everything, her self drowned out of existence by the pure wash of watered fabric.

Suddenly Arthur moved into the room, and ten seconds later had the brocade in his hands. She saw him hold it up, measure it without knowing he measured it, feel its weight, thickness, value. She saw him suddenly as the eternal shopkeeper measuring out the eternal remnants of time: the small tape-measure of his mind like a white worm in the the precious expanse of her own existence.

"If you bought it to-day," Arthur called, "it would cost you every penny of thirty-five bob a yard."

"Let's go," she said.

Half a minute later she turned and walked out of the door, Arthur following, and then past the wind-stunted trees and on down the road, past the estaminet. It was now herself who walked, Louise Bowen, Standard V girls, certificated, deduct so much for superannuation scheme, tired as after a long day in the crowded chalk-smelling class-room. As they passed the estaminet, the place looked more fly-blown and deserted than ever, and they decided to go on to the station, and get a drink there while waiting for the train. As they passed the fig trees her mind tried to grasp again at the thought of the Gadarene swine, her mood blasted into the same barrenness as the tree in the parable.

"Well, you can have your château," Arthur said. "But I've got my mind on one of those houses Sparkes is putting up on Park Avenue. Sixteen and fourpence a week, no deposit, over twenty years. That's in front of any château."

She saw the houses as he spoke, red and white, white and red, millions of them, one like another, sixteen and fourpence a week, no deposit, stretching out to the ends of the earth. She saw herself in them, the constant and never-changing material of her life cut up by a pair of draper's scissors, the day ticketed, the years fretted by the counting up of farthings and all the endlessly incalculable moods of boredom.

"Two coffees please."

At the little station café they sat at one of the outside tables and waited for the train.

"Well, we've been to the château and never found out its name," he said.

"It ought to be Château Bougainvillaea."

"That's silly," he said. "You don't even know what a bougainvillaea is."

She sat stirring the grey coffee. She could feel the sun burning the white iron table and her hands. She looked up at the château, seeing the windows of the turret above the trees.

"Now we can see the château," she said, "as we should have seen ourselves if we'd been sitting down here when—"

It was beyond her, and she broke off.

"What?" he said.

"I didn't mean that," she said.

"What did you mean?"

"I don't know."

"Well, in future," he said, "mind you say what you mean."

The future? She sat silent. Inland the approaching train made its comic little whistle, cutting off another section of the afternoon.

And hearing it, she knew suddenly that the future was already a thing of the past.

THE DISINHERITED

On that station we had pilots from all over the world, so that the sound of the mess, as someone said, was like a Russian bazaar. They came from Holland and Poland, Belgium and Czechoslovakia, France and Norway. We had many French and they had with them brown and yellow men from the Colonial Empire who at dispersal on warm spring afternoons played strange games with pennies in the dry, white dust on the edge of the perimeter. We had many Canadians and New Zealanders, Australians and Africans. There was a West Indian boy, the colour of milky coffee, who was a barrister, and a Lithuanian who played international football. There was a man from Indo-China and another from Tahiti. There was an American and a Swiss and there were Negroes, very black and curly, among the ground-crews. We had men who had done everything and been everywhere, who had had everything and had lost it all. They had escaped across frontiers and over mountains and down the river valleys of Central Europe; they had come through Libya and Iran and Turkey and round the Cape; they had come through Spain and Portugal or nailed under the planks of little ships wherever a little ship could put safely to sea. They had things in common with themselves that men had nowhere else on earth, and you saw on their faces sometimes a look of sombre silence that could only have been the expression of recollected hatred. But among them all there was only one who had something which no one else had, and he was Capek the Czech. Capek had white hair.

Capek was a night fighter pilot, so that mostly in the daytime you would find him in the hut at dispersal. The hut was very pleasant and there was a walnut piano and a radio and a miniature billiard table and easy chairs that had been presented by the mayor of the local town. No one ever played the piano but it was charming all the same. On the walls there were pictures, some in colour, of girls in their underwear and without underwear at all, and rude remarks about pilots who forgot to check their guns. Pilots who had been flying at night lay on the camp-beds, sleeping a little, their eyes puffed, using their flying jackets as pillows; or they played cards and groused and talked shop among themselves. They were bored because they were flying too much. They argued about the merits of a four-cannon job as opposed to those of a single gun that fires through the airscrew. They argued about the climate of New Zealand, if it could be compared with the climate of England. They were restless and temperamental, as fighter pilots are apt to be, and it seemed always as if they would have been happier doing anything but the things they were.

Capek alone did not do these things. He did not seem bored or irritable, or tired or temperamental. He did not play billiards and he did not seem interested in the bodies of the girls on the walls. He was never asleep on the beds. He never played cards or argued about the merits of this or that. It seemed sometimes as if he did not belong to us. He sat apart from us, and with his white hair, cultured brown face, clean fine lips and the dark spectacles he wore sometimes against the bright spring sunlight he looked something like a middle-aged provincial professor who had come to take a cure at a health resort in the sun. Seeing him in the street, the bus, the train or the tram, you would never have guessed that he could fly. You would never have guessed that in order to be one of us, to fly with us and fight with us, Capek had come half across the world.

There was a time when a very distinguished personage came to the station and, seeing Capek, asked how long he had been in the Air Force and Capek replied "Please, seventeen years." This took his flying life far back beyond the beginning of the war we were fighting; back to the years when some of us were hardly born and when Czechoslovakia had become born again as a nation. Capek had remained in the Air Force all those years, flying heaven knows what types of plane, and becoming finally part of the forces that crumbled away and disintegrated and disappeared under the progress of the tanks that entered Prague in the summer of 1939. Against this progress Capek was one of those who disappeared. He disappeared in a lorry with many others and they rode eastward towards Poland, always retreating and not knowing where they were going. With Capek was a man named Machakek, and as the retreat went on Capek and Machakek became friends.

Capek and Machakek stayed in Poland all that summer, until the chaos of September. It is not easy to know what Capek and Machakek did; if they were interned, or how, or where, because Capek's English is composed of small difficult words and long difficult silences, often broken only by smiles. "All time is retreat. Then war start. Poland is in war. Then Germany is coming one way and Russia is coming another." In this way Capek and Machakek had no escape. They could go neither east nor west. It was too late to go south, and in the north Gdynia had gone. And in time, as Germany moved eastward and Russia westward, Capek and Machakek were taken by the Russians. Capek went to a concentration camp, and Machakek worked in the mines. As prisoners they had a status not easy to define. Russia was not then in the war and Czechoslovakia, politically, did not exist. It seemed in these days as if Russia might come into the war against us. It was very confused and during the period of clarification, if you could call it that, Capek and Machakek went on working in the concentration camp and the mine. "We remain," Capek said, "one year and three-quarter."

Then the war clarified and finally Capek was out of the concentration camp and Machakek was out of the mine. They were together again, still friends, and they moved south, to the Black Sea. Standing on the perimeter track, in the bright spring sun, wearing his dark spectacles, Capek had so little to say about this that he looked exactly like a blind man who has arrived somewhere, after a long time, but for whom the journey is darkness. "From Black Sea I go to Turkey. Turkey then to Syria. Then Cairo. Then Aden."

"And Machakek with you?"

"Machakek with me, yes. But only to Aden. After Aden Machakek is going to Bombay on one boat. I am going to Cape Town on other."

"So Machakek went to India?"

"To India, yes. Is very long way. Is very long time."

"And you—Cape Town?"

"Yes, me, Cape Town. Then Gibraltar. Then here, England."

"And Machakek?"

"Machakek is here too. We are both post here. To this squadron."

The silence that followed this had nothing to do with the past; it had much to do with the present; more to do with Machakek. Through the retreat and the mine and the concentration camp, through the journey to Turkey and Cairo and Aden, through the long sea journey to India and Africa, and finally England, Capek and Machakek had been friends. When a man speaks only the small words of a language that is not his own he finds it hard to express the half-tones of hardship and relief and suffering and most of what Capek and Machakek had suffered together was in Capek's white hair. But now something had happened which was not expressed there but which lay in the dark, wild eyes behind the glasses and the long silences of

Capek as he sat staring at the Hurricanes in the sun. His friend Machakek was dead.

The handling of night fighters is not easy. It was perhaps hard for Capek and Machakek that they should come out of the darkness of Czechoslovakia, through the darkness of the concentration camp and the mine, in order to fight in darkness. It was hard for Machakek who, over-shooting the drome, hit a telegraph post and died before Capek could get there. It was harder still for Capek, who was now alone.

But the hardest part of it all, perhaps, is that Capek cannot talk to us. He does not know words that will express what he feels about the end of Machakek's journey. He does not know words like endurance and determination, imperishable and undefeated, sacrifice, and honour. They are the words, anyway, that are never mentioned at dispersals. He does not know the words for grief and friendship, homesickness and loss. They are never mentioned at dispersals either. Above all he does not know the words for himself and what he has done.

I do not know the words for Capek either. Looking at his white hair, his dark eyes and his long hands, I am silent now.

THE GREATEST PEOPLE IN THE WORLD

He was very young, and because he was also very fair, he sometimes looked too young to have any part in the war at all; and more than anything else, as always, he wanted to fly.

It was his fairness that made him look so very much like one of the aristocracy, or at least very upper middle class, and I was very surprised to find that his people were labourers from a village in Somerset. His father was a hedger and ditcher with a fancy for leaving little tufts of hawthorn unclipped above the line of hedge. These tufts would grow into little ornamental balls, and later were clipped, gradually, summer by summer, into the shapes of birds. His father hoped, Lawson would explain to me, that bullfinches would use them for nesting-places. I never met either his father or his mother, but I gathered that they must have been at least forty when he was born. I gathered too that his mother cleaned at the local rectory and that she worked in the fields, harvesting and haymaking and pea-picking and cabbage-planting, whenever she had the chance or the time.

It was not only that Lawson wanted to fly. He had never wanted to do anything else but fly. It was the only life he had had time to know. There must have been thousands of young men like him, all reading the technicalities of the job in flight magazines, all passionately studying new designs, all longing for a flip, all flying Spitfires in imagination. But there were certain circumstances which made the case of Lawson different.

The chief of these circumstances, and the one which was in fact never altered, was that his parents were poor. When Lawson heard other people with incomes of five or six hundred or more a year talking of having no money he thought of his parents. His father knocked up a regular wage of two pounds a week. In summer he managed to increase this by ten or twelve shillings by gardening in the evenings and his mother put in a weekly average of about sixteen hours at sixpence an hour at the rectory. As a boy, Lawson went harvesting and haymaking for about sixpence a day and doing odd jobs on Saturdays in the rectory kitchen. And somehow, out of this, they bought him an education.

I don't know who was at the back of this idea of education. It may have been the rector. Most likely it was the rector and the mother. Lawson's father, I gathered, was a solid, unimaginative man who was rather content to let things remain as they were. He worked hard for three hundred and sixty-two days of the year—he tended his own garden on Sundays—and then got roaring tight on Christmas Eve, Flower Show Saturday, and the local Easter Monday races. It obviously wasn't he who had the idea of education, yet once the idea had been conceived he was behind it wholly and with all the solidity of his nature. For two years he and the mother saved up every extra penny they earned; every pea picked, every potato picked up, every forkful of hay turned over was something extra to the account. The house where they lived was old and damp, with unplastered walls and a brick floor and cracks in the window-frames that were stuffed with paper. The only light they had was a little oil lamp which they carried from room to room if they wanted a light in another place. They bought half a hundred-weight of coal each week and on Friday afternoons the mother wetted the last shovelful of coal and banked up the fire so that it would last till evening.

When Lawson was fourteen they were able to send him to the local grammar school. Or at least they were going to send him. Everything was arranged for him to start in September when one of those little accidents happened that often greatly affect the course of people's lives. Lawson fell off a bridge and broke his left arm. By the time it was better the vacancies in the first school were filled and he was sent instead to a school about fifteen miles away. He travelled there every day by train.

It was at this school that he heard the remark that was to affect, and crystallize, his whole life. The third term he was there, within a week or so of his fifteenth birthday, he heard a lecture in the school hall on the work of the R.A.F. When the lecture began, he told me, he really wasn't very interested. When he came out he could not get out of his mind something the lecturer had said about those who fly. "I often think," the lecturer said, "that they are the greatest people in the world."

When I knew Lawson the war was two years old. He had graduated rather uneventfully in the usual way, up through Moths and Ansons and so to light bombers, until now he was captain of a Stirling. There was even then a kind of premature immobility about him, especially about his eyes, so that the pupils sometimes looked seared, cauterized, burnt out. His first

trouble was to have been made a bomber pilot at all. He had been through
the usual Spitfire complex; all roaring glory and victory rolls. The thought
of long flights of endurance, at night, with nothing to be seen except the flak
coming up at you in slow sinister curls, the earth in the light of a flare, and
then the flare-path at base if you were lucky and the fog hadn't come down,
shook him quite a lot. It may have been this that accounted for what happened afterwards.

He stayed at school until he was eighteen, and had virtually walked
straight out of school into the Air Force. What struck me most was that
there was no disruption, no disloyalty, between himself and his parents.
There might well have been. Their life, simple, bound to earth, lighted by
that cheap paraffin lamp which they carried from room to room, compressed into the simple measure of hard work, saving, and devotion, was like
the life of another age compared with the life they had chosen for him. I
don't know what education exactly meant to them; I don't know what
ambitions they had for him. But neither could have been connected with his
flying a bomber. Yet they never uttered the smallest reproach or protest to
what must have been rather a terrifying prospect to them. They might have
thought that it would be better for him to be ploughing his own good
Somerset clay. They probably did. But if they did they didn't once say so.
They simply knew he wanted to fly and they let him fly because it was the
thing that was nearest his heart.

His own part was just as straightforward and steadfast. As I became
acquainted with it I didn't wonder at all that he had been made a bomber
pilot. The qualities for it were all there in his behaviour towards these two
simple, self-sacrificial people. They had sent him to a pretty expensive
school—to them it must have been fabulous—and he might easily have
turned his back on them. A touch of swollen head and he might easily have
decided that he was too good for that shabby little cottage, with the unplastered walls, the windows stuffed with paper, and the one cheap paraffin
lamp carried from room to room. But I don't suppose he ever dreamed of
it. He not only remained loyal to them but loyal in a positive way. He sent
home to them a third of his pay every month: which for a Pilot Officer
meant practically the same sacrifice as they had made for him.

He couldn't in fact have been more steadfast and careful. Perhaps he was
too steadfast and, if it's possible as the captain of a crew of seven in a very
expensive piece of aircraft, too careful. Yet nothing went right for him.
Before his first big trip with a Stirling he felt the same dry mental tension,

and the same sour wet slackness of the stomach, that you feel before a race. It was a sort of cold excitement. He felt it get worse as he taxied the aircraft across the field. It was winter and there was a kind of smokiness in the falling twilight over the few distant trees, and the hangars, looming up with their red lights burning, looked enormous. The runway seemed foreshortened and it looked practically impossible not to prang something on take-off. He was certain it would be all right once he was up, but it was the idea of lugging thirty-two tons of aircraft off the wet runway, that was soft in places, and in half-light, which worried him.

He was worked up to a very high state of tension, with the kite actually on the runway, when Control informed him that the whole show would be scrubbed. His crew swore and mouthed at everybody and everything all the way back to dispersal. He felt too empty to say anything. He felt as if his stomach had dropped out and that he might be going to pieces. The awful anti-climax of the thing was too much.

That night he didn't sleep very well. He fell asleep and then woke up. His blankets had slipped and he was very cold and he did not know what time it was. He could hear his watch ticking very loudly. Someone had left a light on in the passage outside and it shone through the fan-light of the bedroom door. He lay for hours watching it, sleepless, cold, his mind full of the impression of the wet runway, the hangars looming up in the twilight, the idea that he was about to prang something on take-off.

Then he fell asleep and dreamed that he really did prang something. He was taking off and his port wing hit the control tower, which had wide, deep, circular windows. Through these windows he could see Brand, the control officer, and a little Flying Officer named Danvers, and the two orderlies, one wearing earphones. The two officers were drinking tea and his wing knocked the cups out of their hands. The tea shot up in a brown wave that broke on Brand's tunic, and he saw vividly the look of helpless and terrified indignation on Brand's face a second before he was hit and died.

It was fantastic, but very real also, and he woke in a terrible sweat of fear, scared solely by the happenings of the dream. He was relieved to find it a waking dream; that it was already daylight beyond the drawn curtains. It was in fact already late and he got up hurriedly and went down to breakfast without shaving. After breakfast he went straight over to the hangars and hoped there would be flying that day. But the weather was worse: grey fenland distances, gathering ground mist, spits of cold rain. The Wing Commander usually got the crews running round the perimeter track for training, but that morning the weather was too bad, there was no running and by eleven o'clock the crews were fretting for an afternoon stand-down. Lawson went over to his aircraft, but everything was nicely fixed there and his stooges were sheltering under the wings, out of the rain, smoking. As he walked back in the rain to Control and went up the concrete stairs to the room where, in his dream, he had crashed through the wide windows and had killed Brand and Danvers, he saw at once that Brand and Danvers were not on duty, and by this fact, the fact that Brand and Danvers had been on duty at the time of the dream, he felt the reality of the dream grow brighter instead of fade.

After he had had the orderly bring him a cup of tea he drank it quickly and then went out alone. The trouble was perhaps that he was at that time a stranger in the station. There was no one—and it must have been better if there had been someone—to whom he could say, joking: "Had a hell of a queer dream last night. Dreamt I pranged the control tower. Brand was stooging around as usual and got it in the neck. He looked pretty damned funny when I knocked the tea out of his hands." But he knew no one very well, and could say nothing about the dream. It was like a complex personal problem. Once you had explained it to someone else it was no longer personal; it ceased to be complex and finally it ceased to be a problem at all.

Unfortunately he could not do this, and unfortunately there was a recurrence of the dream that night. It was the same dream precisely, with one important exception. It was now not Brand or Danvers who were killed, but two men named Porter and Evans, the duty officers for that night. The painful brightness of the dream was identical; he could see the brown tea steaming as it splashed on Porter's jacket and he could see on his face, as on Brand's face, the indignant, ridiculous terror.

The next morning the weather was much better, and by noon it was certain there would be ops. that night. At briefing he felt much as if he had a hangover. He concentrated hard on the met. talk, but his head ached and the green and pink and mauve contour lines of the map troubled his eyes. The target was Hamburg, a fairly long hard trip, and his own take-off was at 18:00 hours. By the time he reached his aircraft the light was no longer good, but there was no mist and only thin cloud in a wasting blue sky. For some reason he now felt better: clearer-headed, quite confident. His stomach was dry and tight and the period of distrust in himself was practically over.

Then something else happened. His outer port engine would not start. As he sat there in the aircraft, struggling to get things going, his crew on edge, his engineer bewildered and furious by this inexplicable behaviour of an engine that had been tested only that morning, he felt his confidence breaking down again. The light was dying rapidly on the fringes of the field and he knew what must happen any moment now. "It's just one of these bloody damn things," the engineer said over and over again. "Just one of these damn bloody aggravating bastard things." Some minutes later Lawson, not listening much now to the engineer, heard what he expected to hear from Control. The trip was off; the margin of time was past. "Is it understood?" said Control in the voice of an ironical automatic parrot. "Is it understood?"

After this second disappointment he went through the same nervous agony of not sleeping. Because the breaking of tension at a vital moment was the cause in both cases you might have said he was trying too hard. But the third occasion seemed to have nothing to do with this. He was again on operations, and again it was evening, with the fringes of the drome blue-grey with winter mist, the runway pooled with water, the red lights like beacons on the black mountains of the hangars. This time he actually got up off the runway. He had actually got over the sickening horror that for the third time running some damnable triviality would stop him from getting the kite airborne. But soon that was past, and he was following the others. The sun had already set, leaving huge cloud-broken lakes of pale green and yellow light for miles above the sunset point, and towards these immense spaces of rapidly fading light he watched the black wings of the Stirlings fading into the distance until at last it was too dark and the lakes of light and the planes were no longer there to see. Then for the first time for weeks he felt good: strained but calm, sure of himself, settled.

I suppose they had been flying about an hour when the icing began. They were over the sea when the kite began to make sickening and heavy plunges in the darkness: movements to which there was only one answer. Lawson felt suddenly up against all the old trouble again: the inexplicable bad luck, the frustration, the disastrous break of tension. He felt himself lose heart. His guts became wet and cold and sour and then seemed to drop out of him. His only piece of luck was that he had not flown far, and when he had safely jettisoned his bombs and turned the kite for home he bitterly told himself that it was the only piece of luck he had ever had as a pilot or was ever likely to have. But even that was not all. As he came into land it was as if there were some evil and persistent Jonah in the kite with him: somebody for whom the simplest moments were inexplicably turned into pieces of hellish and ironical misfortune. Lawson landed perfectly in the darkness, but the runway was wet and greasy after rain. He put on the brakes, but nothing happened. The kite drove fast down the runway and then skidded into a ground loop that brought it to a standstill on the grass, the undercarriage smashed. To Lawson it was like the end of everything.

He expected to be grounded any moment after that. His despair was sour and keen and personal; he could tell no one about it. For about a week he did not sleep much. He did not dream either. He re-created the few moments of ill-luck until they were moments of positive and monstrous failure. And as if this were not enough he created new moments, sharp and terrible seconds of stalling, ground-looping, crash-landing, overshooting the drome. He imagined himself coming in too slow, another time too fast. It never mattered much. He was going to prang the control tower in any case, killing the occupants there as they drank their last oversweetened steaming tea.

Then by accident he discovered it possible to get some sleep. He began to sleep with the light on. The Station at that time was not very crowded; later two and even three people slept in a room. But now no one could see him giving way—not that he was ever the only one—to the fear of sleeping in the dark. In this way he slept quite well for about a week; it was fairly peaceful; he was not cold; he did not have the recurrent dream. And above all, they did not ground him.

I don't know if they were ever thinking of it; but it never in fact became necessary. Another thing happened: this time not just ill-luck, frustration, a mistake, a private illusion about something, but a simple and terrible fact. It was a telegram from the Rectory of his village in Somerset. His parents had been killed in a raid.

After that telegram he got compassionate leave and went home. The next morning he stood in the garden of the house, staring at the bony, burnt roof timbers, the red-grey dust and rubble, the bare scorched blue wall-paper, of the two rooms where the cheap little paraffin lamp had once been carried to and fro. It was winter time. Red dust lay on the frozen leaves of the brussels sprouts; the hawthorn twigs, fancifully clipped by his father above the line of hedge, were almost the only things about the place that remained untouched and as before. He did not stay very long; but while he stayed there he thought he saw his mother working in the fields, skirt pinned behind her, and his father with the hedge-hook in his hand and the black twigs flying in the air. He saw for a moment their lives with the simple clearness of grief, the lives remote from his own, so utterly simple and so utterly remote, yet bound to him elementally.

When he went back to the station three days later, he had forgotten about the dreams, the illusions, and all the rest of it; or at least it was as if he had forgotten. All the reality of the bad moments, if it had been reality, was now obscured by the simple reality of the dusty and fire-blackened little house.

All that he had to do now seemed also quite simple and clear; terribly simple and terribly clear. If he ever had been afraid, there was no longer any sign of it as he took off for a daylight raid over Northern Germany two days later. It was a cold, clear winter afternoon; there was just enough power in the sunlight to reveal the colours of the fields. He used to say it was one of those trips where you felt the aircraft had been shot from a gun. You got away clean and smooth and easy; there was no hitch. Instinctively, from the first, you knew it was a piece of cake. You went over and did the job and no matter what came up at you you knew that, ultimately, it would be all right. That afternoon flak tore a strip off his flaps and for about half an hour his crew did nothing but yell gloriously through the intercom that fighters were coming up from everywhere. Cannon fire hit his middle turret and put it out of action and sprayed the fuselage from end to end with raw ugly little holes. Inland over Germany he lost a lot of height chasing and finally shooting down an Me. 109, and he discovered he could not regain his height as he came back over the coast and sea. But even that did not trouble him then. Everything was clear at last. His whole life was clear.

He came over the English coast and then the English fields, at about two or three hundred feet. The sun was still shining, but sometimes there were clouds and then it was light in patches on the fields below and dark in the upper air. He roared over fields and woods and roads and over the little dusty blue towns and over remote farms where he could even see the hens feeding and scuttling in the dark winter grass.

He came so low once that for a second or so he saw people in the fields. For an instant he saw a man and woman working. They raised flat, astonished faces to look at the great plane overhead. The woman perhaps was picking sticks and he thought he saw the man lean for a moment on a fork. They might have been old or young, he could not tell; they lifted their heads and in a second were cut off by the speed of the plane. But in this second, as he saw them transfixed on the earth below him and before the speed of the plane cut them off for ever, he remembered his own people. He remembered them as they lived, simple and sacrificing, living only for him, and he saw them alive again in the arrested figures of the two people in the field below: as if they were the same people, the same simple people, the same humble, faithful, eternal people, giving always and giving everything: the greatest people in the world.

THE MAJOR OF HUSSARS

That summer we lived in the hotel on the lake below the mountains, and Major Martineau, the Major of Hussars, lived on the floor below us, in a room with a eucalyptus tree on the balcony.

The weather was very hot and in the sunlight the lake sparkled like crusty golden glass and in the late afternoon the peaks of the Blümlisalp and the whole range about the Jungfrau glistened in the fine mountain air with fiery rosy snow. The major was very interested in the mountains, and we in turn were very interested in the major, a spare spruce man of nearly sixty who wore light shantung summer suits and was very studious of his appearance generally, and very specially of his smooth grey hair. He also had three sets of false teeth, of which he was very proud: one for mornings, one for evenings, and one for afternoons.

We used to meet the major everywhere: on the terrace, where lunch was served under a long pergola of crimson and yellow roses, and from which you got a magnificent view of the snow caps; and then under the dark shade of chestnut trees on the lake edge, where coffee was served; and then at the tram terminus, where the small yellow trams started their journeys along the hot road by the lake; and then on the white steamers that came up and down the lake, calling at all the little towns with proud peeps of the funnel whistle, several times a day. At all of these places there was the major, very spruce in cool shantung and always wearing the correct set of false teeth for the time of day, looking very correct, very English, and, we thought, very alone.

It must have been at the second or third of these meetings that he told us of his wife. "She'll be out from England any day now." And at the fifth or sixth that he told us of his false teeth. "After all, one has several suits. One has several pairs of shoes. All excellent for rest and change. Why not different sets of teeth?" It did not occur to me then that the teeth and his wife had anything to do with each other.

Sometimes as we walked along the lake we could see a figure marching briskly towards us in the distance.

"The major," I would say.

"It can't be," my wife would say. "It looks much too young."

But always, as he came nearer, we could see that it was the major, sparkling and smart and spruce with all the shine and energy of a younger man. "Sometimes you'd take him for a man of forty," my wife would say.

Whenever we met on these occasions we would talk briefly of the major's wife; then of the lake, the food, the delicious summer weather, the alpine flowers, the snow on the mountains and how we loved Switzerland. The major was very fond of them all and we got the impression, gradually, that his wife was very fond of them too.

"Ah!" he would say, "she will adore all this. She will simply adore it." His correct blue eyes would sparkle delightfully.

"And when do you expect her?"

"Well," he would say, "in point of fact she was to have been here this week. But there seems to have been some sort of hitch somewhere. Bad staff work."

"I hope she'll soon be able to come."

"Oh! any day now."

"Good. And oh! by the way," I said, "have you been up to the Jungfrau yet? The flowers are very lovely now on the way up."

"The Virgin?" the major said. "Oh! not yet. I'm leaving all the conquest of that sort of thing till my wife gets here," and he would laugh very heartily at the joke he made.

"It's just as well," I said.

But the next day, on the steamer, we saw the major making a conquest of the girl who brought the coffee. She had a beautiful Swiss head, with dark coiled hair, and she was wearing a very virginal Bernese bodice in black and white and a skirt striped in pink and blue. She was very young and she laughed very much at whatever it was the major was saying to her. On the voyage the major drank eight cups of coffee and ate four ham rolls. There was so much ham in the rolls that it hung over the side like spaniel's ears, and the major had a wonderful time with his afternoon false teeth, his best pair, champing it in.

"The major is conquering the Jungfrau," I said.

"You take a very low view of life," my wife said. "He's alone and he's simply being friendly."

"Queer how he doesn't notice us to-day."

The major, in fact, did not notice us; he did not notice us in fact for two days, and I wondered if I had said something to offend him. But when at last we met him again under the chestnut trees at noon, with a glass of lager at his table in the shade, he seemed more friendly, more sparkling and more cheerful than ever. The yellow beer, the light shantung suit and the gleaming white teeth were all alight with the trembling silver reflections that sprang from the sunlight on the water.

"Any news of your wife?" we said.

"Coming to-day!"

We said we were very pleased. "What time?"

"Coming by the afternoon boat. Gets in at three."

He looked at the lake, the roses on the terrace, the blue-grey eucalyptus tree shining on the balcony of his room and then at the vast snows towering and glistening beyond the lake. "I can't tell you how she will adore all this," he said. "I can't tell you."

"I'm sure she will," we said. "You must be very excited."

"Just like a kid with a toy!" he said. "You see, I came out first to arrange it all. Choose the place. Choose the hotel. Choose everything. She doesn't know what she's coming to. You see? It's all going to be a great surprise for her."

"Don't forget you have to conquer the Jungfrau," I said. "The soldanella are wonderful above the Scheidegg now."

"Of course," he said. "Well, I must go. Perhaps you'd join us for an *apéritif* about six? I do very much want you to meet her."

We said we should be delighted and he went singing away up to the hotel.

"Your remark about the Jungfrau was very pointed," my wife said.

"I saved it with the soldanella," I said.

"Anyway," she said, "be careful what you say to-night."

From the lower terrace we could watch the steamers come and go. The afternoon was very hot and we stayed under the dark shade of the chestnut trees to watch the three o'clock boat come in. Among the hotel porters with their green and plum-coloured and scarlet and brown caps and uniforms the major stood out, in cool spruce shantung, as a very English, very conspicuous visitor on the quay.

When the white steamer came up the lake at last, tooting in the hot afternoon air, the major had taken up his stand in front of all the porters, by the water's edge. I got up and leaned on the railings of the terrace to get a better view.

The steamer came swinging in with a ring of engine-room bells, with six or seven passengers waiting by the gangway.

"There she is," I said.

"Where?" My wife had come to stand beside me.

"The lady with the green case," I said. "Standing by the captain. She looks about the major's age and about as English."

"She looks rather nice—yes," my wife said, "it could be."

The steamer bounced lightly against the quay and the gangway came down. The hotel porters adjusted their caps and the passengers began to come ashore. In his eagerness the major almost blocked the gangway.

To my astonishment the lady with the green case came down the gangway and went straight past the major, and the porter from the *Hôtel du Lac* raised his green and gold cap and took the case away from her. The major was looking anxiously up the gangway for the figure of his wife, but in less than two minutes all the passengers had come down. When the steamer moved away again the major was standing on the quay alone, still staring anxiously and still waiting for the wife who had not come.

That evening we went down to the terrace for the *apéritif* with the major. "For goodness sake don't make that joke about the Jungfrau," my wife said. "He'll be in no mood for that." The five o'clock steamer had come in, but the major's wife had not arrived.

"It's his joke," I said. "Not mine."

"You twist it round," she said.

On the terrace the major, dressed in a dark grey suit and with his evening false teeth in, had a surprising appearance of ebullient gaiety. He had a peculiar taste in drinks and drank four or five glasses of Kirsch because there was no whisky and after it he did not seem so tired.

"Met a friend in Paris," he explained to us. "Amazing coincidence." He kept waving a rather long telegram about in front of us. "Hadn't seen this friend for years, and then suddenly ran into her. Of course, it's only a night. She'll be here on Thursday."

Three weeks went past, but the major's wife did not arrive. The best of the roses by that time were over on the terrace and long salmon-scarlet lines of geraniums were blooming there instead. In the beds behind the chestnut trees there were purple petunias with interplantings of cherry-pie and in the hot still evenings the scent of them was delicious against the cool night odour of water. "It's a pity for her to be missing all this," we said.

Now when we met the major we avoided the subject of his wife. We went on several excursions to the mountains and sometimes on the steamers the major was to be seen on the first-class deck champing with his false teeth at the spaniel-eared ham sandwiches and drinking many cups of coffee. As he talked to the Swiss girl who served him he laughed quite often. But I did not think he laughed so much. I thought in a way he seemed not only less happy and less laughing, but more alone. He had stopped making explanations, and I thought he seemed like a man who had given up hoping.

And then it all began again. This time she was really coming. There had really been some awful business of a hold-up about her visa. It had taken a long time. It was all over now.

"She'll be here on Sunday," the major said. "Absolutely certain to be on the boat that gets in at three."

The Sunday steamers were always crowded, their decks gay with Swiss families going up the lake for the day, with tourists going to Interlaken. The little landing stages at the lakeside resorts were always crowded too. There were many straw hats and Bernese bodices and much raising of caps by hotel porters.

So when the steamer arrived this time there was no picking out Mrs. Martineau. Crowds of Sunday holiday-makers stood on the steamer deck and pushed down the gangway and more crowds stood on the quay waiting to go on board. Under the trimmed lime trees of the quayside restaurant the Sunday orchestra was playing, and people at little gay white tables were drinking wine and coffee. It was a very simple, very laughing, very bourgeois, very noisy afternoon.

On the quay the major waited in his bright shantung suit, with his best teeth in.

"There she is," I said.

"You said that last time," my wife said.

"You can see her waving, and the major is waving back."

"Several people are waving."

"The lady in the grey costume," I said. "Not the one with the sun-glasses. The one waving the newspaper."

At the steamer rails an amiable, greyish English-woman of sixty was waving in a nice undemonstrative sort of way to someone on shore. Each time she waved I thought the major waved back.

"Anyway," my wife said, "let's go round and meet her."

We walked up through the hotel gardens and across the bridge over the stream that came down and fed the lake with green snow-water from the mountains. It was very hot. The sun-blinds in the hotel were like squares of red and white sugar candy in the sun, and in the hot scented gardens under the high white walls almost the only thing that seemed cool was the grey eucalyptus tree growing on the balcony of the major's room. I had always rather envied the major the eucalyptus tree. Even the steamer whistle seemed stifled as it peeped the boat away.

"Now mind what you say," my wife said. "No references to any Jungfrau."

"If she's that very English lady with the newspaper I shall like her," I said.

Just at that moment we turned the corner of the kiosk that sold magazines and postcards of alpine flowers, and the lady with the newspaper went past us, arm in arm with another English lady carrying a wine-red parasol.

My wife did not take advantage of this situation. At that moment she became, like me, quite speechless.

Up from the landing-stage the major was coming towards us with his wife. She staggered us. She was a black-haired girl of twenty-five, wearing a very smart summer suit of white linen with scarlet cuffs and revers, with lipstick of the same colour. I do not know what it was about her, but even from that distance I could tell by the way she walked, slightly apart from the major and with her head up, that she was blazingly angry.

"A Jungfrau indeed," I said.

"Be quiet!" my wife said. "They're here."

A moment or two later we were face to face with them. The major had lost his habitual cool spruceness, I thought, and looked harassed and upset about something and seemed as if he would have gone past us, if possible, without speaking.

Instead, he stopped and raised his hat. His manners were always very correct and charming, and now they seemed painfully so.

"May I present Mrs. Martineau?" he said.

Across the narrow roadway the orchestra on the restaurant terrace was playing at full blast, with sour-sharp violins and a stinging trumpet. Mingled with the noise came the sound of guitars played on the steamer as it drew away.

We both shook hands with Mrs. Martineau and said we were glad to meet her. She smiled at us in a politely savage sort of way and the major said:

"Had an exhausting journey. Going to get her some tea and let her lie down."

"Not exhausting, darling," she said. "Just tiresome."

"I thought you said you were exhausted, dear."

"I did not say I was exhausted. I am not exhausted."

"Sorry, dear, I thought you did."

"You shouldn't think," she said. "I am not exhausted. The last thing I am is exhausted."

I could see by the way she looked over her shoulder at the restaurant orchestra that she already hated the place.

"Perhaps you will join us this evening for an *apéritif?*" the major said.

We said we should be delighted, but Mrs. Martineau did not speak, and together, walking apart, she and the major went on to the hotel.

"Oh! dear," I said.

"You sum people up so quickly," my wife said. "Too quickly."

"I didn't say a word."

"Then what was behind that oh! dear?"

"She makes up too much," I said.

I really didn't know what lay behind that oh! dear. It may have been that Mrs. Martineau was very tired; it may have been that she was one of those women who, though young, get fretful and unsociable and angered by the trials of a journey alone; it may have been that she was a person of sensitive temperament and ear who could not bear without pain the terrace orchestras of Swiss Sunday afternoons. I did not know. I only knew that she was less than half the major's age and that the major, when he walked beside her, looked like a sorrowful old dog that had just been beaten.

"They didn't say any time for the *apéritif,*" my wife said. "Or where."

It was about six o'clock that same evening and it was still very warm as we went downstairs.

"The major always has his on the terrace," I said. "We'll wait there."

We waited on the terrace. The red and white sun-blinds were still down, casting a rosy-yellow sort of light, and I asked the waiter to pull them up so that we could see the mountains. When he raised the blinds the whole range of the Jungfrau and the Blümlisalp shone, icily rose and mauve above the mountain-green waters of the lake, and in the gardens below us the flowers were rose and mauve too, tender in the evening sun.

It always seemed to me that you could sit there on the terrace for a long time and do nothing more than watch the changing colours of the lake, the flowers and the mountains.

"The major's late," I said.

From across the lake the smaller of the white steamers was coming in, and as it came nearer I could hear once again the sound of the guitars that were played by two Italian Swiss who travelled on the lake every Sunday, playing gay little peasant melodies from the south, earning a glass of bear or a coffee as they played on the boat or at the cafés of the landing-places.

The sound of the guitars over the water was very gay and charming in the still air.

And then suddenly as we sat listening to it the major came hurrying down.

"So sorry." He seemed agitated and begged several times that we should forgive him. "She'll be down in a moment. Waiter! Very exhausted after that journey. Awful long way. Waiter—ah! there you are."

The major insisted on ordering drinks. He drank very rapidly and finished four or five glasses of Kirsch before Mrs. Martineau came down.

"I've been waiting for hours in the lounge," she said. "How was I to know?"

"Let me get you something to drink," I said. "What will it be?"

"Whisky," she said, "if I may."

"There's never any whisky," the major said.

"Good grief!" she said.

I got up. "I think it'll be all right," I said.

I walked to the end of the terrace and found the waiter. The hotel had a bad brandy that tasted spirituous and harsh like poor whisky, and I arranged with the waiter to bring a double one of that.

When I got back to the table my wife and Mrs. Martineau were talking of the mountains. My wife was trying to remember the names of those you could see from the terrace, but she was never very clear as to which they were.

"I think that's Eiger," she said.

"No," the major said, "that's Finsteraarhorn."

"Then which is the one with pigeons on top?" she said, and I knew she was trying to avoid the question of the Jungfrau. "It has bits of snow on all summer that look like white pigeons," she explained.

"You can't see it from here."

"The one straight across," the major said, "the big one is the Jungfrau."

My wife looked at me. Mrs. Martineau looked very bored.

"There's a railway goes almost to the top," my wife said. "You must really go up while you're here."

I knew the major did not think very much of climbing mountains by rail. "I don't think you'd find it very exciting crawling up in that cold little train."

"Oh! don't you?" Mrs. Martineau said. "I think it would be awful fun."

"No sense of conquest that way," the major said.

"Who wants a sense of conquest? The idea is to get to the top."

"Well, in a way—".

"Oh! don't be so vague. Either you want to get to the top or you don't go."

I said something very pointed about the mountain being called the Jungfrau, but it made no impression on her.

"Have you been up there yet?" she said.

"No," I said, "we're always meaning to go. We've been as far as Wengen, that's all."

"Why don't we all go up together?" my wife said. "I think it would be lovely."

"Marvellous idea," Mrs. Martineau said.

"It means being up very early," the major said. "Have to be up by six. Not quite your time."

"Don't be so rude, darling," she said.

"Anyway, you'll be tired to-morrow."

"I shall not be tired. Why do you keep saying I'm tired? I'm not tired. I simply don't know the first thing about being tired, and yet you keep saying so. I can certainly be up by six if you can."

I could see that she was very determined to go. The major drank three more glasses of Kirsch and looked more than ever like a beaten dog. The sound of the guitars came faintly over the lake and Mrs. Martineau said, "What is that ghastly row?" and we ended up by arranging to go to the Jungfrau the following morning, and then went into dinner.

The train to Jungfraujoch goes very slowly up through lovely alpine valleys rich in spring and summer with the flowers of the lower meadows, violet salvia and wild white daisy and pink lucerne and yellow burnished trollius, and peasants everywhere mow the flowery grass in thick sweet swathes. There is a smell of something like clover and butter in the bright snow-lit air. As the train goes higher the flowers by the track grow shorter and finer until on the slopes about Scheidegg there are thousands of white and pale mauve crocus, with many fragile purple soldanellas, and sharp fierce blue gentians among yellow silken anemones everywhere about the short snow-pressed grass.

As we rode up in the little train that morning under the dazzling snow-bright peak, the major was very interested in the flowers and kept asking me what they were. He was quite dazzled by the blueness of the gentians, and kept saying, "Look at that blue, darling, look at it," but I had never seen anyone quite so bored as Mrs. Martineau. Gradually we climbed higher and nearer the snow until at last the air was white with the downward reflection of snow-light from the great peaks above; so that the powder on her cheeks, too heavy and thick for a young girl, looked scaly and blue and dead, and the scarlet of her lips had the flakiness of thin enamel wearing away.

"God, I simply loathe tunnels," she said.

Above the Scheidegg the train goes into the mountain and climbs darkly and coldly inside, with funereal creakings and clankings every yard or so, for a long time. Mrs. Martineau was furious every yard of that cold gloomy climb.

In the half-darkness she said she could not think why the hell the major had not told her it was this kind of train.

"I did tell you," he said. "I said it would be no fun."

"You said absolutely nothing of the kind."

"My dear, indeed I did. Did you expect the train would climb outside the mountain all the time?"

"How the hell did I know what to expect, darling, if you didn't say a word?"

"I said—"

"The whole trouble is, darling, you haven't a clue."

"It isn't far to the top, anyway," he said.

"It seems a hell of a way to me!" she said. She looked terribly restless and shouted something about claustrophobia.

So we climbed up in the cold gloom of the tunnel, with Mrs. Martineau growing more and more furious, exclaiming more and more of claustrophobia, and all the time calling the major darling more often, as her anger grew. In the queer unwordly coldness of the clanking little train it was hard to believe in the pleasant heat of summer shining on the lake below. Mrs. Martineau shivered and stamped her feet at the halts where we changed carriages and in her white and scarlet suit, with her scarlet lips and her white lamb-skin coat thrown over her shoulders she looked like a cold angry animal pacing up and down.

But if she hated the journey up in the wearying little train under the mountain, she hated even more the hotel at the terminus on top.

The hotel was bright and warm and flooded with the brilliant sunlight of high places, snow-sharp as it leapt off the glacier below. There was a pleasant smell of food, and the menu said *potage parmentier* and escallops of veal with spaghetti. But Mrs. Martineau said she was height-sick and did not want to eat.

"In any case I loathe spaghetti!" she said.

"All right, dear," the major said. He had been quite gentle, in an almost frightened way, under the most trying circumstances in the train. "Have the veal alone."

"I'm not so frightfully fond of veal, either. I'm not hungry."

"Try it, dear."

"Why should I try it if I hate it, darling? Why should I eat if I'm not hungry?"

The major looked terribly embarrassed for us and did not know what to do.

"Well, can't you get the waiter, the manager or something? At least we could order a drink!" she said.

The major sent for the manager.

The manager was a very pleasant fat man with glasses who was amiably running about the large pinewood dining-room with two or three bottles of wine in each hand. There was a great popping of corks everywhere and in the high alpine sunlight, with the smell of food and pinewood and sun-warmed air, nothing could have been more pleasant than to eat and drink and talk and watch that amiable man.

In a few moments he spared the time to come over to us. The major explained how Mrs. Martineau did not like the menu. Wasn't there something else? he said.

"It would mean waiting," the manager said. "The veal is very good." He pronounced it weal instead of veal.

"She doesn't like veal. What else could you do?"

"It would mean waiting."

"Isn't there a steak or something?" Mrs. Martineau said.

"A steak, yes."

"All right, dear, if you'd like a steak?"

"Or I could do you a *fritto misto*," the manager said.

"What is that?" Mrs. Martineau said. "What is *fritto misto?*"

The manager explained what *fritto misto* was. I am exceedingly fond of *fritto misto* myself; I like the spaghetti, and the delicate morsels of fried meat of various kinds, including, as the manager said, the small tender escallops of weal. It was, after all, a refined and more poetical version, with Italian variations, of the dish already on the menu.

"It sounds wonderful," Mrs. Martineau said. "I'll have that."

The manager did not smile. "And something to drink? Some wine?"

"Two bottles of the Dôle," the major said.

The manager smiled very nicely and went away.

"These people are always the same," Mrs. Martineau said. "They don't do a damn thing until you tear the place down."

The one thing it is not necessary to do in Switzerland in order to eat is to tear the place down. And when the *fritto misto* arrived, fifteen minutes late and looking not very different from the escallops of veal we had eaten with so much pleasure, I thought Mrs. Martineau ate them with great gusto for a woman who hated spaghetti and veal and was height-sick and not hungry.

Before the train took us back down the mountain the major drank four more glasses of Kirsch after the wine. He drank them too fast; he also had a cognac with his coffee. And by the time we went upstairs to the men's room he was a little stupid and unsteady from the Kirsch, the wine, the cognac and the rarefied Jungfrau air.

In the men's room he took out his false teeth. I had forgotten all about them. He was a little unsteady. And without his teeth he did not look like the spruce proud man we had first known at the hotel on the lake below. The toothless mouth had quite an aged, unhappy, empty look of helplessness.

Swaying about, he wrapped his morning teeth in a small chamois leather bag and then took his afternoon teeth from an identical bag. Both sets were scrupulously clean and white. I had often wondered why he changed his teeth three times a day and now he told me.

"Gives me a feeling of keeping young," he said. "Renews me. One gets stale, you see, wearing the same teeth. One loses a feeling of freshness."

He put his afternoon teeth into his mouth very neatly, and I could understand, seeing him now with the fresh bright teeth, how much younger, fresher and more sprightly he might feel.

"You have your own teeth?" he said.

"Yes."

"It's the one thing I'm awfully sensitive about. Really awfully sensitive. That's why I change them. I am very self-conscious about feeling a little old. You understand?"

I said it was a good idea.

He said he was glad I thought so. For a moment he swayed about in a confidential lugubrious sort of way, so that I thought he might cry. "It would have to be something really frightfully bad to make me forget to change them," he said.

We rumbled down the mountain in the train all afternoon. Slowly out of the dark tunnel we came down into the dazzling flowery light of the Scheidegg, and once again Mrs. Martineau, altogether oblivious of the scenery and the flowers, was height-sick as we waited on the station for the lower train. All the way down through the lovely meadows of high summer grass, rosy with lucerne, the major had a much needed nap, sleeping in the corner of the carriage with his mouth open, so that I thought once or twice that his teeth would fall out. Mrs. Martineau did not speak and the major woke with a start at Interlaken. He looked about him open-mouthed, like a man who had woken in another world, and then he looked at Mrs. Martineau. She looked young enough to be a reprimanding daughter.

"Really, darling. Honestly," she said.

The major worked his teeth up and down as if they were bothering him, or like a dog that has nothing left to bite on.

We parted at the hotel.

"Oh! dear," I said to my wife, and this time she did not ask what lay behind it. She, too, had rather given up. It was one of those excursions on which enemies are made for life, and for some reason or other I thought that neither the major nor Mrs. Martineau would ever speak to us again.

It was Saturday, in fact, five days later, before we came near enough to them to exchange another word. Somehow we always saw them from a distance. We saw the major running back to the hotel with Mrs. Martineau's bag; we saw them on the steamers, where the major no longer enjoyed the pink-eared ham sandwiches or made eye-love to the waitress; we saw them shopping in the town. Mrs. Martineau wore many new dresses; she seemed to go in very particularly for short-skirted, frothy things, or day-frocks with sailor stripes of scarlet and blue, so that she looked more than ever like a young bright girl and the major more than ever like a father too painfully devoted.

On Saturday came the affair of the eucalyptus tree. It was one of those trees that the Swiss are fond of for courtyards and balconies in summer; it was three or four feet high and it had soft tender blue-grey leaves that I always thought looked charming against the red pot on the major's sunny balcony.

At half-past five that afternoon we heard the most awful crash on the floor below. I went to the balcony and looked down. The eucalyptus tree lay shattered in the courtyard below, and on the balcony the major, looking very unspruce and dishevelled and shattered himself, was standing in his undervest and trousers, staring down. For a moment I could not tell whether the major had thrown the eucalyptus tree down there in a terrible fit of despair, or whether Mrs. Martineau had thrown it at him in an equally terrible fit of anger.

A waiter in a white jacket and then the manager came running out of the hotel to see what had happened and at the same moment Mrs. Martineau shouted from the bedroom: "Come inside you decrepit old fool! Stop making an exhibition of yourself, for God's sake!"

"Please!" I heard the major say. "People are coming."

"Well, let them come!" she shouted. "If you've no more sense than to take a room with a eucalyptus tree when you know I loathe eucalyptus, when you know I've a phobia about eucalyptus—"

"It isn't that sort of eucalyptus," the major whispered.

"Any kind of eucalyptus is eucalyptus to me!" she shouted.

"Please," the major said. He leaned over the balcony and called down to the waiter and the manager below.

"An accident! I will pay!"

"Oh! for God's sake come inside!" she shouted. "What's it matter?"

"I will pay!" the major shouted down again.

Back in the room Mrs. Martineau began throwing things. "You're always fussing!" I heard her shout, and then there was the enraged dull noise of things like books and shoes being thrown.

"Please, darling, don't do that," the major said. "Don't do it please."

"Oh! shut up!" she said. "And these damn things too!"

I heard the most shattering crash as if a glass tumbler had been thrown.

"Oh! not my teeth!" the major said. "Please, darling. Not my teeth! For God's sake, not both sets, please!"

He rushed into the bedroom. I went back into my own.

"Whatever in the world?" my wife said.

"Just the eucalyptus tree," I said. "The major will pay."

The following afternoon the major and Mrs. Martineau went away. On the lake the steamers were very crowded and under the lime trees, at the restaurant by the landing-stage, the Sunday orchestra played very loudly to crowds of visitors in the hot afternoon. It was glorious weather, and on the four o'clock steamer as it came in there were crowds of happy Sunday-laughing people.

On the landing-stage neither Mrs. Martineau nor the major looked very happy. The hotel porter with his scarlet cap stood guarding their luggage, three trunks, two brown hide suitcases, a military-looking khaki grip, a pig-skin hat-box and a shooting-stick, and the major, who was no longer wearing his spruce shantung but a suit of grey tweed, did not see us on the quay. Beside us the two Italian Swiss with their guitars were waiting to catch the steamer too.

When the boat came in there was some difficulty about getting the major's luggage aboard. The trunks were fairly large and the porters grew hot and excited and everyone stared. But at last it was all finished, and on the landing-stage the hotel porter raised his scarlet cap in polite farewell.

As the steamer moved away the major stood by the rail, watching the shore. I could not see Mrs. Martineau. Somewhere behind him the two Italian Swiss struck up with their guitars and began to play their little hungry-sweet gay tune.

At that moment the major saw us. He lifted his hand in recognition, and almost eagerly, I thought, in sudden good-bye. He opened his mouth as if to say something, but the steamer was already too far away and his mouth remained open and empty, without a sound. And in that moment I remembered something. I remembered the eucalyptus tree falling from the balcony and the crash of the major's teeth on the bedroom wall.

"How beautiful the Jungfrau is to-day," my wife said.

From the steamer the major, with his wrong teeth in, gave the most painful sort of smile, and sweetly from across the lake came the gay sound of the guitars.

THELMA

The place where she was born was eighty miles from London. She was never to go to London in all her life except in dreams or in imagination, when she lay awake in the top bedroom of the hotel, listening to the sound of wind in the forest boughs.

When she first began to work at *The Blenheim Arms* she was a plump short girl of fourteen, with remarkably pale cream hands and a head of startling hair exactly the colour of autumn beech leaves. Her eyes seemed bleached and languid. The only colour in their lashes was an occasional touch of gold that made them look like curled paint brushes that were not quite dry.

She began first as a bedroom maid, living in and starting at five in the morning and later taking up brass cans of hot shaving water to the bedrooms of gentlemen who stayed over-night. These gentlemen—any guest was called a gentleman in those days—were mostly commercial travellers going regularly from London to the West country or back again and after a time she got to know them very well. After a time she also got to know the view from the upper bedroom windows very well: southward to the village, down the long wide street of brown-red houses where horses in those days were still tied to hitching posts and then westward and northward and eastward to the forest that sheltered the houses like a great horseshoe of boughs and leaves. She supposed there were a million beech-trees in that forest. She did not know. She only knew, because people said so, that you could walk all day through it and never come to the other side.

At first she was too shy and too quiet about her work in the bedrooms. She knocked on early morning doors too softly. Heavy sleepers could not be woken by the tap of her small soft hands and cans of hot water grew cold on landings while other fuming frowsy men lay awake, waiting for their calls. This early mistake was almost the only one she ever made. The hotel was very old, with several long back stair-cases and complicated narrow pas-

sages and still more flights of stairs up which she had to lug, every morning
to attic bedrooms, twenty cans of water. She soon learned that it was stupid
to lug more than she needed. After two mornings she learned to hammer
hard with her fist on the doors of bedrooms and after less than a week she
was knocking, walking in, putting the can of hot water on the wash-stand,
covering it with a towel and saying in a soft firm young voice:

"Half-past six, sir. You've got just an hour before your train."

In this way she grew used to men. It was her work to go into bedrooms
where men were frequently to be startled in strange attitudes, half-dressed,
unshaved, stupid with sleep and sometimes thick-tongued and groping. It
was no use being shy about it. It was no use worrying about it either. She
herself was never thick-tongued, stupid or groping in the mornings and after
a time she found she had no patience with men who had to be called a second time and then complained that their shaving water was cold. Already
she was speaking to them as if she were an older person, slightly peremptory
but not unkind, a little vexed but always understanding.

"Of course the water's cold, sir. You should get up when you're called.
I called you twice. Do you expect people to call you fifty times?"

Her voice was slow and soft. The final syllables of her sentences went singing upward on a gentle and inquiring scale. It was perhaps because of this
that men were never offended by what she had to say to them even as a
young girl and that they never took exception to remarks that would have
been impertinent or forward in other girls.

"I know, Thelma," they would say. "That's me all over, Thelma. Never
could get the dust out of my eyes. I'll be down in five shakes—four and a
half minutes for the eggs, Thelma. I like them hard."

Soon she began to know not only the names of travellers but exactly when
they had to be called, what trains they had to catch and how they liked their
eggs boiled. She knew those who liked two cans of shaving water and a wad
of cotton wool because they always cut themselves. She was ready for those
who groped to morning life with yellow eyes:

"Well, you won't be told, sir. You know how it takes you. You take
more than you can hold and then you wonder why you feel like death the
morning after."

"I know, Thelma, I know. What was I drinking?"

"Cider most of the time and you had three rum and ports with Mr.
Henderson."

"Rum and port!—Oh! my lord, Thelma—"

"That's what I say—you never learn. People can tell you forty times, can't they, but you never learn."

Once a month, on Sunday, when she finished work at three o'clock, she walked in the forest. She was very fond of the forest. She still believed it was true, as people said, that you could walk through it all day and never come to the farther side of it but she did not mind about that. She was quite content to walk some distance into it and, if the days were fine and warm, sit down and look at the round grey trunks of the countless shimmering beeches. They reminded her very much of the huge iron-coloured legs of a troupe of elephants she had once seen at a circus and the trees themselves had just the same friendly sober air.

When she was eighteen a man a named George Furness, a traveller in fancy goods and cheap lines of cutlery, came to stay at the hotel for a Saturday night and a Sunday. She did not know quite how it came about but it presently turned out in the course of casual conversation that Furness was quite unable to believe that the nuts that grew on beech-trees were just as eatable as the nuts that grew on hazel or walnut trees. It was a silly, stupid thing, she thought, for a grown man to have to admit that he didn't know about beech-nuts.

"Don't kid me," Furness said. "They're no more good to eat than acorns."

For the first time, in her country way, she found herself being annoyed and scornful of someone who doubted the truth of her words.

"If you don't believe me," she said, "come with me and we'll get some. The forest is full enough of them. Come with me and I'll show you—I'll be going there tomorrow."

The following day, Sunday, she walked with Furness in the forest, through the great rides of scalded brilliant beeches. In the October sunshine her hair shone in a big coppery bun from under the back of her green straw Sunday hat. Furness was a handsome, light-hearted man of thirty-five with thickish lips and dark oiled hair and a short yellow cane which he occasionally swished, sword-fashion, at pale clouds of dancing flies. These flies, almost transparent in the clear October sun, were as light and delicate as the lashes of Thelma's fair bleached eyes.

For some time she and Furness sat on a fallen tree-trunk while she picked up beech-nuts, shelled them for him and watched him eat them. She did not feel any particular sense of triumph in having shown a man that beech-nuts were good to eat but she laughed once or twice, quite happily, as Furness threw them gaily into the air, caught them deftly in his mouth and said how good they were. His tongue was remarkably red as it stiffened and flicked at the nuts and she noticed it every time. What was also remarkable was that Furness did not peel a single nut himself. With open outstretched hand and poised red tongue he simply sat and waited to be fed.

"You mean you really didn't know they were good?" she said.

"To tell you the honest," Furness said, "I never saw a beech-tree in my life before."

"Oh! go on with you," she said. "*Never?*"

"No," he said. "Honest. Cut my throat. I wouldn't know one if I saw one anyway."

"Aren't there trees in London?"

"Oh! plenty," Furness said. "Trees all over the place."

"As many as this?" she said. "As many as in the forest?"

"Oh! easy," Furness said, "only more scattered. Scattered about in big parks—Richmond, Kew, Hyde Park, places like that—miles and miles. Scattered."

"I like to hear you talk about London."

"You must come up there some time," he said. "I'll show you round a bit. We'll have a day on the spree."

He laughed again in his gay fashion and suddenly, really before she knew what was happening, he put his arms round her and began to kiss her. It was the first time she had ever been kissed by anyone in that sort of way and the lips of George Furness were pleasantly moist and warm. He kissed her several times again and presently they were lying on the thick floor of beech-leaves together. She felt a light crackle of leaves under her hair as George Furness pressed against her, kissing her throat, and then suddenly she felt afraid of something and she sat up, brushing leaves from her hair and shoulders.

"I think we ought to go now," she said.

"Oh no," he said. "Come on. What's the hurry, what's the worry? Come on, Thelma, let's have some fun."

"Not here. Not today—"

"Here today, gone tomorrow," Furness said. "Come on, Thelma, let's make a little hay while the sun shines."

Suddenly, because Furness himself was so gay and light-hearted about everything, she felt that perhaps she was being over-cautious and stupid and something made her say:

"Perhaps some other day. When are you coming back again?"

"Well, that's a point," he said. "If I go to Bristol first I'll be back this way Friday. If I go to Hereford first I'll stay in Bristol over the week-end and be back here Monday."

Sunlight breaking through thinning autumn branches scattered dancing blobs of gold on his face and hands as he laughed again and said:

"All right, Thelma? A little hay-making when I come back?"

"We'll see."

"Is that a promise?"

"We'll see."

"I'll take it as a promise," he said. He laughed again and kissed her neck and she felt excited. "You can keep a promise, Thelma, can't you?"

"Never mind about that now," she said. "What time shall I call you in the morning?"

"Call me early, mother dear," he said. "I ought to be away by six or just after."

She could not sleep that night. She thought over and over again of the way George Furness had kissed her. She remembered the moist warm lips, the red gay tongue flicking at beech-nuts, and how sunlight breaking through thinning autumn branches had given a dancing effect to his already light-hearted face and hands. She remembered the way he had talked of promises and making hay. And after a time she could not help wishing that she had done what George Furness had wanted her to do. "But there's always next week-end," she thought. "I'll be waiting next week-end."

It was very late when she fell asleep and it was after half-past six before she woke again. It was a quarter to seven before she had the tea made and when she hurried upstairs with the tray her hands were trembling. Then after she had knocked on the door of George Furness' bedroom she went inside to make the first of several discoveries. The bed was empty and George Furness had left by motor-car.

Only a few years later, by the time she was twenty-five, almost every gentleman came and went by motor-car. But that morning it was a new and strange experience to know that a gentleman did not need to go by train. It was a revolution in her life to find that a man could pay his bill overnight, leave before breakfast and not wait for his usual can of shaving water.

All that week, and for several weeks afterwards, she waited for George Furness to come back. She waited with particular anxiety on Fridays and Mondays. She found herself becoming agitated at the sound of a motor-car. Then for the few remaining Sundays of that autumn she walked in the forest, sat down in the exact spot where George Furness had thrown beech-nuts into the air and caught them in his red fleshy mouth, and tried intensely to re-experience what it was like to be kissed by that mouth, in late warm sunlight, under a million withering beech-leaves.

All this time, and for some time afterwards, she went about her work as if nothing had happened. Then presently she began to inquire, casually at first, as if it was really a trivial matter, whether anyone had seen George Furness. When it appeared that nobody had and again that nobody even knew what Furness looked like she found herself beginning to describe him, explain him and exaggerate him a little more. In that way, by making him a little larger than life, she felt that people would recognise him more readily. Presently there would inevitably come a day when someone would say "Ah! yes, old George. Ran across him only yesterday."

At the same time she remained secretive and shy about him. She did not mention him in open company. It was always to some gentleman alone, to a solitary commercial traveller sipping a late night whisky or an early morning cup of tea in his bedroom, that she would say:

"Ever see George Furness nowadays? He hasn't been down lately. You knew him didn't you?

"Can't say I did."

"Nice cheerful fellow. Dark. Came from London—he'd talk to you hours about London, George would. Used to keep me fascinated. I think he was in quite a way up there."

And soon, occasionally, she began to go further than this:

"Oh! we had some times, George and me. He liked a bit of fun, George did. I used to show him the forest sometimes. He didn't know one tree from another."

One hot Sunday afternoon in early summer, when she was twenty, she was walking towards the forest when she met another commercial traveller, a man in hosiery named Prentis, sauntering with boredom along the roadside, flicking at the heads of buttercups with a thin malacca cane. His black patent leather shoes were white with dust and something about the way he flicked at the buttercups reminded her of the way George Furness had cut with his cane at dancing clouds of late October flies.

"Sunday," Prentis said. "Whoever invented Sunday? Not a commercial, you bet. If there's one day in the week I hate it's Sunday—what's there to do on Sundays?"

"I generally walk in the forest," she said.

Some time later, in the forest, Prentis began kissing her very much as George Furness had done. Under the thick bright mass of leaves, motionless in the heat of afternoon, she shut her eyes and tried to persuade herself that the moist red lips of Furness were pressing down on hers. The recaptured sensation of warmth and softness excited her into trembling. Then suddenly, feeling exposed and shy in the open riding, she was afraid that perhaps someone from the hotel might walk past and see her and she said:

"Let's take the little path there. That's a nice way. Nobody ever goes up there."

Afterwards Prentis took off his jacket and made a pillow of it and they lay down together for the rest of the afternoon in the thick cool shade. At the same time Prentis' feet itched and he took off his shoes. As he did so and she saw the shoes white with summer dust she said:

"You'd better leave them with me tonight. I'll clean them nicely."

And then presently, lying on her back, looking up at the high bright mass of summer leaves with her bleached far-off eyes, she said:

"Do you like the forest? Ever been in here before?"

"Never."

"I love it here," she said. "I always come when I can."

"By yourself?"

"That would be telling," she said.

"I'll bet you do," he said. He began laughing, pressing his body against her, stringing his fingers like a comb through her sharp red hair. "Every Sunday, eh? What time will you bring the shoes?"

Presently he kissed her again. And again she shut her eyes and tried to imagine that the mouth pressing down on hers was the mouth of George Furness. The experience was like that of trying to stalk a butterfly on the petal of a flower and seeing it, at the last moment, flutter away at the approach of a shadow. It was very pleasant kissing Prentis under the great arch of beech-leaves in the hot still afternoon. She liked it very much. But what she sought, in the end, was not quite there.

By the time she was twenty-five she had lost count of the number of men she had taken into the forest on Sunday afternoons. By then her face had broadened and begun to fill out a lot. Her arms were fleshy and her hips had begun to stand out from her body so that her skirts were always a little too tight and rode up at the back, showing the hem of her underclothes. Her feet from walking up and down stairs all day, had grown much flatter and her legs were straight and solid. In the summer she could not bear to wear her corsets and gradually her figure became more floppy, her bust like a soft fat pillow untidily slept in.

Most of them who came to spend a night or two at the hotel were married men, travellers glad of a little reprieve from wives and then equally glad, after a week or two on the road, to go back to them again. She was a great comfort to such men. They looked forward through dreary days of lugging and unpacking sample cases to evenings when Thelma, pillowy and soft, with her soothing voice, would put her head into their bedrooms and say:

"Had a good week, sir? Anything you want? Something you'd like me to get for you?"

Many of them wanted Thelma. Almost as many of them were content simply to talk with her. At night, when she took up to their bedrooms hot jugs of cocoa, tots of whisky, pots of tea or in winter, for colds, fiery mugs of steaming rum and cinnamon, they liked her to stay and talk for a while. Sometimes she simply stood by the bedside, arms folded over her enlarging bosom, legs a little apart, nodding and listening. Sometimes she sat on the edge of the bed, her skirt riding up over her thick knees, her red hair like a plaited bell-rope as one of the travellers twisted it in his hands. Sometimes a man was in trouble: a girl had thrown him over or a wife had died. Then she listened with eyes that seemed so intent in their wide and placid colourlessness that again and again a man troubled in loneliness gained the impression that she was thinking always and only of him. Not one of them guessed that she was really thinking of George Furness or that as she let them twist her thick red hair, stroke her pale comforting, comfortable arms and thighs or kiss her unaggressive lips she was really letting someone else, in imagination, do these things. In the same way when she took off her clothes and slipped into bed with them it was from feelings and motives far removed from wantonness. She was simply groping hungrily for experiences she felt George Furness, and only George Furness, ought to have shared.

When she was thirty the urge to see George Furness became so obsessive that she decided, for the first and only time in her life, to go to London. She did not really think of the impossibility of finding anybody in so large a place. She had thought a great deal about London and what it would be like there, with George Furness, on the spree. Lying in her own room, listening to the night sounds of a forest that was hardly ever really still all through winter and summer, she had built up the impression that London, though vast, was also composed in large part of trees. That was because George

Furness had described it that way. For that reason she was not afraid of London; the prospect of being alone there did not appal her. And always at the back of her mind lay the comforting and unsullied notion that somehow, by extraordinary chance, by some unbelievable miracle, she would run into George Furness there as naturally and simply as if he were walking up the steps of *The Blenheim Arms*.

So she packed her things into a small black fibre suit-case, asked for seven days off, the only holiday she had ever taken in her life, and started off by train. At the junction twelve miles away she had not only to change trains but she had also to wait for thirty-five minutes for the eastbound London train. It was midday on a warm oppressive day in September and she decided to go into the refreshment room to rest and get herself an Eccles cake, of which she was very fond, and a cup of tea. The cakes in fact tempted her so much that she ordered two.

Just before the cakes and the tea arrived at her table she became uneasily aware of someone looking at her. She looked round the refreshment room and saw, standing with his foot on the rail of the bar, beside a big blue-flamed tea-urn, a man she knew named Lattimore, a traveller in novelty lines for toy-shops and bazaars. Lattimore, a tallish man of thirty-five with fair receding hair and a thick gold signet ring on the third finger of his right hand, was drinking whisky from a tumbler.

She was so used to the state and appearance of men who took too much to drink that she recognised, even at that distance across the railway refreshment room, that Lattimore was not quite sober. She had seen him drunk once or twice before and instinctively she felt concerned and sorry for him as he picked up his glass, wiped his mouth on the back of his free hand and then came over to talk to her.

"Where are you going, Mr. Lattimore?" she said.

"Down to the old *Blenheim*," he said. "Where are *you?*"

She did not say where she was going. In the few moments before her cakes arrived she looked at Lattimore with keen pale eyes. The pupils of his own eyes were dusky, ill-focused and beginning to water.

"What is it, Mr. Lattimore?" she said.

"Blast and damn her," he said. "Blast her."

"That isn't the way to talk," Thelma said.

"Blast her," he said. "Double blast her."

Her cakes and tea arrived. She poured herself a cup of tea.

"A cup of this would do you more good than that stuff," she said.

"Double blast," he said. He gulped suddenly at the glass of whisky and then took a letter from his pocket. "Look at that, Thelma. Tell us what you think of that."

It was not the first time she had read a letter from a wife to a husband telling him that she was finished, fed up and going away. Most of that sort of thing, she found, came right enough in the end. What she chiefly noticed this time was the postmark on the envelope. The letter came from London and it reminded her suddenly that she was going there.

"Have one of these Eccles cakes," she said. "You want to get some food inside you."

He fumbled with an Eccles cake. Flaky crumbs of pastry and loose currants fell on his waistcoat and striped grey trousers. To her dismay he then put the Eccles cake back on the plate and, after a pause, picked up her cake in mistake for his own. Something about this groping mistake of his with the cakes made her infinitely sad for him and she said:

"You never ought to get into a state like this, Mr. Lattimore. It's awful. You'll do yourself no good getting into this sort of state. You're not driving, are you?"

"Train," he said. "Train." He suddenly drained his whisky and, before she could speak, wandered across the refreshment bar to get himself another. "Another double and what platform for Deansborough?" he called. He banged his hand on the counter and then there was a sudden ring of breaking glasses.

Ten minutes later she was sitting with him in the train for Deansborough, going back home, his head on her shoulder. It was warm and oppressive in the carriage and she opened the window and let in fresh air. The wind blowing on his face ruffled his thinning hair and several times she smoothed it down again with her hands. It came to her then that she might have been smoothing down the hair of George Furness and at the same time she remembered London, though without regret.

"What part of London do you come from?" she said.

"Finchley."

"That isn't near the parks is it?" she said. "You don't ever run across a man named George Furness, do you?"

The little local train was rattling slowly and noisily between banks of woodland. Its noises rebounded from trees and cuttings and in through the open window so that for a moment she was not quite sure what Lattimore was saying in reply.

"Furness? George? Old George?—dammit, friend of mine. Lives in Maida Vale."

She sat staring for some time at the deep September banks of woodland, still dark green from summer, streaming past the windows. The whisky breath of Lattimore was sour on the sultry air and she opened the window a little further, breathing fast and deeply.

"When did you see him last?" she said.

"Thursday—no, Wednesday," he said. "Play snooker together every Wednesday, me and George."

Within a month the leaves on the beeches would be turning copper. With her blood pounding in her throat, she sat thinking of their great masses of burning, withering leaf and the way, a long time before, George Furness had held out his hand while she peeled nuts for him and then watched him toss them into the air and catch them on his moist red tongue.

"How is he these days?" she said.

"Old George?—same as ever. Up and down. Up and down. Same as ever."

Once again she stared at the passing woodlands, remembering. Unconsciously, as she did so, she twisted quietly at the big signet ring on Lattimore's finger. The motion began to make him, in his half-drunk state, soothed and amorous. He turned his face towards her and put his mouth against her hair.

"Ought to have married you, Thelma," he said. "Ought to have put the ring on you."

"You don't want me."

"You like the ring?" he said. "You can have it." He began struggling in groping alcoholic fashion to take the ring off his finger. "Have it, Thelma— you put it on."

"No," she said. "No." And then: "How was George Furness when you saw him last Wednesday?"

He succeeded suddenly in taking the ring from his finger and began pressing it clumsily on one of her own.

"There y'are, Thelma. You put it on. You wear it. For me. Put it on and keep it, Thelma. For me."

The ring was on her finger.

"How was George?" she said.

"Getting fat," he said. "Can't get the old pod over the snooker table nowadays. Rest and be thankful—that's what they call George."

Half sleepy, half drunk, Lattimore let his head slip from her shoulder and
the mass of her thick red hair down to the shapeless comforting pillow of
her bosom and she said:

"What's he travel in now? The same old line?"

"Same old line," he said. "Furniture and carpets. Mostly carpets now."

She realised suddenly that they were talking of quite different things,
quite different people. She was listening to a muddled drunk who had
somehow got the names wrong. She stared for a long time at the woods
rushing past the rattling little train. There was no need to speak. Lattimore
was asleep in her bosom, his mouth open, and the rink was shining on
her finger.

Next day Lattimore did not remember the ring and she did not give it
back. She kept it, as she kept a great many other things, as a memento of
experiences that men liked to think were services she had rendered.

A drawer in the wardrobe in her bedroom was full of these things. She
hardly ever used them: handkerchiefs, night-dress cases and bits of underwear from travellers in ladies' wear, bottles of perfume and powder, night-
dresses and dress-lengths of satin, necklaces of imitation pearl and amber;
presents given for Christmas, her birthday or for a passing, comforting week-
end.

Some of the men who had given them came back only once or twice and
she never saw them again. They changed jobs or were moved to other dis-
tricts. But they never forgot Thelma and travellers were always arriving to
say that they had seen Bill Haynes and Charlie Townsend or Bert Hobbs
only the week before and that Bill or Charlie or Bert wished to be remembered. Among themselves too men would wink and say "Never need be
lonely down at *The Blenheim*. What do you say, Harry? Thelma always
looks after you," and many a man would be recommended to stay there,
on the edge of the forest, where he would be well looked after by Thelma,
rather than go on to bigger towns beyond.

By the time she was forty she was not only plumper and more shapeless but her hair had begun to show the first cottony signs of grey. There
was nothing she disliked more than red hair streaked with another colour
and from that time onwards she began to dye her hair. Because she could
never shop anywhere except in the village or at most in Chippingham,
the junction, twelve miles away, she never succeeded in getting quite the
right shade for her hair. The first dye she used was a little too yellow
and gave her hair the appearance of an old fox fur. One day the shop

in the village ran out of this dye and sold her something which, they said, was the nearest thing. This shade made her hair look as if stained with a mixture of beetroot and bay rum. It was altogether too dark for her. Later when the shop got in its new supplies of the yellow dye she uneasily realised that neither tint was suitable. The only thing that occurred to her to do then was to mix them together. This gave a strange gold rusty look to her hair and something in the dye at the same time made it much drier, so that it became unnaturally fuzzier and more difficult to manage than it had been.

The one thing that did not change about her as she grew older was the colour and appearance of her eyes. They remained unchangeably bleached and distant, always with the effect of the mild soft lashes being still wet with a touch of gold paint on them. While the rest of her body grew plumper and older and greyer the eyes remained, perhaps because of their extreme pallor, very young, almost girlish, as if in a way that part of her would never grow up.

It was these still pale, bleached, unnaturally adolescent eyes that she fixed on a man named Sharwood more than ten years later as she took him a tray of early morning tea and a newspaper on a wet late October morning, soon after she was fifty. During the night torrents of rain had hurled through the miles of beeches, bringing down great flying droves of leaves. Through the open bedroom window rain had poured in too on the curtains and as Thelma reached up to shut the window she said:

"Not much of a morning to be out, sir. Which way are you off today?"

"London," he said.

There was no need for him to say any more. Purposely she fussed a little with curtains and then casually, in the same slow, upward-singing voice, asked the inevitable question:

"London? I suppose you never run into George Furness up there?"

Sharwood, a middle-aged man who travelled mainly in woollen goods, put three lumps of sugar into his tea, stirred it and then said:

"As a matter of fact I was thinking of asking you the same question."

"Me?"

"Funny thing," Sharwood said, "it was George who recommended me here."

Her heart began racing, fast and heavily, as it had done on the warm afternoon with Lattimore, drunk in the train.

"Ran across him up in Glasgow about a month ago," Sharwood said.

"You knew he was up there, didn't you?—I mean had been. Been up there for thirty years—settled there. Even got himself a bit of a Scotch accent on the way."

"No, I didn't know," she said. "I never only saw him the once."

She did not know quite why she should admit, for the first and only time, that she had seen him only once, but by now she was so transfixed and over-wrought that she hardly knew what she was saying.

"I know," Sharwood said. "He told me. It's been all those years ago, he said, but if you go to *The Blenheim Arms* ask if Thelma's still there. She'll look after you."

She locked her hands together to prevent them quivering too hopelessly and he said:

"That was the last time he was ever down this way. He moved up to Glasgow the next week. Heard of a good job there with a big wholesale firm of cloth people and there he stopped."

Sharwood paused, drank his tea and stared over the rim of the cup to the October rain slashing on the window beyond.

"He'd have been up there just thirty-five years if he'd lived till November."

Her heart seemed to stop its racing.

She did not know what to say or do. Then after a moment Sharwood said:

"Hand me my wallet off the wash-stand, will you? I've got a cutting about him. Clipped it out of *The Glasgow Herald*."

She stood staring for a few moments longer at the newspaper cutting that Sharwood handed her across the bed. The face of George Furness stared back at her from a photograph and she said simply:

"I don't think he's changed a lot, do you?"

"Same as ever," Sharwood said. "You'd have known him anywhere."

That afternoon, although it was a mid-week afternoon, she left *The Blenheim Arms* about three o'clock, walked up the road and into the forest. The rain had stopped about noon and now it was a day of racing sea-bright cloud, widening patches of high blue sky and a wind that broke from the beeches an endless stream of leaves.

She walked slowly down the long riding. She stopped for a few moments at the place where she and George Furness had eaten beech-nuts and where, some years later, she had tried for the first of many times to recapture the moment with another man. She picked up a few beech-nuts and made an attempt to peel them but the summer that year had been rainy and cool and most of the husks she broke were empty.

Finally she walked on and did something she had never done before. Slowly, in brightening sunlight, through shoals of drenched fallen leaves, she walked the entire width of the forest to the other side. It was really, after all, not so far as people had always led her to believe.

By the time she reached the open country beyond the last of the enormous beeches the sky had been driven almost clear of cloud. The sun was warm and brilliant and as she sat down on a bank of leaves at the forest edge she could feel it burning softly on her face and hands.

After a time she lay down. She lay there for two hours, not moving, her frizzed foxy hair blown against wet leaves, her bleached pale eyes staring upwards beyond the final rim of forest branches to where the sky, completely clear now of cloud, was almost fierce with high washed blue light in the falling afternoon.

That night she did not sleep much. The following night she was restless and there was a sharp, drawing pain in her back whenever she breathed a little hard. The following afternoon the doctor stood by her bed and said, shaking his head, joking with her:

"Now, Thelma, what's all this? What have you been up to? It's getting cool at night this time of year."

"I sat down in the forest," she said. "That's all. I lay down for a while."

"You know, Thelma," he said, "you're getting too old for lying down in the forest. You've got a good warm bed, haven't you?"

"I like the forest."

"You're really getting too old for this sort of thing," he said. "Now be a good girl and take care of yourself a little better. You've had your fling—we all know—but now you'll have to take care a little more. Understand?"

She made no sign that she understood except for a slight flicker of her thin pale gold lashes.

"There comes a time," the doctor said.

She died five days later. On the coffin and on the graveside in the churchyard that lay midway between the village and the forest there were a great many wreaths. Many gentlemen had remembered her, most of them individually, but someone had had the idea of placing a collecting box on the bar of *The Blenheim Arms* so that casual callers, odd travellers passing, could put into it a few coppers or a shilling or two and so pay their last respects.

A good deal of money was collected in this way and because so many people, mostly men, had contributed something it was impossible to indicate who and how many they were. It was thought better instead to put on the big round wreath of white chrysanthemums only a plain white card. "Thelma. R.I.P.," it said. "Loved by all."

GO, LOVELY ROSE

"He is the young man she met on the aeroplane," Mrs. Carteret said. "Now go to sleep."

Outside the bedroom window, in full moonlight, the leaves of the willow tree seemed to be slowly swimming in delicate but ordered separation, like shoals of grey-green fish. The thin branches were like bowed rods in the white summer sky.

"This is the first I heard that there was a young man on the aeroplane," Mr. Carteret said.

"You saw him," Mrs. Carteret said. "He was there when we met her. You saw him come with her through the customs."

"I can't remember seeing her with anybody."

"I know very well you do because you remarked on his hat. You said what a nice colour it was. It was a sort of sage-green one with a turn-down brim—"

"Good God," Mr. Carteret said. "That fellow? He looked forty or more. He was as old as I am."

"He's twenty-eight. That's all. Have you made up your mind which side you're going to sleep?"

"I'm going to stay on my back for a while," Mr. Carteret said. "I can't get off. I heard it strike three a long time ago."

"You'd get off if you'd lie still," she said.

Sometimes a turn of humid air, like the gentlest of currents, would move the entire willow tree in one huge soft fold of shimmering leaves. Whenever it did so Mr. Carteret felt for a second or two that it was the sound of an approaching car. Then when the breath of wind suddenly changed direction and ran across the night landscape in a series of leafy echoes, stirring odd trees far away, he knew always that there was no car and that it was only, once again, the quiet long gasp of midsummer air rising and falling and dying away.

"Where are you fussing off to now?" Mrs. Carteret said.

"I'm going down for a drink of water."

"You'd better by half shut your eyes and lie still in one place," Mrs. Carteret said. "Haven't you been off at all?"

"I can never sleep in moonlight," he said. "I don't know how it is. I never seem to settle properly. Besides it's too hot."

"Put something on your feet," Mrs. Carteret said, "for goodness sake."

Across the landing, on the stairs and down in the kitchen the moonlight was the white starkness of shadowless glare. The kitchen floor was warm to his bare feet and the water warmish as it came from the tap. He filled a glass twice and then emptied it into the sink and then filled it again before it was cold enough to drink. He had not put on his slippers because he could not remember where he had left them. He had been too busy thinking of Sue. Now he suddenly remembered that they were still where he had dropped them in the coal-scuttle by the side of the stove.

After he had put them on he opened the kitchen door and stepped outside and stood in the garden. Distinctly, with astonishingly pure clearness, he could see the colours of all the roses, even those of the darkest red. He could even distinguish the yellow from the white and not only in the still standing blooms but in all the fallen petals, thick everywhere on dry earth after the heat of the July day.

He walked until he stood in the centre of the lawn. For a time he could not discover a single star in the sky. The moon was like a solid opaque electric bulb, the glare of it almost cruel, he thought, as it poured down on the green darkness of summer trees.

Presently the wind made its quickening watery turn of sound among the leaves of the willow and ran away over the nightscape, and again he thought it was the sound of a car. He felt the breeze move coolly, almost coldly, about his pajama legs and he ran his fingers in agitation once or twice through the pillow tangles of his hair.

Suddenly he felt helpless and miserable.

"Sue," he said. "For God's sake where on earth have you got to? Susie, Susie—this isn't like you."

His pet term for her, Susie. In the normal way, Sue. Perhaps in rare moments of exasperation, Susan. He had called her Susie a great deal on her nineteenth birthday, three weeks before, before she had flown to Switzerland for her holiday. Everyone thought, that day, how much she had grown, how firm and full she was getting, and how wonderful it was that she was flying off alone. He only thought she looked more delicate and girlish than ever, quite thin and childish in the face in spite of her lipstick, and he was surprised to see her drinking what he thought were too many glasses of sherry. Nor, in contrast to himself, did she seem a bit nervous about the plane.

Over towards the town a clock struck chimes for a half hour and almost simultaneously he heard the sound of a car. There was no mistaking it this time. He could see the swing of its headlights too as it made the big bend by the packing station down the road, a quarter of a mile away.

"And quite time too, young lady," he thought. He felt sharply vexed, not miserable any more. He could hear the car coming fast. It was so fast that he began to run back to the house across the lawn. He wanted to be back in bed before she arrived and saw him there. He did not want to be caught like that. His pajama legs were several inches too long and were wet with the dew of the grass and he held them up, like skirts, as he ran.

What a damn ridiculous situation, he thought. What fools children could make you look sometimes. Just about as exasperating as they could be.

At the kitchen door one of his slippers dropped off and as he stopped to pick it up and listen again for the sound of the car he discovered that now there was no sound. The headlights too had disappeared. Once again there was nothing at all but the enormous noiseless glare, the small folding echoes of wind dying away.

"Damn it, we always walked home from dances," he thought. "That was part of the fun."

Suddenly he felt cold. He found himself remembering with fear the long bend by the packing station. There was no decent camber on it and if you took it the slightest bit too fast you couldn't make it. Every week there were accidents there. And God, anyway what did he know about this fellow? He might be the sort who went round making pick-ups. A married man or something. Anybody. A crook.

All of a sudden he had a terrible premonition about it all. It was exactly the sort of feeling he had had when he saw her enter the plane, and again when the plane lifted into sky. There was an awful sense of doom about it: he felt sure she was not coming back. Now he felt in some curious way that his blood was separating itself into single drops. The drops were freezing and dropping with infinite systematic deadliness through the veins, breeding cold terror inside him. Somehow he knew that there had been a crash.

He was not really aware of running down through the rose garden to the gate. He simply found himself somehow striding up and down in the road outside, tying his pajama cord tighter in agitation.

My God, he thought, how easily the thing could happen. A girl travelled by plane or train or even bus or something and before you knew where you were it was the beginning of something ghastly.

He began to walk up the road, feeling the cold precipitation of blood take drops of terror down to his legs and feet. A pale yellow suffusion of the lower sky struck into him the astonishing fact that it was almost day. He could hardly believe it and he broke miserably into a run.

Only a few moments later, a hundred yards away, he had the curious impression that from the roadside a pair of yellow eyes were staring back at him. He saw then that they were the lights of a stationary car. He did not know what to do about it. He could not very well go up to it and tap on the window and say, in tones of stern fatherhood, "Is my daughter in there? Susan, come home." There was always the chance that it would turn out to be someone else's daughter. It was always possible that it would turn out to be a daughter who liked what she was doing and strongly resented being interrupted in it by a prying middle-aged stranger in pajamas.

He stopped and saw the lip of daylight widening and deepening its yellow on the horizon. It suddenly filled him with the sobering thought that he ought to stop being a damn fool and pull himself together.

"Stop acting like a nursemaid," he said. "Go home and get into bed. Don't you trust her?" It was always when you didn't trust them, he told himself, that trouble really began. That was when you asked for it. It was a poor thing if you didn't trust them.

"Go home and get into bed, you poor sap," he said. "You never fussed this much even when she was little."

He had no sooner turned to go back than he heard the engine of the car starting. He looked round and saw the lights coming towards him down the road. Suddenly he felt more foolish than ever and there was no time for him to do anything but press himself quickly through a gap in the hedge by the roadside. The hedge was not very tall at that point and he found himself crouching down in a damp jungle of cow parsley and grass and nettles that wetted his pajamas as high as the chest and shoulders. By this time the light in the sky had grown quite golden and all the colours of day were becoming distinct again and he caught the smell of honeysuckle rising from the dew-iness of the hedge.

He lifted his head a second or so too late as the car went past him. He could not see whether Susie was in it or not and he was in a state of fresh exasperation as he followed it down the road. He was uncomfortable because the whole of his pajamas were sopping with dew and he knew that now he would have to change and get himself a good rub-down before he got back into bed.

"God, what awful fools they make you look," he thought, and then, a second later, "hell, it might not be her. Oh! hell, supposing it isn't her?" Wretchedly he felt his legs go weak and cold again. He forgot the dew on his chest and shoulders as the slow freezing precipitation of his blood began. From somewhere the wrenching thought of a hospital made him feel quite faint with a nausea that he could not fight away.

"Oh! Susie, for Jesus' sake don't do this any more to us. Don't do it any more—"

Then he was aware that the car had stopped by the gates of the house. He was made aware of it because suddenly, in the fuller dawn, the red rear light went out.

A second or two later he saw Susie. She was in her long heliotrope evening dress and she was holding it up at the skirt, in her delicate fashion, with both hands. Even from that distance he could see how pretty she was. The air too was so still in the birdless summer morning silence that he heard her distinctly, in her nice fluty voice, so girlish and friendly, call out:

"Good-bye. Yes: lovely. Thank you."

The only thing now, he thought, was not to be seen. He had to keep out of sight. He found himself scheming to get in by the side gate. Then he could slip up to the bathroom and get clean pajamas and perhaps even a shower.

Only a moment later he saw that the car had already turned and was coming back towards him up the road. This time there was no chance to hide and all he could do was to step into the verge to let it go past him. For a few wretched seconds he stood there as if naked in full daylight, trying with nonchalance to look the other way.

In consternation he heard the car pull up a dozen yards beyond him and then a voice called:

"Oh! sir. Pardon me. Are you Mr. Carteret, sir?"

"Yes," he said.

There was nothing for it now, he thought, but to go back and find out exactly who the damn fellow was.

"Yes, I'm Carteret," he said and he tried to put into his voice what he thought was a detached, unstuffy, coolish sort of dignity.

"Oh! I'm Bill Jordan, sir." The young man had fair, smooth-brushed hair that looked extremely youthful against the black of his dinner jacket. "I'm sorry we're so late. I hope you haven't been worried about Susie?"

"Oh! no. Good God, no."

"It was my mother's fault. She kept us."

"I thought you'd been dancing?"

"Oh! no, sir. Dinner with my mother. We did dance a few minutes on the lawn but then we played canasta till three. My mother's one of those canasta fanatics. It's mostly her fault, I'm afraid."

"Oh! that's all right. So long as you had a good time."

"Oh! we had a marvellous time, sir. It was just that I thought you might be worried about Susie—"

"Oh! great heavens, no."

"That's fine, then sir." The young man had given several swift looks at the damp pajamas and now he gave another and said: "It's been a wonderfully warm night, hasn't it?"

"Awfully close. I couldn't sleep."

"Sleep—that reminds me." He laughed with friendly, expansive well-kept teeth that made him look more youthful than ever and more handsome. "I'd better get home or it'll be breakfast-time. Good night, sir."

"Good night."

The car began to move away. The young man lifted one hand in farewell and Carteret called after him:

"You must come over and have dinner with us one evening—"

"Love to. Thank you very much, sir. Good night."

Carteret walked down the road. Very touching, the sir business. Very illuminating and nice. Very typical. It was touches like that which counted. In relief he felt a sensation of extraordinary self-satisfaction.

When he reached the garden gate the daylight was so strong that it showed with wonderful freshness all the roses that had unfolded in the night. There was one particularly beautiful crimson one, very dark, almost black, that he thought for a moment of picking and taking upstairs to his wife. But finally he decided against it and left it where it grew.

By that time the moon was fading and everywhere the birds were taking over the sky.

THE KIMONO

[1]

It was the second Saturday of August, 1911, when I came to London for the interview with Kersch and Co. I was just twenty-five. The summer had been almost tropical.

There used to be a train in those days that got into St. Pancras, from the North, about ten in the morning. I came by it from Nottingham, left my bag in the cloakroom and went straight down to the City by bus. The heat of London was terrific, a white dust heat, thick with the smell of horse dung. I had put on my best suit, a blue serge, and it was like a suit of gauze. The heat seemed to stab at me through it.

Kersch and Co. were very nice. They were electrical engineers. I had applied for a vacancy advertised by them. That morning I was on the short list and Mr. Alexander Kersch, the son, was very nice to me. We talked a good deal about Nottingham and I asked him if he knew the Brownsons, who were prominent Congregationalists there, but he said no. Everyone in Nottingham, almost, knew the Brownsons, but I suppose it did not occur to me in my excitement that Kersch was a Jew. After a time he offered me a whisky and soda, but I refused. I had been brought up rather strictly, and in any case the Brownsons would not have liked it. Finally, Mr. Kersch asked me if I could be in London over the week-end. I said yes, and he asked me at once to come in on Monday morning. I knew then that the job was as good as settled and I was trembling with excitement as I shook hands and said good-bye.

I came out of Kersch and Co. just before twelve o'clock. Their offices were somewhere off Cheapside. I forget the name of the street. I only remember, now, how very hot it was. There was something un-English about it. It was a terrific heat, fierce and white. And I made up my mind to go straight back to St. Pancras and get my bag and take it to the hotel the Brownsons had recommended to me. It was so hot that I didn't want to eat. I felt that if I could get my room and wash and rest it would be enough. I could eat later. I would go up West and do myself rather well.

Pa Brownson had outlined the position of the hotel so well, both in conversation and on paper, that when I came out of St. Pancras with my bag I felt I knew the way to the street as well as if it had been in Nottingham. I turned east and then north and went on turning left and then right, until finally I came to the place where the street with hotel ought to have been. It wasn't there. I couldn't believe it. I walked about a bit, always coming back to the same place again in case I should get lost. Then I asked a baker's boy where Midhope Street was and he didn't know. I asked one or two more people, and they didn't know either. "Wade's Hotel," I would say, to make it clearer, but it was no good. Then a man said he thought I should go back towards St. Pancras a bit, and ask again, and I did.

It must have been about two o'clock when I knew that I was pretty well lost. The heat was shattering. I saw one or two other hotels but they looked a bit low class and I was tired and desperate.

Finally I set my bag down in the shade and wiped my face. The sweat on me was filthy. I was wretched. The Brownsons had been so definite about the hotel and I knew that when I got back they would ask me if I liked it and all about it. Hilda would want to know about it too. Later on, if I got the Kersch job, we should be coming up to it for our honeymoon.

At last I picked up my bag again. Across the street was a little sweet shop and café showing ices. I went across to it. I felt I had to have something.

In the shop a big woman with black hair was tinkering with the ice-cream mixer. Something had gone wrong. I saw that at once. It was just my luck.

"I suppose it's no use asking for an ice?" I said.

"Well, if you wouldn't mind *waiting*."

"How long?"

"As soon as ever I get this nut fixed on and the freezer going again. We've had a breakdown."

"All right. You don't mind if I sit down?" I said.

She said no, and I sat down and leaned one elbow on the tea-table, the only one there was. The woman went on tinkering with the freezer. She was a heavy woman, about fifty, a little swarthy, and rather masterful to look at. The shop was stifling and filled with a sort of yellowish-pink shade cast by the sun pouring through the shop blind.

"I suppose it's no use asking you where Midhope Street is?" I said.

"Midhope Street," she said. She put her tongue in her cheek, in thought. "Midhope Street, I ought to know that."

"Or Wade's Hotel."

"Wade's Hotel," she said. She wriggled her tongue between her teeth. They were handsome teeth, very white. "Wade's Hotel. No. That beats me." And then: "Perhaps my daughter will know. I'll call her."

She straightened up to call into the back of the shop. But a second before she opened her mouth the girl herself came in. She looked surprised to see me there.

"Oh, here you are, Blanche! This gentleman here is looking for Wade's Hotel."

"I'm afraid I'm lost," I said.

"Wade's Hotel," the girl said. She too stood in thought, running her tongue over her teeth, and her teeth too were very white, like her mother's. "Wade's Hotel. I've seen that somewhere. Surely?"

"Midhope Street," I said.

"Midhope Street."

No, she couldn't remember. She had on a sort of kimono, loose, with big orange flowers all over it. I remember thinking it was rather fast. For those days it was. It wouldn't be now. And somehow, because it was so loose and brilliant, I couldn't take my eyes off it. It made me uneasy, but it was an uneasiness in which there was pleasure as well, almost excitement. I remember thinking she was really half undressed. The kimono had no neck and no sleeves. It was simply a piece of material that wrapped over her, and when suddenly she bent down and tried to fit the last screw on to the freezer the whole kimono fell loose and I could see her body.

At the same time something else happened. Her hair fell over her shoulder. It was the time of very long hair, the days when girls would pride themselves that they could sit on their pigtails, but hers was the longest hair I had ever seen. It was like thick jet-black cotton-rope. And when she bent down over the freezer the pigtail of it was so long that the tip touched ice.

"I'm so sorry," the girl said. "My hair's always getting me into trouble."

"It's all right. It just seems to be my unlucky day, that's all."

"I'm so sorry."

"Will you have a cup of tea?" the woman said. "Instead of the ice? Instead of waiting?"

"That's it, Mother. Get him some tea. You *would* like tea, wouldn't you?"

"Very much."

So the woman went through the counter-flap into the back of the shop to get the tea. The girl and I, in the shop alone, stood and looked at the freezer. I felt queer in some way, uneasy. The girl had not troubled to tighten up her kimono. She let it hang loose, anyhow, so that all the time I could see part of her shoulder and now and then her breasts. Her skin was very white, and once when she leaned forward rather farther than usual I could have sworn that she had nothing on at all underneath.

"You keep looking at my kimono," she said. "Do you like it?"

"It's very nice," I said. "It's very nice stuff."

"Lovely stuff. Feel of it. Go on. Just feel of it."

I felt the stuff. For some reason, perhaps it was because I had had no food, I felt weak. And she knew it. She must have known it. "It's lovely stuff. Feel it. I made it myself." She spoke sweetly and softly in invitation. There was something electric about her. I listened quite mechanically. From the minute she asked me to feel the stuff of her kimono I was quite helpless. She had me, as it were, completely done up in the tangled maze of the orange and green of its flowers and leaves.

"Are you in London for long? Only today?"

"Until Monday."

"I suppose you booked your room at the hotel?"

"No. I didn't book it. But I was strongly recommended there."

"I see."

That was all, only "I see." But in it there was something quite maddening. It was a kind passionate veiled hint, a secret invitation.

"Things were going well," I said, "until I lost my way."

"Oh?"

"I came up for an interview and I got the job. At least I think I got the job."

"A bit of luck. I hope it's a good one?"

"Yes," I said. "It is. Kersch and Co. In the City."

"Kersch and Co.?" she said. "Not really? Kersch and Co.?"

"Yes," I said. "Why, do you know them?"

"Know them? Of course I know them. Everybody knows them. That *is* a bit of luck for you."

And really I was flattered. She knew Kersch and Co.! She knew that it was a good thing. I think I was more pleased because of the attitude of the Brownsons. Kersch and Co. didn't mean anything to the Brownsons. It was just a name. They had been rather cold about it. I think they would have liked me to get the job, but they wouldn't have broken their hearts if I hadn't. Certainly they hadn't shown any excitement.

"Kersch and Co.," the girl said again. "That really *is* a bit of luck."

Then the woman came in with the tea. "Would you like anything to eat?"

"Well, I've had no dinner."

"Oh! No wonder you look tired. I'll get you a sandwich. Is that all right?"

"Thank you."

So the woman went out to get the sandwich, and the girl and I stayed in the shop again, alone.

"It's a pity you booked your room at the hotel," she said.

"I haven't booked it," I said.

"Oh! I thought you said you'd *booked* it. Oh! My fault. You *haven't* booked it?"

"No. Why?"

"We take people in here," she said. "Over the café. It's not central of course. But then we don't charge so much."

I thought of the Brownsons. "Perhaps I ought to go to the hotel," I said.

"We charge three and six," she said. "That isn't much, is it?"

"Oh, no!"

"Why don't you just come up and see the room?" she said. "Just come up."

"Well—"

"Come up and see it. It won't eat you."

She opened the rear door of the shop and in a moment I was going upstairs behind her. She was not wearing any stockings. Her bare legs were beautifully strong and white. The room was over the café. It was a very good room for three and six. The new wall-paper was silver-leaved and the bed was white and looked cool.

And suddenly it seemed silly to go out into the heat again and wander about looking for Wade's Hotel when I could stay where I was.

"Well, what do you think of it?" she said.

"I like it." She sat down on the bed. The kimono was drawn up over her legs and where it parted at her knees I could see her thighs, strong and white and softly disappearing into the shadow of the kimono. It was the day of long rather prim skirts and I had never seen a woman's legs like that. There was nothing between Hilda and me beyond kissing. All we had done was to talk of things, but there was nothing in it. Hilda always used to say that she would keep herself for me.

The girl hugger her knees. I could have sworn she had nothing on under the kimono.

"I don't want to press you," she said, "but I do wish you'd stay. You'd be our first let."

Suddenly a great wave of heat came up from the street outside, the fierce, horse-smelling, dust-white heat of the earlier day, and I said:

"All right. I'll stay."

"Oh, you angel!"

The way she said that was so warm and frank that I did not know what to do. I simply smiled. I felt curiously weak with pleasure. Standing there, I could smell suddenly not only the heat but the warmth of her own body. It was sweetish and pungent, the soft odour of sweat and perfume. My heart was racing.

Then suddenly she got up and smoothed the kimono over her knees and thighs.

"My father just died, you see," she said. "We are trying this for a living. You'll give us a start."

Somehow it seemed too good to be true.

[2]

I know now that it was. But I will say more of that later, when the time comes.

That evening I came down into the shop again about six o'clock. I had had my tea and unpacked my things and rested. It was not much cooler, but I felt better. I was glad I had stayed.

The girl, Blanche, was sitting behind the counter, fanning herself with the broken lid of a sweet-box. She had taken off her kimono and was wearing a white gauzy dress with a black sash. I was disappointed. I think she must have seen that, because she pouted a bit when I looked at her. In turn I was glad she pouted. It made her lips look full-blooded and rich and shining. There was something lovely about her when she was sulky.

"Going out?" she said.

"Yes," I said. "I thought of going up West and celebrating over Kersch and Co."

"Celebrating? By yourself?"

"Well," I said. "I'm alone. There's no one else."

"Lucky you."

I knew what she meant in a moment. "Well," I said, almost in a joke, "why don't you come?"

"Me?" she said, eyes wide open. "You don't mean it. Me?"

"I do," I said. "I do mean it."

She got up. "How long can you wait? I'll just change my dress and tell mother."

"No hurry at all," I said, and she ran upstairs.

I have said nothing about how old she was. In the kimono she looked about twenty, and in the white dress about the same age, perhaps a little younger. When she came down again that evening she looked nearer twenty-six or twenty-seven. She looked big and mature. She had changed from the white dress into a startling yellow affair with a sort of black coatee cut away at the hips. It was so flashy that I felt uneasy. It was very tight too: the skirt so tight that I could see every line of her body, the bodice filled tight in turn with her big breasts. I forgot what her hat was like. I rather fancy I thought it was rather silly. But later she took it off.

"Well, where shall we go?" she said.

"I thought of going up West and eating and perhaps dropping in to hear some music."

"Music. Isn't that rather dull?"

"Well, a play then."

"I say," she said, "don't let's go up West. Let's go down to the East End instead. We can have some fun. It'll do you good to see how the Jews live. If you're going to work for a firm of Jews you ought to know something about them. We might have some Jewish food. I know a nice place."

So we took a bus and went. In the Mile End Road we had a meal. I didn't like it. The food didn't smell very nice. It was spiced and strong and rather strange to eat. But Blanche liked it. Finally she said she was thirsty. "Let's go out of here and have a drink somewhere else," she said. "I know a place where you can get beautiful wine, cheap." So we went from that restaurant to another. We had some cheese and a bottle of wine—asti, I think it was. The place was Italian. The evening was stifling and everywhere people were drinking heavily and fanning themselves limply against the heat. After the wine I began to feel rather strange. I wasn't used to it and I hardly knew what I was doing. The cheese was rather salty and made me thirsty. I kept drinking almost unconsciously and my lips began to form syllables roundly and loosely. I kept staring at

Blanche and thinking of her in the kimono. She in turn would stare back and we played a kind of game, carrying on a kind of conversation with glances, burning each other up, until at last she said:

"What's your name? You haven't told me yet."

"Arthur," I said. "Arthur Lawson."

"Arthur."

The way she said it set my heart on fire. I just couldn't say anything: I simply sat looking at her. There was an intimacy then, at that moment, in the mere silences and glances between us, that went far beyond anything I had known with Hilda.

Then she saw something on the back of the menu that made her give a little cry.

"Oh, there's a circus! Oh, let's go! Oh, Arthur, you must take me."

So we went there too. I forget the name of the theatre and really, except for some little men and women with wizened bird faces and beards, there is nothing I remember except one thing. In the middle of the show was a trapeze act. A girl was swinging backwards and forwards across the stage in readiness to somersault and the drum was rolling to rouse the audience to excitement. Suddenly the girl shouted "I can't do it!" and let loose. She crashed down into the stalls and in a minute half the audience were standing up in a pandemonium of terror.

"Oh! Arthur, take me out."

We went out directly. In those days women fainted more often and more easily than they do now, and I thought Blanche would faint too. As we came out into the street she leaned against me heavily and clutched my arm.

"I'll get a cab and take you home," I said.

"Something to drink first."

I was a bit upset myself. We had a glass of port in a public house. It must have been about ten o'clock. Before long, after the rest and the port, Blanche's eyes were quite bright again.

Soon after that we took the cab and drove home. "Let me lean against you," she said. I took her and held her. "That's it," she said. "Hold me. Hold me tight." It was so hot in the cab that I could hardly breathe and I could feel her face hot and moist too. "You're so hot," I said. She said it was her dress. The velvet coatee was too warm. "I'll change it as soon as I get home," she said. "Then we'll have a drink. Some ice-cream in lemonade. That'll be nice."

In the cab I looked down at her hair. It was amazingly black. I smiled at it softly. It was full of odours that were warm and voluptuous. But it was the blackness of it that was so wonderful and so lovely.

"Why do they call you Blanche?" I said. "When you're so black. Blanche means white."

"How do you know I'm not white underneath?" she said.

I could not speak. No conversation I had ever had with a woman had ever gone within miles of that single sentence. I sat dazed, my heart racing. I did not know what to do. "Hold me tight," she said. I held her and kissed her. I got out of the cab mechanically. In the shop she went straight upstairs. I kept thinking of what she had said. I was wild with a new and for me a delicious excitement. Downstairs the shop was in darkness and finally I could not wait for her to come down again. I went quietly upstairs to meet her.

She was coming across the landing as I reached the head of the stairs. She was in the kimono, in her bare feet.

"Where are you?" she said softly. "I can't see you." She came a second later and touched me.

"Just let me see if mother has turned your bed back," she whispered.

She went into my bedroom. I followed her. She was leaning over the bed. My heart was racing with a sensation of great longing for her. She smoothed the bed with her hands and, as she did so, the kimono, held no longer, fell right apart.

And as she turned again I could see, even in the darkness, that she had nothing on underneath it at all.

[3]

On the following Monday morning I saw Kersch and Co. again and in the afternoon I went back to Nottingham. I had been given the job.

But curiously, for a reason I could not explain, I was no longer excited. I kept thinking of Blanche. I suppose, what with my engagement to Hilda Brownson and so on, I ought to have been uneasy and a little conscience-stricken. I was uneasy, but it was a mad uneasiness and there was no con-science at all in it. I felt reckless and feverish, almost desperate. Blanche was the first woman I had known at all on terms of intimacy, and it shattered me. All my complacent values of love and women were smashed. I had slept

with Blanche on Saturday night and again on Sunday and the effect on me
was one of almost catastrophic ecstasy.

That was something I had never known at all with Hilda: I had never
come near it. I am not telling this, emphasizing the physical side of it and
singling out the more passionate implications of it, merely for the sake of
telling it. I want to make clear that I had undergone a revolution: a revolution brought about, too, simply by a kimono and a girl's bare body underneath it. And since it was a revolution that changed my whole life it seems
to me that I ought to make the colossal effect of it quite clear, now and for
always.

I know, now, that I ought to have broken it off with Hilda at once. But
I didn't. She was so pleased at my getting the Kersch job that to have told
her would have been as cruel as taking away a doll from a child. I couldn't
tell her.

A month later we were married. My heart was simply not in it. I wasn't
there. All the time I was thinking of and, in imagination, making love to
Blanche. We spent our honeymoon at Bournemouth in September. Kersch
and Co. had been very nice and the result was that I was not to take up the
new appointment until the twenty-fifth of the month.

I say appointment. It was the word the Brownsons always used. From the
very first they were not very much in love with my going to work in
London at all and taking Hilda with me. I myself had no parents, but Hilda
was their only child. That put what seemed to me a snobbish premium on
her. They set her on a pedestal. My job was nothing beside Hilda. They
began to dictate what we should do and how and where we ought to live,
and finally Mrs. Brownson suggested that we all go to London and choose
the flat in which we were to live. I objected. Then Hilda cried and there was
an unpleasant scene in which Pa Brownson said that he thought I was unrea-
sonable and that all Mrs. Brownson was trying to do was to ensure that I
could give Hilda as good a home as she had always had. He said something
else about God guiding us as He had always guided them. We must put our
trust in God. But God or no God, I was determined that if we were going
to live in a flat in London the Brownsons shouldn't choose it. I would
choose it myself. Because even then I knew where, if it was humanly possible, I wanted it to be.

In the end I went to London by myself. I talked round Hilda, and Hilda
talked round her mother, and her mother, I suppose, talked round her
father. At any rate I went. We decided on a flat at twenty-five shillings a

week if we could get it. It was then about the twentieth of September.
I went straight from St. Pancras to Blanche. It was a lovely day, blue and
soft. It was a pain for me merely to be alive. I got to the shop just as Blanche
was going out. We almost bumped into each other.

"Arthur!"

The way she said it made me almost sick with joy. She had on a tight fawn
costume and a little fussy brown hat. "Arthur! I was just going out. You just
caught me. But mother can go instead. Oh! Arthur." Her mother came out
of the back room and in a minute Blanche had taken off her hat and costume
and her mother had gone out instead of her, leaving us alone in the shop.

We went straight upstairs. There was no decision, no asking, no consent
in it at all. We went straight up out of a tremendous equal passion for each
other. We were completely in unison, in desire and act and consummation
and everything. Someone came in the shop and rang the bell loudly while
we were upstairs, but it made no difference. We simply existed for each
other. There was no outside world. She seemed to me then amazingly rich
and mature and yet sweet. She was like a pear, soft and full-juiced and over-
flowing with passion. Beside her Hilda seemed like an empty eggshell.

I stayed with the Hartmans that night and the next. There were still three
days to go before the Kersch job began. Then I stayed another night. I tel-
egraphed Hilda, "Delayed. Returning certain tomorrow."

I never went. I was bound, heart and soul, to Blanche Hartman. There
was never any getting away from it. I was so far gone that it was not until
the second day of that second visit that I noticed the name Hartman at all.

"I'm going to stay here," I said to Blanche. "Lodge here and live with
you. Do you want me?"

"Arthur, Arthur."

"My God," I said. "Don't." I simply couldn't bear the repetition of my
name. It awoke every sort of fierce passion in me.

Then after a time I said: "There's something I've got to tell you."

"I know," she said. "About another girl. It doesn't matter. I don't want
to hear. I could tell you about other men."

"No, but listen," I said. "I'm married." I told her all about Hilda.

"It doesn't matter," she said. "It makes no difference. You could be a
Mormon and it wouldn't matter."

And after that, because it mattered nothing to her, it mattered nothing to
me. There is no conscience in passion. When I did think of Hilda and the
Brownsons it was like the squirt of a syphon on to a blazing furnace. I really

had no conscience at all. I walked out of one life into another as easily as from one room into another.

The only difficulty was Kersch and Co. It was there that Hilda would inquire for me as soon as I failed to turn up.

Actually I got out of the Kersch difficulty as easily as I got out of the rest. I didn't go back there either.

[4]

I went on living with Blanche until the war broke out. I got another job. Electrical engineers were scarcer in those days. Then, as soon as the war broke out, I joined up.

In a way it was almost a relief. Passion can go too far and one can have too much of it. I was tired out by a life that was too full of sublimity. It was not that I was tired of Blanche. She remained as irresistible to me as when I had first seen her in the green and orange kimono. It was only that I was tired of the constant act of passion itself. My spirit, as it were, had gone stale and I needed rest.

The war gave it me. As soon as I came home for my first leave I knew it was the best thing that could have happened to me. Blanche and I went straight back to the almost unearthly plane of former intimacy. It was the old almost catastrophic ecstasy.

I say almost catastrophic. Now, when I think of it, I see that it was really catastrophic. One cannot expect a woman to feed off the food of the gods and then suddenly, because one man among a million is not there, to go back on a diet of nothing at all. I am trying to be reasonable about this. I am not blaming Blanche. It is the ecstasy between us that I am blaming. It could not have been otherwise than catastrophic.

I always think it odd that I did not see the catastrophe coming before it did. But perhaps if I had seen it coming it would have ceased to be a catastrophe. I don't know. I only know that I came home in 1917, unexpectedly, and found that Blanche was carrying on with another man.

I always remembered that Mrs. Hartman looked extraordinarily scared as I walked into the shop that day. She was an assured, masterful woman and it was not at all like her to be scared. After a minute or so I went upstairs and in my bedroom a man was just buttoning up his waistcoat. Blanche was not there, but I understood.

I was furious, but the fury did not last. Blanche shattered it. She was a woman to whom passion was as essential as bread. She reminded me of that. But she reminded me also of something else. She reminded me that I was not married to her.

"But the moral obligation!" I raged.

"It's no good," she said. "I can't help it. It's no more than kissing to me. Don't be angry, honey. If you can't take me as I am you're not bound to take me at all."

And in the end she melted my fury. "What's between us is different from all the rest," she said. I believe her and she demonstrated it to me too. And I clung to that until the end of the war.

But when I came home finally it had gone farther than that. There was more than one man. They came to the shop, travellers in the sweet-trade, demobilized young officers with cars. They called while I was at my job.

I found out about it. This time I didn't say anything. I did something instead. I gave up what the Brownsons would have called my appointment.

"But what have you done that for?" Blanche said.

"I can't stand being tied by a job anymore," I said. "I'll work here. We'll develop the shop. There's money in it."

"Who's going to pay for it?"

"I will."

Just before I married Hilda I had nearly a hundred and fifty pounds in the bank. I had had it transferred to a London branch and it was almost all of it still there. I drew it out and in the summer of 1919 I spent nearly £80 of it on renovating the Hartman's shop. Blanche was delighted. She supervised the decorations and the final colour scheme of the combined shop and café was orange and green.

"Like your kimono," I said. "You remember it? That old one?"

"Oh! Arthur. I've got it."

"Put it on," I said.

She went upstairs and put it on. In about a minute I followed her. It was like old times. It brought us together again.

"Tell me something," I said. "That first day, when I came in. You hadn't anything on underneath, had you?"

"No," she said. "I'd just had a bath and it was all I had time to slip on."

"By God, kiss me."

She kissed me and I held her very tight. Her body was thicker and heavier now, but she was still lovely. It was all I asked. I was quite happy.

Then something else happened. I got used to seeing men in the shop. Most of them shot off now when they saw me, but one day when I came back from the bank there was a man in the livingroom.

He was an oldish chap, with pepper and salt hair cut rather short.

"Hello," I said, "what's eating you?" I got to be rather short with any man I saw hanging about the place.

"Nothing's eating me," he said. "It's me who wants something to eat."

"Oh! Who are you?"

"My name's Hartman," he said.

I looked straight at his hair. It was Blanche's father. And in a minute I knew that he was out of prison.

I don't know why, but it was more of a shock to me than Blanche's affairs with other men. Blanche and I could fight out the question of unfaithfulness between ourselves, but the question of a criminal in the house was different.

"He isn't a criminal," Blanche said. "He's easily led and he was led away by others. Be kind to him, honey."

Perhaps I was soft. Perhaps I had no right to do anything. It was not my house, it was not my father. Blanche was not even my wife. What could I possibly do but let him stay?

That summer we did quite well with the new café. We made a profit of nine and very often ten or eleven pounds a week. Hartman came home in May. In July things began to get worse. Actually, with the summer at its height, they ought to have been better. But the takings dropped to six and even five pounds. Blanche and her mother kept saying that they couldn't understand it.

But I could. Or at least I could after a long time. It was Hartman. He was not only sponging on me, but robbing the till too. All the hard-earned savings of the shop were being boozed away by Hartman.

I wanted to throw him out. But Blanche and her mother wouldn't hear of it. "He's nothing but a damned scoundrel," I shouted.

"He's my father," Blanche said.

That was the beginning of it. I date the antagonism between us and also the estrangement between us from that moment. It was never the same afterwards. I could stand Blanche being nothing more or less than a whore, but it was the thought of the old man and the thought of my own stupidity and folly that enraged me and finally almost broke me up.

Perhaps, I shouldn't have written the word whore, and I wouldn't have done if it wasn't for the fact that, as I sit here, my heart is really almost broken.

[5]

I am sitting in what used to be my bedroom. We have changed it into a sitting-room now. We ought to have it done up. We haven't had new paper on it for seven or eight years.

I am just fifty. I think Blanche is just about fifty, too. She is out somewhere. It's no use thinking where. Passion is still as essential to her as bread. It means no more to her and I have long since given up asking where she goes. And somehow—and this is the damnable part of it all—I am still fond of her, but gently and rather foolishly now. What I feel for her most is regret. Not anger and not passion. I couldn't keep up with her pace. She long since outdistanced me in the matter of emotions.

Mrs. Hartman is dead. I am sorry. She was likeable and though sometimes I didn't trust her I think she liked me. Hartman still hangs on. I keep the till-money locked up, but somehow he picks the locks, and there it is. He's too clever for me and I can't prove it. I feel as if, now, I am in a prison far more complete than any Hartman was ever in. It is a bondage directly inherited from that first catastrophic passion for Blanche. It's that, really, that I can't escape. It binds me irrevocably. I know that I shall never escape.

Last night, for instance, I had a chance to escape. I know of course that I'm a free man and that I am not married to Blanche and that I could walk out now and never come back. But this was different.

Hilda asked for me. I was in the shop, alone, just about six o'clock. I was looking at the paper. We don't get many people in the café now, but I always have the evening paper, in case. This district has gone down a lot and the café of course has gone down with it. We don't get the people in that we did. And as I was reading the paper the wireless was on. At six o'clock, the dance band ended and in another moment or two someone was saying my name.

"Will Arthur Lawson, last heard of in London twenty-five years ago, go at once to the Nottingham Infirmary, where his wife, Hilda Lawson, is dangerously ill."

That was all. No one but me, in this house I mean, heard it. Afterwards no one mentioned it. Round here they think my name is Hartman. It was as thought it had never happened.

But it was for me all right. When I heard it I stood stunned, as though something had struck me. I almost died where I stood, at the foot of the stairs.

Then after a bit I got over it enough to walk upstairs to the sitting-room. I did not know quite what I was doing. I felt faint and I sat down. I thought it over. After a minute I could see that there was no question of going. If it had been Blanche—yes. But not Hilda. I couldn't face it. And I just sat there and thought not of what I should do but what I might have done.

I thought of that hot day in 1911, and the Kersch job and how glad I was to get it. I thought about Hilda. I wondered what she looked like now and what she had done with herself for twenty-five years and what she had suffered. Finally I thought of that catastrophic ecstasy with Blanche, and then of the kimono. And I wondered how things might have gone if the Hartmans' ice-cream freezer had never broken and if Blanche had been dressed as any other girl would have been dressed that day.

And thinking and wondering, I sat there and cried like a child.

LOVE IN A WYCH ELM

When I was a boy the Candleton sisters, seven of them, lived in a large gabled house built of red brick that gave the impression of having been muted by continual sunlight to a pleasant shade of orange-rose. The front face of it had a high, benign open appearance and I always felt that the big sash windows actually smiled down on the long gravel terrace, the iron pergola of roses and the sunken tennis lawn. At the back were rows of stables, all in the same faded and agreeable shade of brick, with lofts above them that were full of insecure and ancient bedsteads, fire-guards, hip-baths, tennis rackets, croquet hammers, rocking horses, muscle-developers, Indian clubs, travelling trunks and things of that sort thrown out by Mr. and Mrs. Candleton over the course of their fruitful years.

I was never very sure of what Mr. Candleton did in life; I was not even sure in fact if he did anything at all except to induce Mrs. Candleton, at very regular intervals, to bear another daughter. In a town like Evensford there were at that time very few people of independent means who lived in houses that had stables at the back. The Candletons were, or so it seemed to me, above our station. There was at one time a story that Mr. Candleton was connected with wine. I could well believe this. Like his house, Mr. Candleton's face had toned to a remarkably pleasant shade of inflammable rose. This always seemed perhaps brighter than it really was because his eyes were so blue. They were of that rare shade of pale violet blue that always seems about to dissolve, especially in intoxication. This effect was still further heightened by hair of a most pure distinguished shade of yellow: a thick oat-straw yellow that was quite startling and remarkable in a male.

All the Candleton sisters too had their father's pale violet dissolving eyes and that exceptional shade of oat-straw hair.

At first, when they were very small children, it was white and silky. Then as they grew up its characteristic shining straw-colour grew stronger. A stranger seeing them for the first time would have said that they were seven dolls who had been dipped in a solution of something several shades paler than saffron. The hair was very beautiful when brushed and as children they all wore it long.

On hot days in summer Mr. Candleton wore cream flannel trousers with a blue pin stripe in them, a blazer with red and orange stripes, and a straw hat with a band of the same design. Round his waist he wore a red silk cummerbund. All his shirts were of silk and he always wore them buttoned at the neck. In winter he wore things like Donegal tweeds: roughish, sporting, oatmeal affairs that were just right for his grained waterproof shooting brogues. He wore smart yellow gloves and a soft tweed hat with a little feather in the band. He always seemed to be setting off somewhere, brisk and dandyish and correct, a man of leisure with plenty of time to spare.

It was quite different with Mrs. Candleton. The house was big and rambling and it might well have been built specially to accommodate Mrs. Candleton, who was like a big, absent-minded, untidy, roving bear. My mother used to say that she got up and went to bed in a pinafore. It wasn't a very clean pinafore either. Nor were her paper hair-curlers, which were sometimes still in her rough unruly black hair at tea time. She always seemed to be wearing carpet slippers and sometimes her stockings would be slipping down. She was a woman who always seemed to be catching up with life and was always a day and a half behind.

The fact was, I suppose, that with seven children in something like a dozen years Mrs. Candleton was still naturally hazy in some of her diurnal calculations. Instead of her catching up with life, life was always catching up with her.

Meals, for example, made the oddest appearances in the Candleton household. If I went on a school-less day to call on Stella—she was the one exactly of my own age, the one I knew best—it was either to find breakfast being taken at eleven-thirty, with Mr. Candleton always immaculate behind the silver toast-rack and Mrs. Candleton looking like the jaded mistress of a rag-and-bone man, or dinner at half-past three or tea at seven. In a town like Evensford everybody was rigidly governed by factory hours and the sound of factory hooters. At various times of the day silences fell on the town that were a hushed indication that all honest people were decently at work. All this meant that breakfast was at seven, dinner at twelve-thirty and tea at half-past five. That was how everybody ate and lived and ran their lives in Evensford: everybody, that it, except the Candletons.

These characteristics of excessive and immediate smartness on the one hand and the hair-curler and pinafore style on the other had been bequeathed by him and Mrs. Candleton in almost exactly equal measure to their children. The girls were all beautiful, all excessively dressy as they grew up and, as my mother was fond of saying, not over clean.

"If they get a cat-lick once a week it's about as much as they do get," was one of her favourite sayings.

But children do not notice such things very acutely and I cannot say that I myself was very interested in the virtues of soap and water. What I liked about the Candletons was not only a certain mysterious quality of what I thought was aristocracy but a feeling of untamed irresponsibility. They were effervescent. When the eldest girl, Lorna, was seventeen she ran off with a captain in the Royal Artillery who turned out to be a married man. I thought it might well have been the sort of thing that would have ruined a girl, temporarily at least, in Evensford, but Stella simply thought it a wild joke and said:

"She had a wonderful time. It was gorgeous. They stayed at a marvellous hotel in London. She told us all about it. I thought Mother would die laughing."

Of laughing, not shame: that was typical of the Candleton standard, the Candleton approach and the Candleton judgement on such things.

The four eldest girls, two of them twins, were called Lorna, Hilda, Rosa and Freda. This habit of giving names ending in the same letter went on to Stella, with whom I played street-games in winter in front of the gas-lit windows of a pork-pie and sausage shop and games in summer in the Candleton garden and among the muscle-developers and bedsteads of the Candleton loft, and then on to the two youngest, who were mere babies as I knew them, Wanda and Eva. Mrs. Candleton's Christian name was Blanche, which suited her perfectly.

It was a common tendency in all the Candleton girls to develop swiftly. At thirteen they were filling out; at fifteen they were splendidly and handsomely buxom and were doing up their hair. Hilda appeared to me to be a goddess of marbled form long before she was eighteen and got engaged to a beefy young farmer who bred prize cattle and called for her in a long open sports car.

Hilda had another characteristic not shared by any of the rest of the family except her mother. She sang rather well. At eighteen she began to have her pleasant, throaty, contralto voice trained. Mr. Candleton was a strict Sunday morning churchgoer in pin-stripe trousers, bowler hat and spats, and Hilda went with him to sing in the choir. Her voice was trained by a Mr.

Lancaster, a rather bumptious pint-sized tenor who gave her lessons three evenings a week. It was generally known that Mr. Lancaster was, as a singer at any rate, past his best, but it was not long before the engagement between Hilda and the farmer was broken.

At that time Stella and I were nine. I, at least, was nine and Stella, physically, was twelve or thirteen. What I liked about her so much in those days was her utter freedom to come and go as she pleased. Other children had errands to run, confirmation classes to attend, catechisms to learn, aunts to visit, restrictive penances like shoes to clean or knives to rub up with bath-brick.

In the Candleton way she had never anything to do but play, enjoy herself, indulge in inconsequential make-believe and teach me remarkable things about life and living.

"What shall we do? Let's be married. Let's go up to the loft and be married."

"We were married the day before yesterday."

"That doesn't matter. You can be married over and over again. Hilda's going to be. Come on, let's be married."

"All right. But not in the loft. Let's have a new house this time."

"All right. Let's be married in the wych-elm."

The Candleton garden extended beyond the stables into a rough orchard of old damson trees, with a few crooked espalier pears. A pepper-pot summer house in rustic work with a thatched roof stood in one corner, almost obliterated by lilac trees. In summer damsons and pears fell into the deep grass and no one picked them up. A sense of honeyed rotting quietness spread under the lurching trees and was compressed and shut in by a high boundary line of old, tapering wych-elms.

Rooks nested in the highest of the elms and when summer thickened the branches the trees were like a wall. The house was hidden and shut away. On a heavy summer day you would hear nothing there but the sound of rooks musing and croaking and fruit falling with a squashy mellow plop on the grass and paths.

Up in the wych-elms the peculiar structure of boughs made a house for us. We could walk about it. We crawled, like monkeys, from tree to tree. In this paradise we stayed for entire afternoons, cocooned with scents, hidden away in leaves. We made tea in ancient saucepans on flameless fires of elm twigs and prepared dinners of potatoes and gravy from fallen pears. And up here, on a soft August afternoon, we were married without witnesses and

Stella, with her yellow hair done up for the first time, wore a veil of lace curtains and carried a bunch of cow-parsley.

But before that happened I had caught, only the day before, another glimpse of the Candleton way of living.

I had called about six o'clock in the evening for Stella but although the door of the house was open nobody, for some time at any rate, answered my ring at the bell. That was not at all unusual at the Candleton household. Although it never seemed possible for nine such unmistakable people to disappear without trace it was frequently happening and often I went to the door and rang until I was tired of ringing and then went away without an answer.

I remember once ringing the bell and then, tired of it, peeping into the kitchen. It was one of those big old-fashioned kitchens with an enormous iron cooking range with plate racks above it and gigantic dressers and vast fish-kettles and knife-cleaners everywhere. In the middle of it all Mrs. Candleton sat asleep. Not normally asleep, I could see. A quarter-full bottle of something for which I had no definition stood on the table in front of her, together with a glass and, beside the glass, most astonishing thing of all, her false teeth.

Blowsily, frowsily, comfortably, toothlessly, Mrs. Candleton was sleeping away the afternoon in her hair-curlers and her pinafore.

But on the evening I called for Stella the kitchen was empty. I rang the bell four or five times and then, getting no answer, stepped into the hall.

"Hullo," someone said.

That very soft, whispered throaty voice was Hilda's. She was standing at the top of the stairs. She was wearing nothing but her petticoat and her feet were bare. In her hands she was holding a pair of stockings, which she had evidently been turning inside out in readiness to put on.

"Oh! it's you," she said. "I thought I heard someone."

"Is Stella here?"

"They're all out. They've all gone to the Robinsons' for tea. It's Katie's birthday."

"Oh! I see," I said. "Well, I'll come again tomorrow—"

"I'm just going to a dance," she said. "Would you like to see my dress? Would you?—come on, come up."

Standing in the bedroom, with the August sunlight shining on her bare shoulders, through the lace of her slip and on her sensational yellow Candleton hair, she was a magnificent figure of a girl.

"Just let me put my stockings on and then you can see my dress."

She sat down on the bed to put on her stockings. Her legs were smooth and heavy. I experienced an odd sensation as the stockings unrolled up her legs and then were fastened somewhere underneath the petticoat. Then she stood up and looked at the back of her legs to see if her stockings were straight. After that she smoothed the straps of her petticoat over her shoulders and said:

"Just wait till I give my hair one more brush."

I shall never forget how she sat before the dressing mirror and brushed her hair. I was agreeably and mystically stunned. The strokes of the brush made her hair shine exactly, as I have said before, like oat-straw. Nothing could have been purer and more shining. It was marvellously burnished and she laughed at me in the mirror because I stood there so staring and speechless and stunned.

"Well, do I look nice? You think I shall pass in a crowd?"

"Yes."

"That's good. It's nice to have a man's opinion."

She laughed again and put on her dress. It was pure white, long and flouncy. I remember distinctly the square low collar. Then she put on her necklace. It was a single row of pearls and she couldn't fasten it.

"Here, you can do this," she said.

She sat on the bed and I fastened the necklace. The young hair at the nape of her neck was like yellow chicken down. I was too confused to notice whether she had washed her neck or not and then she said:

"That's it. Now just a little of this and I'm ready."

She sprayed her hair, her arms and the central shadow of her bosom with scent from a spray.

"How about a little for you?"

She sprayed my hair and in a final moment of insupportable intoxication I was lost in a wave of wallflowers.

"That's the most expensive scent there is," she said. "The most difficult to make. Wallflowers."

Perhaps it was only natural, next day, as I came to be married to Stella high at the altar of the wych-elms, that I found myself oppressed by a sensation of anticlimax. Something about Stella, I felt, had not quite ripened. I had not the remotest idea as to what it could be except that she seemed, in some unelevating and puzzling way, awkward and flat.

"What do you keep staring at me for?"

"I'm just going to spray you with scent," I said. "There—piff! pish! piff—"

"Whatever made you think of that?"

I was afraid to speak of Hilda and I said:

"All girls have to have scent on when they're married."

"Do I look nice?"

She didn't really look nice. The lace curtain was mouldy in one corner and had holes down one side. I didn't like the odour of cow-parsley. But the soft golden oat-straw hair was as remarkable as ever and I said:

"You look all right."

Than we were married. After we were married she said:

"Now you have to make love to me."

"Why?"

"Everybody has to make love when they're married."

I looked at her in utter mystification. Then suddenly she dropped the cow-parsley and pushed back her veil and kissed me. She held me in an obliterating and momentary bondage by the trunk of the wych-elm, kissing me with such blistering force that I lost my cap. I was rather upset about my cap as it fell in the nettles below but she said:

"Sit down. We're in bed now. We have to be in bed now we're married. It's the first thing people do."

"Why?"

"Don't you know?"

I did not know; nor, as it happens, did she. But one of the advantages of being born one of a family of seven sisters is that you arrive much earlier at the approximation of the more delicate truths than you do if you are a boy. Perhaps in this respect I was a backward boy, but I could only think it was rather comfortless trying to make love in a wych-elm and after a time I said:

"Let's go and play in the loft now."

"What with?"

"I don't know," I said. "Let's have a change. We've been married an awful lot of times—"

"I know," she said. "We'll play with the chest-developers."

While we played in the loft with the chest-developers she had an original thought.

"I think if I practise a lot with these I shall get fat up top more quickly."

"You will?"

"I think I shall soon anyway."

Like Hilda, I thought. A renewed sensation of agreeable and stupefying delight, together with a scent of wallflowers, shot deliciously through me and I was half-way to the realisation of the truth that girls are pleasant things when she said:

"One day, when we're big, let's be really married, shall us?"

"All right."

"Promise?"

"Yes," I said.

"You know what you'll be when you're married to me, don't you?" she said.

I couldn't think.

"You'll be a viscount," she said.

"What's a viscount?"

"It's the husband of a viscountess."

"How shall I come to be that?"

"Because a viscountess is the daughter of a lord."

"But," I said, "your father isn't a lord."

"No," she said, "but his brother is. He lives in a castle in Bedfordshire. It has a hundred and forty rooms in it. We go there every summer. And when he dies my father will be a lord."

"Is he going to die?"

"Soon."

"Supposing your father dies before he does?"

"Oh! he won't," she said. "He's the youngest son. The oldest always die first."

She went on to tell me many interesting things about our life together. Everything in that life would be of silk, she said, like her father's shirts. Silk sheets on the bed, silk pillows, silk tablecloths, silk cushions. "And I shall always wear silk drawers," she said. "Even on week-days."

Altogether, it seemed, we should have a marvellous life together.

"And we shall drink port wine for supper," she said. "Like my father does. He always drinks port wine for supper."

"Is it nice?"

"Yes," she said. "I'm allowed to have it sometimes. You'll like it. You can get drunk as often as you like then. Like my father does."

"Does he get drunk?"

"Not as often as my mother does," she said, "but quite a lot."

I suppose I was shocked.

"Oh! that's all right," she said. "Lords always get drunk. That's why people always say 'drunk as a lord.' That's the proper thing to do."

Armed with the chest-developers, we spent an ecstatic afternoon. I was so filled with the golden snobbery of being a viscount that it was a cold and dusty sort of shock when she told me that anyway we couldn't be married for years and years, not until she was fatter, like Hilda was.

The recollection of Hilda, all burnished and magnificent and intoxicating and perfumed, inflamed and inspired me to greater efforts with the chest-developers.

"We must work harder," I said.

I wanted so much to be a lord, to live in a castle, to drink port wine and to be married to someone with silk drawers that I was totally unprepared for the shock my mother gave me.

"The little fibber, the little story-teller, the little liar," she said.

"But she said so," I said. "She told me."

"I went to board school with Reggie Candleton," she said. "He was in my class. They came from Gas Street."

Nothing in the world was worse than coming from Gas Street. You could not go lower than Gas Street. The end of the respectable world was Gas Street.

"It's she who had the money," my mother said. "Mrs. Candleton. Her father was a brewer and Reggie Candleton worked there. He was always such a little dandy. Such a little masher. Always the one for cutting such a dash."

I decided it was wiser to say nothing about the prospect of marrying, or about Stella's urgent efforts with the chest-developers, or the silk drawers.

"All top show," my mother said. "That's what it is. All fancy fol-di-dols on top and everything dropping into rags underneath. Every one of them with hair like a ten-guinea doll and a neck you could sow carrots in."

I don't suppose for a moment that Stella remembers me; or that, on an uncomfortable, intimate occasion, we were married in a wych-elm. It is equally unlikely that Hilda remembers me; or that, with her incomparable yellow hair, her white dance dress, her soft blonde flesh and her rare scent of wallflowers, she once asked me to give her my opinion as a man. I believe Stella is married to a bus-conductor. The rest of the Candletons have faded from my life. With the summer frocks, the summer straw hats and the summer flannels, the cummerbunds, the silk shirts, the elegant brogues, the chest-developers and the incomparable yellow hair they have joined Mr. Candleton in misty, muted, permanent bankruptcy.

Love in a wych-elm is not an easy thing; but like the Candletons it is unforgettable.

LET'S PLAY SOLDIERS

The yellow strings of laburnum flower had already faded that afternoon when I stood on sentry for the 1st Battalion Albion Street Light Infantry and Mrs. Strickland came out of her kitchen door wearing a sack apron and a man's check cap pinned on her spindly curling rags by a long black hat pin and started shaking mats against the garden fence, not three yards from the tent made of split sacks and old lace curtains where we of the battalion held councils of war before going into battle.

Upstairs across the yard Mrs. Rankin was sitting at a window with a bottom like a pumpkin hanging over the sill, huffing energetically on a glass already as pure as crystal and then scrupulously polishing the vapour off again with a spotless yellow rag.

The face of Mrs. Rankin, smooth and clean as porcelain, looked as if it had been polished too but the face of Mrs. Strickland, like her curl-ragged hair, had nothing but greyness in it, a dopey salty greyness at the same time hard so that the skin looked like scoured pumice stone.

I was only six at the time and still a private; but I thought I detected a smell of parsnip wine in the air. Mangled dust and shreds of coco-matting rose in dense brown clouds as Mrs. Strickland beat the decaying mats against the fence but I stood unshakably at attention under the laburnum tree, head up, eyes straight ahead, right hand firmly on the umbrella we were using as a rifle because Jeddah Clarke, our Captain, had the air-gun, the only other weapon we possessed.

I knew that if I stood firm on guard and didn't flinch and saluted properly and challenged people and didn't let them pass until they gave the password, I might become, in time, a lance corporal. There was nothing on earth I wanted more than to be a lance corporal: except perhaps to kill a soldier.

"I wisht Albie was here," Mrs. Strickland said. "I wisht Albie was here."

It wasn't only that morning that her voice had that pumice-dry melancholy in it. It was always there, like the curling rags. Sometimes Mrs. Strickland didn't take out the curling rags until after Bill Strickland came home for his bloater tea at six o'clock and sometimes she didn't take them out at all.

"Ain't got a spare Daisy Powder, gal, I reckon?"

Mrs. Strickland, staring with diffused and pleading eyes through the dust she had raised, groping up towards the sumptuous pumpkin of Mrs. Rankin on the window sill, ran a dreary hand several times across her aching brow.

"Ain't got nivry one left," Mrs. Rankin said. "You had the last one yisty."

Daisies were a brand of headache powder guaranteed to refresh and free you from pain in five minutes. Mrs. Strickland was taking them all day.

"Ain't Bill a-workin' then?"

"Bad a-bed. Can't lift 'isself orf the piller. I wisht Albie was here."

I knew Albie couldn't be here. Albie, who was eighteen, a private too like me, was in France, fighting the Germans. I liked Albie; he had a ginger moustache and was my friend. Every other day or so I asked Mrs. Strickland if and when Albie was going to become a lance corporal, but somehow she never seemed to think he was.

"Ain't you got nivry one tucked away, gal, somewheer?"

"Nivry one," Mrs. Rankin said. "Nivry one."

Despair wrapped Mrs. Strickland's face in a greyer, dustier web of gloom.

"Me 'ead's splitten'. It'll split open. I wisht Albie was here."

"Won't the boy nip and get y' couple? Ask the boy."

Mrs. Strickland, seeming to become aware of me for the first time, turned to my impassive sentinel figure with eyes of greyest supplication.

"Nip down the shop and fetch us a coupla Daisies, there's a good boy. Nip and ask your mother to lend us a thrippenny bit, there's a good boy. I left my puss upstairs."

It was funny, my mother always said, how Mrs. Strickland was always leaving, losing or mislaying her purse somewhere.

"And a penn'orth o' barm too, boy, while you're down there. I gotta make a mite o' bread, somehow," she called up to Mrs. Rankin. "Aain't got a mite in the place, gal. Not so much as a mossel."

Mrs. Rankin, who would presently be hurrying down to the yard to scour and white-wash the kitchen steps to blinding glacier whiteness and who, as my mother said, almost polished the coal before putting it on the fire, merely turned on Mrs. Strickland a rounder, blanker, completely unhelpful pumpkin.

I didn't move either; I was on guard and Jeddah Clarke said you could be shot if you moved on guard.

"Nip and ask your mother to lend us a thrippenny bit, boy. Tanner if she's got it, boy—"

"I can't go, Mrs. Strickland. I'm on sentry," I said. "I'll get shot."

"Kids everywhere," Mrs. Strickland said, "and nivry one on 'em to run of arrant for you when you want. I wisht Albie was here."

Mrs. Strickland dragged the decaying mats to the middle of the yard. The smell of parsnip wine went with her and she called up to Mrs. Rankin:

"Ain't got 'arf a loaf I can have for a goin' on with gal, I reckon? Jist till the baker gits here? Jist 'arf? Jist the top?"

"You want one as'll fit on the bottom I lent you the day afore yisty? or will a fresh 'un do?"

Fiery, tempestuous white curls seemed to fly suddenly out of Mrs. Strickland's mournful, aching head.

"What's a matter wi' y'? Askt y' a civil question, dint I? Askt y' civil question. What's a matter wi' y' all of a pop?"

"Sick on it,' Mrs. Rankin said. 'About sick to death on it."

"Go on, start maungin'! Start yelpin'!"

"Yelpin', yelpin'? Ain't got nothing to yelp about, I reckon, have I? When it ain't bread it's salt. When it ain't salt it's bakin' powder. Enough to gie y' the pip. When it ain't—"

"Keep on, keep on!" Mrs. Strickland said. "It'll do your fat gullet good. And me with 'im in bed. And the damn war on. And Albie not here."

Suddenly she dropped the mats, picked up a bucket from the kitchen drain and started beating and rattling it like a war-gong. In a flash Mrs. Rankin's pumpkin darted through the window, dragging the sash down behind it. Behind the crystal glass Mrs. Rankin's face remained palely distorted, mouthing furiously.

Down below in the yard, Mrs. Strickland rattled the bucket again, shaking her curling rags, and yelled:

"Mag, mag. Jaw, jaw. That's all folks like you are fit for. Mag, jaw, mag, jaw—"

Mrs. Rankin's face, ordinarily so polished and composed, splintered into uncontrollable furies behind the glass as Mrs. Strickland started to fill the bucket with water from the stand-pipe in the yard.

In a second Mrs. Rankin had the window up with a shrilling squeak of the sash and was half leaping out:

"And don't you start your hanky-pankies. Don't you start that!—I oiled and polished my door!—"

An arc of white water struck Mrs. Rankin's back door like a breaker. Mrs. Rankin slammed down the window and started beating the panes with her fists. Mrs. Strickland screamed that she wisht Albie was here, Albie would let some daylight into somebody, and threw the bucket with a crashing roll across the yard.

A moment later a bedroom window shot open in the Strickland house and an unsober chin of black stubble leaned out and bawled:

"What the bloody 'ell's going on down there? If you two don't shut your yawpin' chops I'll come down and lay a belt acrosst the pair on y'—"

"I wisht Albie was here!" Mrs. Strickland said. "I wisht Albie was here!"

Drearily she slammed away into the house and after that it was silent for some minutes until suddenly from the street beyond the yard I could hear the inspiring note of war cries. A minute later the 1st Battalion Albion Street Light Infantry came triumphantly pounding down the path between the cabbage patches, led by Jeddah Clarke, carrying the air-gun, Wag Chettle, bearing the standard, a red handkerchief tied to a bean-pole, and Fred Baker, beating a drum he had had for Christmas.

Fred and Jeddah were actually in khaki uniforms. Jeddah, besides the air-gun, wore a bandolier across his chest with real pouches and two clips of spent cartridges; Fred had a peaked khaki cap on, with the badge of the Beds & Bucks Light Infantry on one side and that of the Royal Welch Fusiliers on the other. At that time the Fusiliers were billeted in the town and we had an inspired admiration for them because they kept a white goat as mascot. The goat ate anything you gave it, even cigarettes.

What now surprised me about the battalion was not its air of triumph but its size. Usually it was no more than eight strong. Now it was twenty. Those bringing up the rear were even flying a second flag. It was a square of blue-and-white football shirt. I caught the gleam of a second and even a third air-gun and then suddenly Jeddah Clarke, our Captain, raised his air-gun and yelled:

"Gas Street are on our side! They're in the battalion! Gas Street have come in with us! Charge!"

We all cheered madly and charged. The little hairs of my neck stuck up in pride, excitement and admiration as we thundered dustily into the summer street outside.

"Charge!" we all shouted. "Charge! Capture 'em! Charge!"

Heady with thought of battle, we wheeled like thunder into Winchester Street: completely unnoticed by a milk float, two bakers' carts, a chimney sweep on a bicycle and two women pushing prams.

"Charge!" I yelled, and was stunned to hear the blast of a bugle, suddenly blown at my side by a boy named Charley Fletcher, who was in the Lads' Brigade.

This new note, defiant above the roll of Fred Baker's drum, had us all in a frenzy of battle just as we surged past a railway dray loading piles of bulky leather outside a factory, where the crane swung out from its fourth storey door like a gallows and dropped its thirty-feet of rippling chain down to the shining hot pavement below.

"Charge!" I yelled, bringing up the rear with the umbrella under my arm and pointing it forward as if it had a bayonet in the end, exactly as I had seen in pictures of soldiers charging from the trenches. There was nothing we didn't know about soldiers and the trenches. We knew all about Vimy Ridge, Ypres, Hill 60 and Verdun too. We had seen them all in pictures.

The voice of our Captain, Jeddah Clarke, tore the air with fresh challenge as we whipped out of Winchester Street into Green's Alley. Continually Charley Fletcher's bugle ripped the quiet of the afternoon to shreds with raucous notes that were almost hysterical, rallying both us and the reinforcements of Gas Street, and I wondered suddenly where we were going and where the attack would be made.

Jeddah, yelling, told us all a moment later:

"Down to The Pit! We'll git'em in The Pit!"

My heart went absolutely icy, turned sour and dropped to my stomach.

The Pit was a terrible place. You never went to The Pit. No one ever did. If you did you never came out alive. The people there, who lived in sordid back-to-back hovels with sacks at the windows, captured you, tied you up, locked you in satanic privies and let you suffocate to death. If they didn't do that they starved you, took away all your clothes and sold you naked in slavery. They were the most awful people in the world. People like Mrs. Strickland were respectable by comparison. They were always dirty, drunk and fighting. They were always stinking and they were full of bugs and fleas.

I suddenly wanted to turn back, stand guard in the cabbage patch and dream quietly about being a lance corporal one day.

"Charge!" everyone yelled. "Charge! Git the stones ready!"

Out of Green's Alley we swung on the tide of battle into The Jetty, a narrow track of dried mud and stone. There the triumphant column broke up for a moment or two and we began to hack stones from the dust with the heels of our boots. By this time my legs and knees were shaking: so much so that all I could hack out were two pebbles and the stopper of a broken beer bottle. But Fred Baker, seeing this, took pity on me and armed me with half a brick.

The bugle sounded again, shrill as a cornet.

"Air-guns in front!" Jeddah yelled. "Git ready when I say charge!"

We thundered on. We had been joined now by a butcher's boy on a bicycle and for some reason I found myself clinging to his saddle. Suddenly in the excitement the butcher's boy started pedalling madly and I could hardly keep up with the column as it pounded along.

Less than a minute later we were facing the jaws of The Pit. They were nothing more than a gap between two rows of derelict gas-tarred fences but beyond them I could see the little one-storey hovels with sacks at their windows, the horrible squat brick prisons of outdoor privies and a few dirty flags of shirt on a washing line.

It was impossible for my heart to turn cold a second time; it was frozen stiff already. But the paralysis that kept it stuck at the pit of my stomach now affected my legs and I stopped running.

This, as it turned out, was a purely instinctive reaction. Everyone else had stopped running too.

"Charge!" someone yelled and this time it was not our Captain, Jeddah.

The order came from behind us and as we turned in its direction we found ourselves the victims of the oldest of all battle manoeuvres. We were being attacked in the rear.

This time my eyes froze. The Pit Brigade stood waiting for us: eight or ten of them, headed by a black-mouthed deaf-mute armed with five-foot two-pronged hoe. Another had an ugly strip of barrel hoop sharpened up like a sword and another a catapult with a black leather sling big enough to hold an egg. He was smoking a cigarette. Two others were manning a two-seater pram armoured with rusty plates of corrugated iron and this, we all realised, was an armament we did not possess. It was the first tank we had encountered.

The deaf-mute started showing his black teeth, gurgling strange cries. He made vigorous deaf-and-dumb signs with his hands and the snarling faces about him jabbered. The entire Pit Brigade, older, bigger, dirtier and better armed than we were, stood ready to attack.

It was too late to think about being a lance corporal now and a moment later they were on us.

"Charge!" everyone shouted from both sides. "Charge!" and we were locked in an instant clash of bricks, stones, catapults, flags, sticks and air-guns that would not fire. Above it all the unearthly voice of the deaf mute gurgled like a throttled man, mouthing black nothings.

I threw my brick. It fell like the legendary sparrow through the air. Someone started to tear the coat off my back and I thrashed madly about me with the umbrella. I could see our two flags rocking ship-mast fashion in the centre of battle and Charley Fletcher using the bugle as a hammer. The two-pronged hoe fell like a claw among us and the armour plates fell off the pram-tank as it ran into Fred Baker and cut his legs, drawing first blood.

Soon we actually had them retreating.

"We're the English!" I heard Jeddah shouting. "We're the English! The Pit are the bloody Germans," and this stirring cry of patriotism roused us to fresh thrills of battle frenzy.

"We're the English!" we all yelled. "We're the English!"

Suddenly as if a trap door had opened the Pit Brigade, under sheer weight of pressure, fell backward into the jaws of The Pit, hastily slamming the door behind them as a barricade and leaving outside a single stray soldier armed with a rusty flat iron suspended on a piece of cord and dressed as a sergeant of the Royal Artillery, complete with spurs and puttees.

Cut off from the tide of battle, this soldier gave several rapid and despairing looks about him, dropped the flat iron and bolted like a hare.

"Prisoner!" Jeddah yelled. "Prisoner! Git him! Take him prisoner!"

In a moment Fred Baker, Charley Fletcher and myself were after him. We caught him at the top to The Jetty. At first he lay on his back and kicked out at us with the spurs, spitting at the same time, but soon I was sitting on his face, Fred Baker on his chest and Charley Fletcher, who was the eldest, on his legs. For a long time he kept trying to spit at us and all the time there was a strong, putrid, stinking, funny smell about him.

We kept him prisoner all afternoon. Then we decided to strip him. While Fred and I sat on his face and chest Charley unrolled the puttees and took off the spurs.

"You always have spoils of war when you take prisoners," Charley explained. "Soldiers call it a bit of buckshee."

We spent some time arguing about how the buckshee should be divided and finally Charley was awarded the puttees, because he was the eldest, and Fred Baker and I each had a spur. Having the spur was even better than being a lance corporal and I couldn't remember ever having had anything that made me feel more proud.

It was almost evening before Jeddah and the rest of the Battalion got back, fifty strong, from telling of our victory in far places, in Lancaster Street, Rectory Street, Bedford Row, King's Lane and those parts of the town who could not be expected to hear of our triumph other than by word of mouth and from us. "We still got the prisoner, Captain," we said. "What shall we do with him?"

"Shoot him," Jeddah said.

Orders were orders with Jeddah and we asked if we could have the air-gun.

He handed it over.

"I leave it to you," Jeddah said. He was now wearing a forage cap, three long service stripes, a leather belt and a Welch black flash he had captured. "Charge!"

The sound of returning triumph from the fifty-strong battalion had hardly died away before we set to work to shoot the flat-iron boy.

First of all we made him stand up by the fence, among a pile of junk and nettles. By this time we had tied his hands and legs with the cord off the flat-iron and had taken off his shoes so that he found it hard to run. But he still spat at us as he stood waiting to be shot and he still had that funny, sickening smell.

Fred Baker shot him first. The unloaded air-gun made a noise rather like a damp squib. Then Charley Fletcher shot him and the gun made a noise like a damp squib a second time. Then I shot him and as I did so I made a loud, realistic noise that was more like the crack of a bursting paper bag. I aimed between the eyes of the flat-iron boy as I shot and I was very thrilled.

"Now you're dead," we said to him. "Don't you forget. Don't you move—you're dead. You can't fight no more."

He didn't look very dead when we left him but we knew he was. We told the Captain so when we rejoined the battalion in Gas Street, Fred Baker blowing the bugle and wearing the artillery puttees, Charley Fletcher and I taking turns to carry the air-gun and both of us waving a spur.

Jeddah was drunk with victory. "Tomorrow we're goin' to charge The Rock!" he said. The Rock was even worse than The Pit but now none of us was appalled and all of us cheered. There was no holding us now.

"We'll kill 'em all!" Jeddah said. "We'll burn ole Wag Saunders at the stake." Wag was their Captain. "Just like Indians. We'll win 'em. We ain't frit. Who are we?"

"We're the English!" we yelled.

It was already growing dark when I trotted home through the streets with my spur. In the back yard there were no lights in Mrs. Rankin's neat, white-silled windows and in Mrs. Strickland's house all the blinds were drawn although all the lights were on.

"Where have you been all this long time?" my father said.

He sat alone in the kitchen, facing a cold rice pudding. My father was very fond of cold rice pudding but tonight he did not seem to want it. Under the green gaslight the brown nutmeg skin of it shone unbroken.

"Fighting with our battalion," I said.

I told him how the battle had been won and how I had captured the spur.

"That spur doesn't belong to you," he said. "Tomorrow morning you must take it back."

I felt sick with disappointment and at the way grown-up people didn't understand you.

"Can I keep it just for tonight?"

"Just for tonight," he said. "But you must take it back tomorrow."

Then I remembered something and I told him how the boy I'd got it from was dead.

"How is that?" he said. "Dead?"

"We shot him."

"Oh! I see," he said. "Well: tomorrow you go and find the dead boy and give him back his spur."

Looking round the kitchen I now remembered my mother and asked where she was.

"She's with Mrs. Strickland," my father said. "Mrs. Rankin's with her too. I expect you noticed that all the blinds were drawn?"

I said I had noticed and did it mean that someone was dead?

"It's your friend—your friend Albie's not going to come back," my father said.

After that my father didn't seem to want to speak very much and I said: "Could I go and play in the tent until mother comes home?"

"You can go and play in the tent," he said.

"With a candle?" I said. "It's dark now outside."

"Take a candle if you like," he said.

I took a candle and sat in the tent all by myself, looking at my spur. It was shaped something like a handcuff to which was attached a silver star. The candlelight shone down on the spur with wonderful brilliance and as

I looked at it I remembered the voices of Mrs. Strickland and Mrs. Rankin squabbling with bitterness over a loaf of bread in the afternoon and how Mrs. Strickland wisht that Albie would come back, and now I listened again for their voices coming from the outer darkness but all I could hear was the voice from the afternoon:

"I wisht Albie was here. I wisht Albie was here."

There is nothing much you can do with a solitary candle and a single spur. The spur can only shine like silver and the candlelight with a black vein in the heart of it.

Early next morning I took the spur back to The Pit. I ran all the way there and I was glad that no one saw me. The sun was coming up over the gas-tarred fences, the little hovels, the privies and the wishing lines and all I did was to lay the spur on a stone in the sunlight, hoping that someone would come and find it there.

I ran all the way home, too, as hard as I could: afraid of the enemy we had conquered and the solider I had killed.

GREAT UNCLE CROW

Once in the summer time, when the water-lilies were in bloom and the wheat was new in ear, his grandfather took him on a long walk up the river, to see his Uncle Crow. He had heard so much of Uncle Crow, so much that was wonderful and to be marvelled at, and for such a long time, that he knew him to be, even before that, the most remarkable fisherman in the world.

"Masterpiece of a man, your Uncle Crow," his grandfather said. "He could git a clothes-line any day and tie a brick on it and a mossel of cake and go out and catch a pike as long as your arm."

When he asked what kind of cake his grandfather seemed irritated and said it was just like a boy to ask questions of that sort.

"Any kind o' cake," he said. "Plum cake. Does it matter? Caraway cake. Christmas cake if you like. Anything. I shouldn't wonder if he could catch a pretty fair pike with a cold baked tater."

"Only a pike?"

"Times," his grandfather said, "I've seen him sittin' on the bank on a sweltering hot day like a furnace, when nobody was gittin' a bite not even off a bloodsucker. And there your Uncle Crow'd be a-pullin' 'em out by the dozen, like a man shellin' harvest beans."

"And how does he come to be my Uncle Crow," he said, "if my mother hasn't got a brother? Nor my father."

"Well," his grandfather said, "he's really your mother's own cousin, if everybody had their rights. But all on us call him Uncle Crow."

"And where does he live?"

"You'll see," his grandfather said. "All by hisself. In a little titty bit of a house, by the river."

The little titty bit of a house, when he first saw it, surprised him very much. It was not at all unlike a black tarred boat that had either slipped down a slope and stuck there on its way to launching or one that had been washed up and left there in a flood. The rood of brown tiles had a warp in

131

it and the sides were mostly built, he thought, of tarred beer-barrels.

The two windows with their tiny panes were about as large as chessboards and Uncle Crow had nailed underneath each of them a sill of sheet tin that was still a brilliant blue, each with the words "Backache Pills" in white lettering on it, upside down.

On all sides of the house grew tall feathered reeds. They enveloped it like gigantic whispering corn. Some distance beyond the great reeds the river went past in a broad slow arc, on magnificent kingly currents, full of long white islands of water-lilies, as big as china breakfast cups, shining and yellow-hearted in the sun.

He thought, on the whole, that that place, the river with the water-lilies, the little titty bit of a house, and the great forest of reeds talking between soft brown beards, was the nicest place he had ever seen.

"Anybody about?" his grandfather called. "Crow!—anybody at home?"

The door of the house was partly open, but at first there was no answer. His grandfather pushed open the door still farther with his foot. The reeds whispered down by the river and were answered, in the house, by a sound like the creak of bed springs.

"Who is't?"

"It's me, Crow," his grandfather called. "Lukey. Brought the boy over to have a look at you."

A big gangling red-faced man with rusty hair came to the door. His trousers were black and very tight. His eyes were a smeary vivid blue, the same colour as the stripes of his shirt, and his trousers were kept up by a leather belt with brass escutcheons on it, like those on horses' harness.

"Thought very like you'd be out a-pikin'," his grandfather said.

"Too hot. How's Lukey boy? Ain't seed y' lately, Lukey boy."

His lips were thick and very pink and wet, like cow's lips. He made a wonderful erupting jolly sound somewhat between a belch and a laugh.

"Comin' in it a minute?"

In the one room of the house was an iron bed with an old red check horse-rug spread over it and a stone copper in one corner and a bare wooden table with dirty plates and cups and a tin kettle on it. Two osier baskets and a scythe stood in another corner.

Uncle Crow stretched himself full length on the bed as if he was very tired. He put his knees in the air. His belly was tight as a bladder of lard in his black trousers, which were mossy green on the knees and seat.

"How's the fishin'?" his grandfather said. "I bin tellin' the boy—"

Uncle Crow belched deeply. From where the sun struck full on the tarred wall of the house there was a hot whiff of baking tar. But when Uncle Crow belched there was a smell like the smell of yeast in the air.

"It ain't bin all that much of a summer yit," Uncle Crow said. "Ain't had the rain."

"Not like that summer you catched the big 'un down at Archer's Mill. I recollect you a-tellin' on me—"

"Too hot and dry by half," Uncle Crow said. "Gits in your gullet like chaff."

"You recollect that summer?" his grandfather said. "Nobody else a-fetching on 'em out only you—"

"Have a drop o' neck-oil," Uncle Crow said.

The boy wondered what neck-oil was and presently, to his surprise, Uncle Crow and his grandfather were drinking it. It came out of a dark-green bottle and it was a clear bright amber, like cold tea, in the two glasses.

"The medder were yeller with 'em," Uncle Crow said. "Yeller as a guinea."

He smacked his lips with a marvellously juicy, fruity sound. The boy's grandfather gazed at the neck-oil and said he thought it would be a corker if it was kept a year or two, but Uncle Crow said:

"Trouble is, Lukey boy, it's a terrible job to keep it. You start tastin' on it to see if it'll keep and then you taste on it again and you go on tastin' on it until they ain't a drop left as 'll keep."

Uncle Crow laughed so much that the bed springs cackled underneath his bouncing trousers.

"Why is it called neck-oil?" the boy said.

"Boy," Uncle Crow said, "when you git older, when you git growed-up, you know what'll happen to your gullet?"

"No."

"It'll git sort o' rusted up inside. Like a old gutter pipe. So's you can't swaller very easy. Rusty as old Harry it'll git. You know that, boy?"

"No."

"Well, it will, I'm tellin', on y'. And you know what y' got to do then?"

"No."

"Every now and then you gotta git a drop o' neck-oil down it. So's to ease it. A drop o' neck-oil every once in a while—that's what you gotta do to keep the rust out."

The boy was still contemplating the curious prospect of his neck rusting up inside in later years when Uncle Crow said: "Boy, you go outside and

jis' round the corner you'll see a bucket. You bring handful o' cresses out
on it. I'll bet you're hungry, ain't you?"

"A little bit."

He found the watercresses in the bucket, cool in the shadow of the little
house, and when he got back inside with them Uncle Crow said:

"Now you put the cresses on that there plate there and then put your nose
inside that there basin and see what's inside. What is't, eh?"

"Eggs."

"Ought to be fourteen on 'em. Four-apiece and two over. What sort are
they, boy?"

"Moor-hens'."

"You got a knowin' boy here, Lukey," Uncle Crow said. He dropped the
scaly red lid of one eye like an old cockerel going to sleep. He took another
drop of neck-oil and gave another fruity, juicy laugh as he heaved his body
from the bed. "A very knowin' boy."

Presently he was carving slices of thick brown bread with a great horn-
handled shut-knife and pasting each slice with summery golden butter. Now
and then he took another drink of neck-oil and once he said:

"You get the salt pot, boy, and empty a bit out on that there saucer, so's
we can all dip in."

Uncle Crow slapped the last slice of bread on to the buttered pile and then
said:

"Boy, you take that there jug there and go a step or two up the path and
dip yourself a drop o' spring water. You'll see it. It comes out of a little bit
of a wall, jist by a doddle-willer."

When the boy got back with the jug of spring water Uncle Crow was
opening another bottle of neck-oil and his grandfather was saying: "God
a-mussy man, goo steady. You'll have me agooin' one way and another—"

"Man alive," Uncle Crow said, "and what's wrong with that?"

Then the watercress, the salt, the moor-hens' eggs, the spring water, and
the neck-oil were all ready. The moor-hens' eggs were hard-boiled. Uncle
Crow lay on the bed and cracked them with his teeth, just like big brown
nuts, and said he thought the watercress was just about as nice and tender
as a young lady.

"I'm sorry we ain't got the gold plate out though. I had it out a-Sunday."

He closed his old cockerel-lidded eye again and licked his tongue backwards
and forwards across his lips and dipped another peeled egg in salt. "You
know what I had for my dinner a-Sunday, boy?"

"No."

"A pussy-cat on a gold plate. Roasted with broad-beans and new taters. Did you ever heerd talk of anybody eatin' a roasted pussy-cat, boy?"

"Yes."

"You did?"

"Yes," he said, "that's a hare."

"You got a very knowin' boy here, Lukey," Uncle Crow said. "A very knowin' boy."

Then he screwed up a big dark-green bouquet of watercress and dipped it in salt until it was entirely frosted and then crammed it in one neat whole-sale bite into his soft pink mouth.

"But not on a gold plate?" he said.

He had to admit that.

"No, not on a gold plate," he said.

All that time he thought the fresh watercress, the moor-hens' eggs, the brown bread-and-butter, and the spring water were the most delicious, won-derful things he had ever eaten in the world. He felt that only one thing was missing. It was that whenever his grandfather spoke of fishing Uncle Crow simply took another draught of neck-oil.

"When are you goin' to take us fishing?" he said.

"You et up that there egg," Uncle Crow said. "That's the last one. You et up that there egg up and I'll tell you what."

"What about gooin' as far as that big deep hole where the chub lay?" Grandfather said. "Up by the back-brook—"

"I'll tell you what, boy," Uncle Crow said, "you git your grandfather to bring you over September time, of a morning, afore the steam's off the winders. Mushroomin' time. You come over and we'll have a bit o' bacon and mushroom for breakfast and then set into the pike. You see, boy, it ain't the pikin' season now. It's too hot. Too bright. It's too bright of afternoon, and they ain't a-bitin'."

He took a long rich swig of neck-oil.

"Ain't that it, Lukey? That's the time, ain't it, mushroom time?"

"Thass it," his grandfather said.

"Tot out," Uncle Crow said. "Drink up. My throat's jist easin' orf a bit."

He gave another wonderful belching laugh and told the boy to be sure to finish up the last of the watercress and the bread-and-butter. The little room was rich with the smell of neck-oil, and the tarry sun-baked odour of the beer-barrels that formed its walls. And through the door came, always, the sound of reeds talking in their beards, and the scent of summer meadows drifting in from beyond the great curl of the river with its kingly currents and its islands of full-blown lilies, white and yellow in the sun.

"I see the wheat's in ear," his grandfather said. "Ain't that the time for tench, when the wheat's in ear?"

"Mushroom time," Uncle Crow said. "That's the time. You git mushroom time here, and I'll fetch you a tench out as big as a cricket bat."

He fixed the boy with an eye of wonderful watery, glassy blue and licked his lips with a lazy tongue, and said:

"You know what colour a tench is, boy?"

"Yes," he said.

"What colour?"

"The colour of the neck-oil."

"Lukey," Uncle Crow said, "you got a very knowin' boy here. A very knowin' boy."

After that, when there were no more cresses or moor-hens' eggs or bread-and-butter to eat, and his grandfather said he'd get hung if he touched another drop of neck-oil, he and his grandfather walked home across the meadows.

"What work does Uncle Crow do?" he said.

"Uncle Crow? Work?—well, he ain't—Uncle Crow? Well, he works, but he ain't what you'd call a reg'lar worker—"

All the way home he could hear the reeds talking in their beards. He could see the water-lilies that reminded him so much of the gold and white inside the moor-hens' eggs. He could hear the happy sound of Uncle Crow laughing and sucking at the neck-oil, and crunching the fresh salty cresses into his mouth in the tarry little room.

He felt happy, too, and the sun was a gold plate in the sky.

THE WATERCRESS GIRL

The first time he ever went to that house was in the summer, when he was seven, and his grandfather drove him down the valley in a yellow trap and all the beans were in flower, with skylarks singing so high above them in the brilliant light that they hung trembling there like far-off butterflies.

"Who is it we're going to see?" he said.

"Sar' Ann."

"Which one is Sar' Ann?"

"Now mek out you don' know which one Sar' Ann is," his grandfather said, and then tickled the flank of the pony with the end of the plaited whip—he always wanted to plait reeds like that himself but he could never make them tight enough—so that the brown rumps, shorn and groomed for summer, quivered like firm round jellies.

"I don't think I've ever seen her," he said.

"You seen her at Uncle Arth's," his grandfather said. "Mek out you don't remember that, and you see her a time or two at Jenny's." He pronounced it Jinny, but even then the boy could not remember who Jinny was and he knew his grandfather wouldn't tell him until he remembered who Sar' Ann was and perhaps not even after that.

He tried for some moments longer to recall what Sar' Ann was like and remembered presently a square old lady in a pork-pie lace cap and a sort of bib of black jet beads on a large frontal expanse of shining satin. Her eyes were watering. She sat on the threshold of a house that smelled of apples and wax polish. She was in the sun, with a lace pillow and bone bobbins in a blue and ivory fan on her knees. She was making lace and her hands were covered with big raised veins like the leaves of cabbages when you turned them upside down. He was sure that this was Sar' Ann. He remembered how she had touched his hands with her big cold cabbagy ones and said she would fetch him a cheese cake, or if he would rather have it a piece of toffee, from the cupboard in her kitchen. She said the toffee was rather sugary and

that made him say he preferred the cheese cake, but his grandfather said:
"Now don't you git up. He's ettin' from morn to night now. His eyes are
bigger'n his belly. You jis sit still," and he felt he would cry because he was
so fond of cheese cake and because he could hardly bear his disappointment.

"She's the one who wanted to give me cheese cake," he said, "isn't she?"

"No, she ain't," his grandfather said. "That's your Aunt Turvey."

"Then is she the one who's married to Uncle Arth? Up the high steps?"
he said.

"Uncle Arth ain't married," his grandfather said. "That's jis the widder-
woman who looks after him."

His Uncle Arth was always in a night-shirt, with a black scarf round his
head. He lived in bed all the time. His eyes were very red. Inside him, so
his grandfather said, was a stone and the stone couldn't go up or down but
was fixed, his grandfather said, in his kitney, and it was growing all the time.

The stone was an awful nightmare to him, the boy. How big was it? What
sort of stone was it? he would say, a stone in the kitney?

"Like a pibble," his grandfather said. "Hard as a pibble. And very like as
big as a thresh's egg. Very like bigger'n that by now. Very like as big as a
magpie's."

"How did it get there?"

"You're arstin' on me now," his grandfather said. "It'd be a puzzle to
know. But it got there. And there it is. Stuck in his kitney."

"Has anybody ever seen it?"

"Nobody."

"Then if nobody's ever seen it how do they know it's there?"

"Lean forward," his grandfather said. "We're gittin' to Long Leys hill.
Lean forward, else the shafts'll poke through the sky."

It was when they climbed slowly up the long wide hill, already white with
the dust of early summer, that he became aware of the beans in flower and
the skylarks singing so loftily above them. The scent of beans came in soft
waves of wonderful sweetness. He saw the flowers on the grey sunlit stalks
like swarms of white, dark-throated bees. The hawthorn flower was nearly
over and was turning pink wherever it remained. The singing of the skylarks
lifted the sky upward, farther and farther, loftier and loftier, and the sun
made the blue of it clear and blinding. He felt that all summer was pouring
down the hill, between ditches of rising meadowsweet, to meet him. The
cold quivering days of coltsfoot flower, the icy-sunny days of racing cloud-
shadow over drying ploughland, the dark-white days of April hail, were all

behind him, and he was thirsty with summer dust and his face was hot in the sun.

"You ain't recollected her yit, have you?" his grandfather said.

They were at the top of the hill now and below them, in its yellow meadows, he could see the river winding away in broad and shining curves. He knew that that river was at the end of the earth; that the meadows, and with them the big woods of oak and hornbeam and their fading dusty spangles of flower, were another world.

"Take holt o' the reins a minute," his grandfather said. He put on the brake a notch and the brake shoes scraped on the metal tires. The boy held the thin smooth reins lightly between his fingers, the way he had been taught to do. He sat forward on the high horse-hair cushions and looked down the long black tramlines of the dead level reins to the brown pony's ears and felt himself, for one moment, high on the hill, to be floating in air, level with all the skylarks above the fields below.

"I'll jis git me bacca going," his grandfather said. "We'll be there in about a quartern of hour. You keep holt on her steady."

He wanted to say to his grandfather that that was a funny word, quartern; his schoolteacher never used that word; and then as he turned he saw the brown, red-veined face softened by the first pulls of tobacco. All the mystery of it was dissolved in a blue sweet cloud. Then his grandfather began coughing because the bacca, he said, had gone down wrong way and was tiddling his gills. His eyes were wet from coughing and he was laughing and saying:

"You know who she is. She's the one with the specs like glarneys."

Then he knew. She was a little woman, he remembered clearly now, with enormous spy-glass spectacles. They were thick and round like the marbles he played with. She was always whisking about like a clean starched napkin. Hi had seen her at Uncle Arth's and she had jolted Uncle Arth about the bed with a terrible lack of mercy as she re-made his pillows, smacking them with her lightning hands as if they were disobedient bottoms. The colossal spectacles gave the eyes a terrible look of magnification. They wobbled sometimes like masses of pale floating frog-spawn. He did not like her; he was held in the spawn-like hypnotism of the eyes and dared not speak. She had a voice like a jackdaw's which pecked and mocked at everybody with nasty jabs. He knew that he had got her mixed up somehow and he said:

"I thought the one with the glass eye was Aunt Prunes."

"Prudence!" his grandfather said. "They're sisters. She's the young 'un, Prudence." He spat in a long liquid line, with off-hand care, over the side of the trap. "Prunes?—that was funny. How'd you come to git holt o' that?"

"I thought everybody else called her Prunes."

"Oh! You did, simly? Well, it's Prudence. Prudence—that's her proper name."

Simly was another funny word. He would never understand that word. That was another word his schoolteacher never used.

"Is she the one with the moustache?"

"God alive," the man said. "Don't you say moustache. You'll git me hung if you say moustache. That's your Aunt Prudence you're talking about. Females don't have moustaches—you know that."

He knew better than that because Aunt Prunes had a moustache. She was a female and it was quite a long moustache and she had, what was more, a few whiskers on the central part of her chin.

"Why doesn't she shave it off?" he said.

"You watch what you're doing," his grandfather said. "You'll have us in the duck-pond."

"How do you spell it?" he said. "Her name—Prunes?"

"Here, you gimme holt o' the reins now," his grandfather said. "We'll be there in five ticks of a donkey's tail."

His grandfather took the reins and let the brake off, and in a minute the pony was trotting and they were in a world of high green reeds and grey drooping willows by the river.

"Is it the house near the spinney?" he said.

"That's it," his grandfather said. "The little 'un with the big chimney."

He was glad he remembered the house correctly: not because he had ever seen it but because his grandfather always described it with natural familiarity, as if taking it for granted that he had seen it. He was glad too about Aunt Prunes. It was very hard to get everyone right. There were so many of them, Aunt Prunes and Sar' Ann and Aunt Turvey and Uncle Arth and Jenny and Uncle Ben Newton, who kept a pub, and Uncle Olly, who was a fat man with short black leggings exactly like polished bottles. His grandfather would speak of these people as if they were playmates who had always been in his life and were to be taken for granted naturally and substantially like himself. They were all very old, terribly old, and he never knew, even afterwards, if they were ordinary aunts or uncles or great ones or only cousins some stage removed.

The little house had two rooms downstairs with polished red bricks for floors and white glass vases of dried reeds from the river on the mantelpiece. His grandfather and Aunt Prunes and Sar' Ann and himself had dinner in the room where the stove was, and there were big dishes of potatoes, mashed with thick white butter sauce. Before dinner he sat in the other room with his grandfather and Aunt Prunes and looked at a large leather book called *Sunday at Home*, a prize Aunt Prunes had won at Bible Class, a book in which there were sandwiches, between steel-cuts of men in frock coats and sailors in sailing ships and ladies in black bonnets, pressings of dried flowers thin as tissue from the meadows and the riverside. His contemplation of the flat golden transparencies of buttercup and the starry eyes of bull-daisy and the wooly feathers of grass and reed was ravaged continually by the voice of Sar' Ann, the jackdaw, pecking and jabbing from the kitchen:

"There's something there to keep you quiet. That's a nice book, that is. You can look at that all afternoon."

"You tell me," Aunt Prunes said softly, "when you want another."

He liked Aunt Prunes. She was quiet and tender. The moustache, far from being forbidding, brushed him with friendly softness, and the little room was so hot with sun and cooking that there were beads of sweat on the whiskers which he made the mistake of thinking, for some time, were drops of the cowslip wine she was drinking. His grandfather had several glasses of cowslip wine and at the third or fourth of them he took off his coat and collar.

At the same time Aunt Prunes bent down and took the book away from him and said:

"You can take off your coat too. That's it. That's better. Do you want to go anywhere?"

"Not yet."

"When you do it's down the garden and behind the elderberry tree." Her eyes were a modest brown colour, the same colour as her moustache, and there were many wrinkles about them as she smiled. He could smell the sweetish breath, like the yeast his grandmother used for baking, of the fresh wine on her lips, and she said:

"What would you like to do this afternoon? Tell me what you'd like to do."

"Read this book."

"I mean really."

"I don't know."

"You do what you like," she said. "You go down to the back-brook or in the garden or into the spinney and find snails or sticklebacks or whatever you like."

She smiled delicately, creating thousands of wrinkles, and then from the kitchen Sar' Ann screeched:

"I'm dishing up in two minutes, you boozers. You'd guzzle there till bulls'-noon if I'd let you."

Bulls'-noon was another word, another strange queer thing he did not understand.

For dinner they had Yorkshire pudding straight out of the pan and on to the plate, all by itself, as the opening course. Sometimes his grandfather slid slices of the creamy yellow pudding into his mouth on the end of his knife and said he remembered the days when all pudding was eaten first and you had your plate turned upside down, so that you could turn it over when the meat came. Sar' Ann said she remembered that too and she said they were the days and she didn't care what anybody said. People were happier. They didn't have so much of everything but they were happier. He saw Aunt Prunes give a little dry grin whenever Sar' Ann went jabbing on and once he thought he saw her wink at his grandfather. All the time the door of the little room was open so that he could see into the garden with its white pinks and stocks and purple iris flags and now and then he could hear the cuckoo, sometimes near, sometimes far off across the meadows, and many blackbirds singing in endless call and answer in the oak trees at the end of the garden, where rhubarb and elderberry were in foaming flower together.

"You can hear nightingales too," Aunt Prunes said. "Would you like more pudding? You can have more pudding if you want it."

But his grandfather said again that his eyes were always bigger than his belly and the pudding was put away. "Ets like a thacker," his grandfather said and Aunt Prunes said, "Let him eat then. I like to see boys eat. It does your heart good," and she smiled and gave him cloudy piles of white potatoes and white sauce from a blue china boat and thin slices of rich beef with blood running out and washing against the shores of his potatoes like the little waves of a delicate pink sea.

"How's Nance and Granny Houghton?" Sar' Ann said, and his grandfather said they were fair-to-mid and suddenly there was great talk of relatives, of grown-ups, of people he did not know, of Charley and a man he thought was named Uncle Fuggles and Cathy and Aunt Em and Maude Rose and two people called Liz and Herbert from Bank Top. His grandfather, who had begun the meal with three or four glasses of cowslip wine and a glass of beer, now helped himself to another glass of beer and then dropped gravy down his waistcoat. Aunt Prunes had beer too and her eyes began to look warm and sleepy and beautifully content.

Afternoon, cuckoo-drowsy, very still and full of sun, seemed to thicken like a web about him long before the meal was over. He thought with dread of the quietness when all of them would be asleep and he himself in the little room with a big boring book and its rustling transparencies of faded flowers. He knew what it was to try to move in the world of grown-up sleep. The whisper of the thinnest page would wake them. Night was the time for sleeping and it was one of the mysteries of life that people could also sleep by day, in chairs, in summertime, in mouth-open attitudes, and with snorting noises and legs suddenly jumping like the legs of horses when the flies were bad.

Then to his joy Aunt Prunes remembered and said:

"You know what I said. You run into the garden and have a look in the spinney for nests. Go down as far as the back-brook if you like."

"That's it," his grandfather said. "You'll very like see a moor-hen's or a coot's or summat down there. Else a pike or summat. Used to be a rare place for pike, a-layin' there a-top o' the water—"

"Don't you git falling in," Sar' Ann said. "Don't you git them feet wet. Don't you git them gooseberries—they'll give you belly-ache summat chronic—"

"You bring me some flowers," Aunt Prunes said. "Eh?—how's that? You stay a long time, as long as you like, and bring me some flowers."

There were no nests in the spinney except a pigeon's high up in a hazel-tree that was too thin to climb. He was not quite sure about the song of a nightingale. He knew the blackbird's, full and rich and dark like the bird itself and deep like the summer shadow of the closing wood, and with the voices of thrushes the blackbirds' song filled all the wood with bell-sounds and belling echoes.

Beyond the wood the day was clear and hot. The grass was high to his knees and the ground, falling away, was marshy in places, with mounds of sedge, as it ran down towards the back-brook and the river. He walked with his eyes on the ground, partly because of oozy holes among the sedge, partly because he hoped to see the brown ring of a moor-hen's nest in the marshier places.

It was because of his way of walking that he did not see, for some time,

a girl standing up to her knees in red-ochre mud, among half-floating beds
of dark-green cresses. But suddenly he lifted his head and saw her standing
there, bare-legged and bare-armed, staring at him as if she had been watching
him for a long time. Her brown osier cress-basket was like a two-bushel
measure and was slung over her shoulder with a strap.

"You don't live here," she said.

"No," he said. "Do you?"

"Over there," she said. "In that house."

"Which house?" He could not see a house.

"You come here and you can see it," she said.

When he had picked his way through tufts of sedge to where she was
standing in the bed of cresses he still could not see a house, either about the
wood or across the meadows on the rising ground beyond.

"You can see the chimney smoking," she said.

"It's not a house. It's a hut," he said.

"That's where we live."

"All the time?"

"Yes," she said. "You're sinking in."

The toes of his boots were slowly drowning in red-ochre water.

"If you're coming out here you'd better take your shoes and stockings
off," she said.

A moment or two later his bare feet were cool in the water. She was gathering cresses quickly, cutting them off with an old shoe-knife, leaving young
sprigs and trailing skeins of white root behind. She was older than himself,
nine or ten, he thought, and her hair hung ribbonless and uncombed, a
brown colour, rather like the colour of the basket, down her back.

"Can I gather?" he said, and she said, yes, if he knew what brook-lime
was.

"I know brook-lime," he said. "Everybody knows brook-lime."

"Then which is it? Show me which it is. Which is brook-lime?"

That was almost as bad, he thought, as being nagged by Sar' Ann. The
idea that he did not know brook-lime from cress seemed to him a terrible
insult and a pain. He snatched up a piece in irritation but it did not break
and came up instead from the mud-depths in a long rope of dripping red-
black slime, spattering his shirt and trousers.

She laughed at this and he laughed too. Her voice, he thought, sounded
cracked, as if she were hoarse from shouting or a cold. The sound of it carried a long way. He heard it crack over the meadows and the river with a

coarse broken sort of screech that was like the slitting of rag in the deep oppressive afternoon.

He never knew till long afterwards how much he liked that sound. She repeated it several times during the afternoon. In the same cracked voice she laughed at questions he asked or things he did not know. In places the water, shallower, was warm on his feet, and the cresses were a dark polished green in the sun. She laughed because he did not know that anyone could live by gathering cresses. He must be a real town boy, she said. There was only she and her father, she told him, and she began to tell what he afterwards knew were beautiful lies about the way they got up every other day at two in the morning and tramped out to sell cresses in Evensford and Bedford and towns about the valley.

"But the shops aren't open then," he said and that made her laugh again, cracked and thin, with that long slitting echo across the drowsy meadows.

"It's not in the shops we sell them," she said. "It's in the streets—don't you know that?—in the streets—"

And suddenly she lifted her head and drew back her throat and yelled the cry she used in the streets. He had heard that cry before, high and long and melancholy, like a call across lonely winter marshes in its slow fall and dying away, and there was to be a time in his life when it died for ever and he never heard it again:

"Watercree-ee-ee-ee-ee-s! Fresh cre-ee-ee-ee-ee-ee-s! Lovely fresh watercree-ee-ee-ee-ee-ee-s!"

Standing up to his knees in water, his hands full of wet cresses and slimy skeins of roots dripping red mud down his shirt and trousers, he listened to that fascinating sound travelling like a bird-cry, watery and not quite earthly, down through the spinney and the meadows of buttercup and the places where the pike were supposed to lie.

His eyes must have been enormous and transfixed in his head as he listened, because suddenly she broke the note of the cry and laughed at him again and then said:

"You do it. You see if you can do it—"

What came out of his mouth was like a little soprano trill compared with her own full-throated, long-carrying cry. It made her laugh again and she said:

"You ought to come with us. Come with us tomorrow—how long are you staying here?"

"Only today."

"I don't know where we'll go tomorrow," she said. "Evensford, I think. Sometimes we go forty or fifty miles—miles and miles. We go to Buckingham market sometimes—that's forty miles—"

"Evensford," he said. "That's where I come from. I could see you there if you go."

"All right," she said. "Where will you be? We come in by The Waggon and Horses—down the hill, that way."

"I'll be at The Waggon and Horses waiting for you," he said. "What time?"

"You be there at five o'clock,"she said. "Then I'll learn you how to do it, like this—watercree-ee-ee-ee-ee-ee-ee-s! Fresh cree-ee-ee-ee-ee-ee-ee-s! Lovely fresh watercree-ee-ee-ee-ee-ee-s!"

As the sound died away it suddenly seemed to him that he had been there, up to his knees in water, a very long time, perhaps throughout the entire length of the sultry, sun-flushed afternoon. He did not know what time it was. He was cut off from the world of Aunt Prunes and Sar' Ann and his grandfather, the little house and the white pinks and the gooseberry trees, the big boring book whose pages and dead flowers turned over in whispers.

He knew that he ought to go back and said:

"I got to go now. I'll see you tomorrow though—I'll be there. Five o'clock."

"Yes, you be there," she said. She wiped a may-fly from her face with her forearm, drawing water and mud across it, and then remembered something. "You want some cresses for tea? You can take some."

She plunged her hands into the basket and brought them out filled with cresses. They were cool and wet; and he thought, not only then but long afterwards, that they were the nicest things perhaps anyone had ever given him.

"So long," she said.

"So long." That was another funny expression, he thought. He could never understand people who said so long when they seemed to mean, as he did, soon.

She waved her hands, spilling arcs of water-drops in the sun, as he climbed the stile into the spinney and went back. He did his best to wave in answer, but his shoes and stockings were too wet to wear and his hands were full with them and the cresses. Instead he simply stood balanced for a moment on the top bar of the stile, so that she could see him well and then call to him for the last time:

"Cree-ee-ee-ee-ee-es! Lovely fresh cree-ee-ee-ee-ee-es!"

It was only Aunt Prunes who was not angry with him. His grandfather called him "A young gallus," and kept saying, "Where the Hanover've you bin all the time? God A'mighty, you'll git me hung. I'll be burned if I don't git hung," and Sar' Ann flew about the kitchen with the squawks of a trapped hen, telling him:

"You know what happens to little boys what git wet-foot? And look at your shirt! They git their death, they catch their death. And don't you know who them folks are? Gyppos—that's all they are. Gyppos—they steal things, they live on other folks. That's the sort of folks they are. Don't you go near such folks again—they'll very like keep you and take you away and you'll never see nobody who knows you again. Then we'll find you in the bury-hole."

But he was not afraid of that and Aunt Prunes only said:

"You didn't bring me my flowers, did you? I like watercress though. I'm glad you brought the watercress. I can have it with my tea."

I was late before they could start for home again. That was because his socks and shirt took a long time to dry and his shirt had to have an iron run over it several times in case, Sar' Ann kept saying, his mother had a fit. Before getting up into the trap he had to kiss both Sar' Ann and Aunt Prunes, and for some moments he was lost in the horror of the big globular spectacles reflecting and magnifying the evening sun, and then in the friendliness of the dark moustaches below which the warm mouth smiled and said:

"How would you like to stay with me one day? Just you and me in the summer. Would you?"

"Yes," he said.

"Then you come and see me again, won't you, soon?"

He said Yes, he would see her soon. But in fact he did not see her soon or later or at any time again. He did not go to that house again until he was grown up. That was the day they were burying her and when the cork of silence that passed over the grave had blown out again he felt he could hear nothing but the gassy voice of Sar' Ann, who was old by then but still with the same fierce roving globular eyes, shrilly reminding him of the day he had gathered cresses.

'I'll bet you would never know her now," she said, "that girl, would you? Would you ever know that this was her?"

Then she was by his side and he was talking to her: the girl who had gathered the cresses, the same girl who had called with that screeching, melan-

choly, marshy cry across the summer afternoon. She was not fat but she had
a great puffy placidity. She was all in black and her hat had a purple feather
in the crown. He remembered the little hut and the brown osier basket on
her lithe thin shoulders and he asked her where she lived and what she was
doing now. "In the new houses," she said. "I'm Mrs. Corbett now." She
took him to the garden hedge and pointed out to him blocks of bricks, like
the toys of gigantic children, red and raw and concrete fenced, lining the
road above the valley. That was the road where he and his grandfather had
driven down on that distant summer morning, when the beans were in
flower and he had got so mixed with his relatives and had wondered how
Aunt Prunes had spelled her name.

"That's us," she said. She pointed with stout and podgy finger, a trifle
nervously but with pride, across the fields. "The second one. The one with
the television. Have you got television?"

"No."

"You ought to have it," she said. "It's wonderful to see things so far away.
Don't you think it's wonderful?"

"Wonderful," he said.

But on the night he drove home as a boy, watching the sky of high summer turn from blue to palest violet and then more richly to purple bronze
and the final green-gold smokiness of twilight, he did not know these things.
He sat still on the cushions of the trap, staring ahead. The evening was full
of the scent of bean flowers and he was searching for early stars.

"Shall we light the lamps?" he said.

And presently they lit the lamps. They too were golden. They seemed to
burn with wonderful brightness, lighting the grasses of the roadside and the
flowers of the ditches and the crowns of fading may. And though he did not
know it then they too were fading, for all their brightness. They too were
dying, along with the things he had done and seen and loved: the little
house, the cuckoo day, the tender female moustaches and the voice of the
watercress girl.

COCONUT RADIO

Across plates of raw fish, steaming dishes of suckling pig, crabs and liver, fried plantain, curries of prawn and fresh-water shrimp, bowls of bread-fruit, sweet potatoes and rice, Mr. Pilgrim raised his gin glass to me and looked over the edge of it with his pink, under-cooked eyes.

"Those fellows in Africa have the right idea," he said. "They're out to keep Africa for the white man."

"Pass the bread-fruit, Freddy," Linda said, "and stop yattering."

Mr. Pilgrim ignored the request for bread-fruit and picked up a rib of suckling pig, warm fat dripping from his fingers. The girl named Linda, splendidly American in rose-coloured shorts, blue silk shirt and a peach-yellow hibiscus in her fair hair, leaned across me, took the bread-fruit dish and said:

"How are you doing? Don't you like bread-fruit? Try some raw fish."

"Take the Chinks," Mr. Pilgrim said. "You're interested in people." He waved the rib of suckling pig at me, dropped it on his plate and picked up another. "Take the Chinks, now. Here in Tahiti—"

"Anybody ready for wine?" a man said. His name was George. He was tall, with a head like a bald domed white rock and a shirt of orange and purple design that fell outside his copper-coloured trousers. "Speak up. Take a little wine for thy stomach's sake. Where's Bill Rockley?"

"Entertaining his new *vahini*," Linda said.

"Who said? Who said? What *vahini* is this?" George said. "Since when? Who told you?"

"Coconut radio!" a dozen voices said. "Coconut radio!"

Everybody sucked at pig-bones, laughing.

"Anybody seen her? What's she like?" George said. He moved down the long table of food, pouring red wine into tumblers. "Gentleman over there, I've forgotten your name. Have some wine? Like the suckling pig? I'm so sorry I've forgotten your name."

"Matthews."

"Call him Morgenthau," a girl said. She was pert, dark, quick-tongued. "We all call him Morgenthau. He came on the plane with us, didn't you, Morgenthau? He lends us money, don't you, Morgenthau?"

"Well—"

Shyly the young man called Morgenthau, blushing a little, was trying to cut a rib of suckling pig with his knife and fork.

"Saved our lives, Morgenthau did, when the banks weren't open," the pert, quick-tongued girl said.

"Where are you from, Mr. Morgenthau?" Mr. Pilgrim asked.

"New Zealand, but—"

"Take the Chinks here," Mr. Pilgrim said. "You come from a white country, Mr. Morgenthau. You don't need to be hit over the head with a sledge-hammer to see which way the wind is blowing, do you?"

"I actually work in Fiji—"

"Another example!" Mr. Pilgrim said. "Worse if anything. Take the Indians in Fiji—"

"I wonder where Bill Rockley is?" Linda said. "Bill is fun. I miss Bill."

"He'll be here," George said. "He knows about the suckling pig. Come to that, where's that man of yours? Where's Henry?"

"Must you ask?" she said. "Somewhere between here and Bora-Bora. As usual. With that damned out-board put-put. Catching tuna. One day a shark—"

"Reminds me," a man said. He was hairy-chested, but otherwise bald too. His open shirt was sulphur yellow, with a design of green sword-fish across it. His slacks were pale blue, the top buttons of the front undone, letting his paunch protrude.

Beside him sat a thin, blank-eyed Tahitian girl drinking gin. She did not, I noticed, eat very much. Sometimes she took up a rib of suckling pig, held it absent-eyed for a time in her fingers and then, equally absent-eyed, gave it to the man beside her. She did not look young and the listless skin of her face, something the colour of old, faded straw, was deeply pock-marked.

"Reminds you of what?" George said. "Don't be so damned secretive. Don't feed the animal, Marcelle, if he won't talk."

The girl, Marcelle, did not smile.

"I hear the new *vahini* comes from Bora-Bora, that's all. I don't know, I just heard—"

"Where from? Who said?"

"Coconut radio again!" they all said. "Coconut radio!"

"Everywhere this same pattern," Mr. Pilgrim said to me, "is manifesting itself. Have some raw fish? Try the shrimps—the shrimps are delicious. Take the Indians in Fiji. Eh, Mr. Morgenthau, you know all about the Indians in Fiji. What were they, fifty, sixty years ago?"

"Coolies mostly. Indentured labour—"

"Exactly. And what are they now? Rich. Prosperous. Prolific as flies. Outnumbering everybody." He helped himself to large portions of raw fish and curried prawns. "And the Chinks. Take the Chinks. Not only here in Tahiti, but in Honolulu. In San Francisco. And the Japs. Take the Japs in San Francisco. Three generations back—"

"How long have you been here, Mr. Morgenthau?" a voice said. "Your first visit?"

"Well, just—"

Mr. Morgenthau blushed, still trying to cut ribs of suckling pig with his knife and fork, and looked mildly and shyly about him.

"Mr. Morgenthau's too wild!" someone said. "He needs taming. Can't we get him a *vahini*? What about it, Mr. Morgenthau? Stay here and settle down and pick yourself a nice *vahini*."

"What exactly," Mr. Morgenthau said, "is a *vahini*?"

Mr. Pilgrim, who was now cracking crabs' claws, took advantage of the rising gust of laughter to turn round, screen his mouth with one arm and address me confidentially.

"You know, I suppose, that among themselves they are largely infertile?" he said. "You appreciate that?"

"No, I hadn't—"

"The Tahitians I mean. These girls. With whites, even with Chinese, right as rain." Already very flushed, his eyes cooked to a deeper, moister pink, he reached out, took up a bottle and poured himself more wine. "But among themselves—phut!"

"If Bill doesn't hurry soon," someone said, "there'll be no more suckling pig."

"The real truth is of course," Mr. Pilgrim said, and again he addressed me confidentially, cracking a crab's claw, "that the whole place is ruined. Travesty. You hear all this talk about the paradise? The paradise has gone, old boy. It's finished. They've ruined it completely."

"You mean the whites?"

"Not the whites. Good God, the French."

Large dishes of glowing water-melon, frosty-pink, came down the table, followed by pineapple, banana and passionfruit. Mr. Pilgrim, though not yet finished with crabs, chose a passionfruit and began to press it to his lips, giving it quick sucking kisses.

"How do they strike you?" he said. "What's your honest opinion? Looks, I mean."

"Some are nice."

"But on the whole? Disappointing, wouldn't you say?"

"Not disappointing," I said. "Only lost. Only very sad."

"Sad? Perhaps you're right," Mr. Pilgrim said. He sucked loudly at his fruit. "Though that doesn't alter—"

"Bill!" someone shouted. "Bill!" everyone began to say. "Bill! Where were you? What happened? Don't tell!—we know. Everybody knows—"

"Can't a man keep anything to himself?—"

"Coconut radio again!" they all shouted. "Coconut radio!"

"For those who don't know this fellow already," George said, "this is Bill Rockley."

A sombre, tallish man, brown, dark-haired, looking a little more than forty, smiled down the table and said, "Hullo" several times. His shirt was blue-black check and this, perhaps, together with a dark moustache, made him seem older than he was.

"Like to introduce Michele to everybody," he said. "Everybody—Michele."

The girl who stood beside him smiled down at us with wide dark eyes. Her hair was plaited. It fell over her bare shoulders in two thick blue-black ropes, reaching below her hips. She was perhaps fourteen or fifteen and under the vermilion hibiscus-pattern of her pereu her breasts were beautiful, taut and high. With shyness and grace she stood with one knee gently overlapping the other, one hand fingering the yellow hibiscus in her hair.

"Fine!" George said. "Get the man some suckling pig."

Grinning rinds of melon were now littered about the table. Mr. Pilgrim helped himself to another passionfruit. The shy Mr. Morgenthau fingered the last of his pig's bones. Mr. Pilgrim, unable to focus his reddening eyes correctly on the passionfruit, bit it at one edge, squirting juice, flesh and seeds down his chin. And then, as music suddenly flooded about the room, the pert, dark, quick-tongued girl laughed and shouted:

"Good, a record. Marvellous. I love that tune. I adore that Tahitian tune. Isn't somebody going to dance? Mr. Pilgrim, dance with me!"

Mr. Pilgrim, his chin still covered with passionfruit, staggered to his feet for dancing.

"Good idea!" Linda said. "Morgenthau! Dance with me! Lend me your arms!"

Soon everybody was dancing. Even the shy Mr. Morgenthau was dancing.

Only the girl with the yellow hibiscus in her hair and myself were left at the table, staring at the wreckage of pigs' ribs, the grinning rinds of melon, the crabs and their claws.

THE WORLD UPSIDE-DOWN

The first time Miss Olive Stratton put on odd stockings, one a green-ish brown, the other a shade of rusty red, was purely by accident, as she hurriedly dressed herself in the twilight of a winter morning. But when daylight came and she could see better it suddenly struck her how curiously attractive, even striking, the odd stockings were. They might even be a reason, she thought, for making men look at her legs more often, more closely and perhaps with more appreciation. They were not very good legs and the more she could do to improve them, she felt, the better.

Nor was her face at all an exceptional one. It resembled, as much as anything, a piece of rather coarse yellowish flannel. The grey eyes were dark, as if with bruises, underneath. For this reason she wore tinted spectacles of a smoky-rose colour. Her black hair was also coarse and would in fact have been slightly grey if she hadn't regularly tinted that too.

After the discovery of the stockings she began to go to work every morn-ing wearing one stoking of one colour and one of another. Sometimes she chose blue and green; sometimes red and yellow; once purple and brown. On one occasion she even went so far as to wear a green stocking and a red shoe on one leg and a red stocking and a green shoe on the other. On another occasion, a morning of black snowy slush, she wore odd calf-length boots, one white and one black, with a pair of gloves matching them but as it were in opposition.

In spite of all this the desired effect of making men take more than a momentary interest in her legs never seemed to come about. Her legs con-tinued to produce an effect neither elegant nor exciting. Men merely passed her in the street as if she were some sort of female crank. This went on for several weeks until one perishingly cold rainy morning she was slightly late for her train, found every second class seat filled and was obliged to travel first.

The only other person in the carriage was a man of about her own age and it immediately struck her that he too had dressed in a hurry. One half of his blue necktie was inside his shirt collar and the other half outside. This aroused in her a strong and growing desire not only to tell him of the fact but also to get up and re-arrange the tie nearer, as it were, to her heart's desire.

While this feeling mounted she kept crossing and uncrossing her legs, revealing a blue-stockinged knee for a few minutes and then a green one for a time. All the while she tried reading her *Times* and then, finding herself unable to concentrate, put it down on the seat beside her.

About a minute later the man coughed, leaned forward and said with great politeness:

"I wonder if I might borrow your *Times*? I couldn't get one myself."

"Oh! certainly. Certainly. By all means."

"It's most awfully kind of you."

Miss Stratton gave a polite smile and handed over *The Times*. In the instant before the man lifted up the paper to begin reading it she caught another glimpse of the blue necktie protruding from under its collar and she felt she knew, with certainty, that the man was unmarried. No woman would ever have let a man out of the house, she was sure, with collar and tie so painfully dishevelled.

As she pondered on this thought, at the same time wondering if she dared mention the curious state of the necktie, she stared out of the window, watching the black bare winter landscape slipping past, every field rain-soaked under a sky of driving cloud.

When she turned her glance to the man again it was to be confronted with an immense surprise. At first she found it impossible to believe what she saw. Then a second, third and finally a prolonged fourth look convinced her that she wasn't dreaming.

The man was reading *The Times* completely upside down.

"The necktie," she told herself, "I can understand. That's just a slip in the hurry of getting ready. Like my stockings. Anyone could do a thing like that. But reading the paper upside down—that simply can't be an accident. That simply can't be."

At once it seemed to her imperative that she must do something about this curious state of affairs and she suddenly leaned forward and said:

"Oh! excuse me."

"Yes?"

"I hope—I don't know if you know, but you're reading *The Times* upside down."

"Yes, I do know."

Miss Stratton sat open-mouthed, too flabbergasted to speak.

"Yes, I do know. I prefer it that way."

"You actually—you mean—but isn't it frightfully difficult?"

"Not at all. I've been doing it for years."

"But isn't it a strain? Wouldn't it be easier the right way up?"

"It's more fun this way. Besides I've got used to it." He gave a quick shy smile, a gesture that struck her as being rather squirrel-like. "I've been doing it ever since I was a boy. I got awfully interested in codes and that sort of thing. You know how boys are—turning words round, dropping letters, making X stand for one vowel and Y for another. I started to write sentences backwards and then of course it was only another step to reading things upside down."

Again Miss Stratton was too surprised to speak.

"Have a try yourself." The man held out *The Times* to her. "It's extraordinarily easy once you—it's really a simple matter of concentration."

"Oh! I don't think I could possibly—"

"Try."

Suddenly Miss Stratton was aware of the man sitting next to her. They were holding *The Times* together, upside down.

"Try the headline. This one."

Miss Stratton stared for fully half a minute at the paper, eyes groping behind her smoky-rose spectacles, like a child trying to read for the first time.

"I simply can't make head or tail of it. It looks sort of like Russian."

"Oh! it's easy. It says *U.S. Lose More Helicopters in Vietnam. Vietcong Casualties Reported Heavy.*"

"Oh! so it does. I see now. I must be very stupid."

"Not at all. It just needs practice." The man gave a short treble laugh that Miss Stratton found most engaging. It struck her as being quite boyish. "The curious part is that when you've been reading upside down for ages it seems most odd when you start reading right way up."

"Yes, I suppose *that* could happen."

"It's all a question of viewpoint. After all the world's pretty well upside down as it is, wouldn't you think?"

Miss Stratton laughed too and said she would indeed.

"You know," he suddenly went on, "but you're the first person who's ever drawn my attention to the fact that I read upside down. Hundreds of people every year see me doing it in the train but not one has ever said a word. I suppose they're either too shy or they think I'm mad. Do you think I'm mad?"

"Oh! not at all. Not at all."

"It's merely a question of reversing convention—"

"Can you do it with figures?"

"Oh! with figures, yes. I can add up backwards and so on—it's a mental exercise, you see. A challenge."

For some five minutes or more the train had been running slowly. With slight irritation the man took his watch from his waistcoat pocket—it hung from a thin gold chain—and looked at it.

"Thought so. Running late again. It's a confounded nuisance, this line. Every day last week we were late by ten minutes or more."

"The evening trains are worse."

"I know. Which one do you catch? The 6.10?"

Yes, she always caught the 6.10, Miss Stratton said. In fact she invariably caught the 5.20.

"I don't think I've ever run across you before, have I?" He looked quickly down at Miss Stratton's legs, encased as they always were in odd stockings, one green and one blue. "I'm sure I'd remember if I had."

Miss Stratton felt herself flush very slightly, without a word to say.

"I used to come on the 5.20" he said, "but the thing was a madhouse. A terrible bun-fight."

"I think it's because I usually travel second that you haven't seen me."

"Ah! possibly, possibly."

Again he took a quick hard look at Miss Stratton's stockings. The matter of the stockings struck him as being no less unusual than Miss Stratton found his reading *The Times* upside down. Why did a woman go to work in stockings that didn't match? Most curious. You might well think her mad.

"I always stop off across the road at Porter's Wine Bar for a sherry," he said. "I allow myself that bit of extra time. It's a good relaxer. You wouldn't care to join me, I suppose, this evening?"

Totally ignorant of what prompted her to say so Miss Stratton suddenly said she really didn't know. It all depended on her friend.

"Oh! I see."

Miss Stratton, who had invented the friend on the spur of the moment purely because she was rather flummoxed, now found herself trapped with the problem of getting rid of the friend.

"Well, perhaps some other evening. By the way my name's Fletcher."

"It's very nice of you, Mr. Fletcher. I daresay I could phone my friend."

"Oh! could you? That would be nice. The sherry's awfully good at this place. Of course one can have something else. A glass of burgundy. They have champagne by the glass too."

As he said this Miss Stratton found herself unaccountably inspired to laughter.

"I suppose," she said, "you don't by any chance drink upside down too?"

"That's a thought," Mr. Fletcher said and was unaccountably inspired to laughter too.

That evening, on the 6.10 train, Miss Stratton found herself deeply flushed and panting as she flopped into the corner of the first carriage, with Mr. Fletcher opposite her. The fact that they had had to run for the train, together with two large glasses of sherry—they were called schooners, Mr. Fletcher informed her—occasionally made her giggle briefly as she sought to recover breath.

"Well, that was a close-run thing," Mr. Fletcher said. "Still, if we'd missed it we'd have had an excuse for another schooner."

"Oh! those schooners. They must be trebles."

Having finally got his breath back too Mr. Fletcher took a rapid glance at Miss Stratton's legs, only to find a further interesting surprise awaiting him there. During her lunch hour, in a sudden unpremeditated rush of abandon, Miss Stratton had bought herself some new stockings and was now wearing one of a bright raspberry rose and another of a shade of muted violet. They contrasted and yet blended very well, she thought.

Mr. Fletcher was impelled to think so too but was far too shy to look at them for more than a few seconds or to say so.

He really wanted to say something else but it was only after reading his evening paper upside down for another half hour that he at last found courage enough to do so.

"Do you know this place, Purland Court?" he said. "They've turned it into flats."

No, Miss Stratton said, she didn't think she did.

"It used to be the old Bradfield house. Big Victorian thing, in its own park. I've got one of the flats. Oh! it's only one of the very small ones. Right at the top. A maid's box room originally, I suppose."

"It's not the place with the huge wrought iron gates?"

"That's it. Marvellously beautiful in spring. Big avenue of limes with millions and millions of aconites blooming underneath. As early as February. All gold."

"What are aconites? I'm afraid I'm awfully bad about flowers."

Mr. Fletcher explained about aconites and how he loved them. To him, he didn't know why, they represented something Grecian. They brought spring into winter, he said, and as he spoke of them Miss Stratton was touched into thinking that his voice took on a certain urgent but at the same time bemused note of tenderness.

"Will you be on the train tomorrow?" he finally said.

"Oh! I'm on it every day," Miss Stratton again found herself briefly giggling. "Always on the treadmill."

"I'll look out for you. Perhaps we could indulge in another schooner."

Something about the word indulge instantly illuminated the otherwise drab atmosphere of the railway carriage. There was something intimate and warm about it too: a feeling that almost brought Miss Stratton to the point of saying something about Mr. Fletcher's necktie, which had evidently remained half in, half outside his collar all day. Instead she merely gazed at it with her own air of bemusement. And then Mr. Fletcher said:

"Just in case I miss you in the morning shall we say we'll meet in the wine bar at half past five? That is unless you have to see your friend."

Oh! she didn't think she had to see her friend tomorrow, said Miss Stratton, now under the vexatious impression that Mr. Fletcher understood her friend to be a man.

"Oh! Good." Mr. Fletcher gave her a shy smile and went on to say how pleasant it had all been, meeting her and the sherry and everything.

Miss Stratton said it had been pleasant too and finally went home to an early bed, where for some considerable time she sat reading her newspaper upside down, an experience that troubled her so much that she afterwards didn't sleep well.

The next morning Mr. Fletcher arrived on the train with a small posy of fifteen or twenty yellow aconites wrapped in tissue paper. Miss Stratton, amazed that flowers of such delicacy, and so Grecian in feeling, as Mr. Fletcher maintained, could produce their cool fresh beauty in the darkest hours of winter, kept them all day, and then for the rest of the week, on her office desk, in a small blue plastic tumbler.

Every time she gazed at them she saw Mr. Fletcher's necktie, the knot of which, that morning, was somewhere in the region of his left ear.

After that they started to meet every evening in the wine bar, religiously repeating the ritual of indulging in schooners. Each evening too Miss Stratton went home to read her newspaper upside down, thereby experiencing a curious intimate thrill, almost as if Mr. Fletcher were in bed with her.

All this might have gone on quite uninterrupted if Miss Stratton hadn't happened to remark one evening "Oh! I don't see my friend now—I—well, let's not talk about it."

Mr. Fletcher seemed to think this at last released him from some obligation or other and after some minutes of apparent contemplation said:

"I've been wondering if you might care to come and see my little place sometime. It's very modest, but—"

"Oh! I should love to."

"You couldn't by some remote chance come to lunch? Say on Sunday."

Miss Stratton said she would be quite absolutely delighted and immediately started to wonder what she would wear. For several days she went on wondering, finally coming to the conclusion that since Mr. Fletcher lived in a flat in a Victorian mansion she had better dress accordingly. As a result she bought herself an entirely new outfit, a two piece linen suit in pale green that made her look unusually neat, even a little elegant. She also decided to discard, for once, the odd stockings and instead wore perfectly ordinary nylons in a flesh-pink shade.

"The trouble is there's no lift. I do hope you're not completely fagged out, climbing the stairs."

Miss Stratton, more than a little flustered after climbing four flights of stairs, the last narrow and very steep, eventually found herself contemplating the crazy cell of what Mr. Fletcher called his little place. A gas stove piled with books, a divan bed on which slept three white cats, a bicycle draped with bundles of dried beech leaves, a sewing machine of the old treadle kind on which stood plates, wine-glasses, and bottles of tomato ketchup, a bowl of bananas and custard and an unopened tin of sardines, a bureau littered with a mass of papers, some of them held down with pots of crocuses, others with pots of jam, jars of fish paste and even, in one instance, a half eaten currant loaf: the whole appeared to her to have come out of some lunatic dream. She was also strongly aware of an odour of stale fish combined with the sort of dusty pungency that comes of floors long unswept and windows long unopened.

"I'm afraid I'm a bit tucked for space," Mr. Fletcher said.

Quite unable to make any sort of comment on this, Miss Stratton found herself mournfully distressed for Mr. Fletcher, who was also attired to match the shabby confusion of his little place. His clothes, consisting of a pair of flabby plus-fours the colour of horse manure and a polo-necked sweater that appeared to have been dipped in a solution of stale beer and axle grease, threw her own new pale green suit into such relief that she was now almost ashamed for having put it on.

While Mr. Fletcher poured out sherry into a pair of chipped tooth-glasses Miss Stratton could only wonder what lunch was going to consist of. Mr. Fletcher soon informed her:

"I did knock up a pigeon and steak pie. I normally do it rather well. But I went down into the park to look for primroses and left the gas too high and the thing burnt to a cinder. I hope you don't mind sardines? They ought to marry fairly well with the wine."

Jammed between gas stove and bureau was a low couch, from which Mr. Fletcher presently removed a basket of swede turnips, a portable radio, two empty sherry bottles, a shooting bag and a box of gramophone records, so that he and Miss Stratton could sit down.

"These are the first primroses. They're very early this year. I wanted awfully to get a few to put on the lunch table."

The primroses were in an egg-cup. Miss Stratton, again mournfully touched, held them to her face, breathing in the delicate velvet scent of them.

"I always think you get the whole of spring in the scent of primroses," Mr. Fletcher said. "It takes you back through all the springs of your life."

Such remarks of Mr. Fletcher's always affected her deeply. It was almost as if Mr. Fletcher had stroked her hand or put his face against hers. They had an intolerable, elusive intimacy.

In the intervals of pouring and drinking sherry Mr. Fletcher got up to cut thick slices of brown bread and butter. Miss Stratton, wondering continually about the lunch table, of which she could so far see no sign, was prompted to ask if she could by any chance help?

"I generally eat on the sewing machine," Mr. Fletcher said. "The thing folds in and you get a flat top. It's about right for two."

"Shall I arrange it a bit?"

"Oh! would you? That's awfully nice of you."

Miss Stratton did her best to arrange the lunch table. The plain white tablecloth, much creased, had several holes in it and these she covered with pepper and salt pots, plates and the bowl of bananas and custard. While she was doing this Mr. Fletcher opened the tin of sardines and said:

"I rather fancy the sardines should be good. They're very old. Did you know that sardines improved with age? Like wine?"

Miss Stratton said no, she wasn't aware of that. She herself had no great fondness for sardines, though she was too embarrassed to say so, and now secretly wondered if Mr. Fletcher wouldn't allow her to poach some eggs or make an omelette or something of that sort.

Emboldened by a third glass of sherry, she at last made up her mind to suggest this. It would be the easiest thing in the world. And which did he prefer? Poached eggs or omelette?

"I adore omelettes actually."

Very well, Miss Stratton said, she would do omelettes. She in fact rather prided herself on her omelettes. Had Mr. Fletcher any sort of thing to flavour them with? Cheese or ham or something?

"I've got a tin of mushrooms somewhere," Mr. Fletcher said and started to search for them in the jungle of his little place, eventually finding them in the bureau, mixed up with tins of cat food.

"I know it's the right one," Mr. Fletcher said, "because it's the one without the label."

Miss Stratton, at once revolted by the thought of cat food, profoundly hoped it was. In the end it proved to be and Miss Stratton proceeded to make the omelette, the excellence of which Mr. Fletcher praised with a typically shy enthusiasm throughout the meal.

After lunch Mr. Fletcher sat on the couch and read the Sunday newspaper upside down. Once he looked up to see Miss Stratton reading hers upside down too and said:

"I see you're getting the knack of it. It really isn't all that difficult, is it?"

No, Miss Stratton said, it wasn't, and then caught Mr. Fletcher in the act of gazing at her knees, above which her skirt had ridden up some inches. She hoped that this might mean that Mr. Fletcher was taking a greater and more intimate interest in her legs and that in consequence he might even suggest that she sit on the sofa with him. But nothing of the kind happened at all.

During subsequent weeks nothing happened either. Mr. Fletcher was always kind, polite, considerate, attentive, anxious to please. On the train he brought Miss Stratton little nosegays of violets, once a bunch of cowslips, a pot of white cyclamen for her office desk and in due course a bunch of roses. In the evenings they drank sherry together. On Sundays she cooked lunch for him among the shambles of the sewing machine, the cats, the strewn papers and the clinging odour of fish.

But of the things she wanted most there was no sign. She longed for Mr. Fletcher to make a gesture of something more than mere friendship: to touch her knee, to rest his face against hers, to make a gesture of affection, even love. At night, alone in bed, she even entertained the wild notion that one day Mr. Fletcher might suddenly lose his head and kiss her, even approach her with passion. In such moods she was always ready to surrender.

But by midsummer nothing had happened; and Miss Stratton, half in despair, at last decided to do something about it.

She decided to re-introduce her friend.

Her friend, she reasoned, might arouse in Mr. Fletcher a keener interest in herself, even jealousy.

"Well, I'm awfully afraid I can't meet you tonight. You see, my friend—"

Curiously enough her increasing refusals had on Mr. Fletcher an effect quite opposite from that she hoped and intended. Far from becoming more attentive, passionate or even jealous, Mr. Fletcher became more and more depressed, turning more and more in upon himself, painfully spurned. Finally, on a hot, humid Sunday in July, they quarrelled.

An unexpectedly prolonged beautiful spell of weather had inspired Mr. Fletcher to suggest a picnic in the park. At this time of year the long avenue of limes was in full flower: a great heavenly cathedral of perfume, the whole essence of summer.

Mr. Fletcher had suggested one o'clock for the picnic but it was in fact past two o'clock when Miss Stratton arrived. When Mr. Fletcher uttered some mild remonstrance about this, slightly agitated that some accident might have befallen her, she said:

"Well, I had a phone call from my friend—I couldn't very well not talk—"

In addition to being deliberately late Miss Stratton had also bought herself a new summer dress: a pale yellow short-sleeved shantung, purposely low at the neck. She had been inspired to do this by reading an article in a magazine which had examined the age-old causes of the things by which women attracted men. It seemed that the mode of attraction by the exposure of the legs was comparatively recent; until modern times the legs had been scrupulously concealed. The bosom, on the other hand, especially in the 18th century, had long been exposed.

She and Mr. Fletcher sat in the shade of a huge old lime tree to eat a picnic of ham, green salad, cheese, tomatoes and finally strawberries and cream, together with a bottle of white Alsatian wine. The scent of limes drenching the air was heavy and exotic. The taste of the wine, flowery too, matched it perfectly.

After the strawberries and cream Miss Stratton lay back on the grass, legs carelessly exposed, the slightest curve of her bosom faintly revealed. Now and then she gave a replete, indulgent sigh, breathing in the scent of limes with a sound that expressed a sleepy, dreamy, ecstasy. All Mr. Fletcher did in response was to read his newspaper upside down.

"*Must* you read your newspaper?"

"Well, I always do. There isn't much point in having one if one doesn't read it."

"This heavenly day and all you can think of is to bury your head in a lot of stocks and shares or something."

"Well, I'm sorry. Of course if it offends you—"

"I didn't say it offended me. I said this heavenly day and all you can do is to turn into a book-worm—a newspaper-worm—or something."

"I don't think I care for the word worm. Whatever's come over you?"

"Nothing has come over me, as you fondly put it."

"You shock me. I've never heard you speak like this."

For some minutes Miss Stratton lay grimly, resolutely silent. Then she suddenly uttered a peremptory, whispered "My God!"

"And what, pray, was that in aid of?" Mr. Fletcher said.

"Oh! read your wretched newspaper!"

"Really."

Miss Stratton, silent and impotent, stared up through the great canopy of leaves and keys of lime flower above her head. Only the minutest fragments of sky, like segments of bright blue broken glass, were visible beyond.

"What am I expected to do?" Mr. Fletcher said.

"Do? Well, you could admire my new dress, for one thing. Or even notice it."

"I have noticed it. I like it."

"Like it! My friend went into raptures about it."

"Am I to take it that you'd rather be with your friend?"

"I didn't say that. All I said was—Oh! never mind."

For more than another half hour they were completely silent. Once Miss Stratton, as if half-suffocated by the drenching heat of afternoon, loosened still further the neck of her dress and wiped the damp upper curves of her neck and bosom with a handkerchief.

At last Mr. Fletcher said in a flat, almost morbid monotone:

"We seem to have wasted a whole afternoon."

"We!" Miss Stratton could bear it no longer and suddenly sprang to her feet. "We, for Heaven's sake! Include me out, as they say."

"Oh! my dear, I never thought we'd come to this."

"Don't 'my dear' me!"

To Mr. Fletcher's utter astonishment Miss Stratton was already walking away.

"Where on earth are you going?"

"Going? Where do you think I'm going? I'm going to see my friend. Note the word. Friend—friend!"

Head high in the air, under the blazing July sun, Miss Stratton stormed away across the park.

For nearly two months after this she never saw Mr. Fletcher on the train. Nor did she ever see him in the wine bar, where she sometimes lingered in the evenings, sipping sherry and hoping that by some sort of miracle he might appear.

Finally, unable to bear it any longer, she went over to Mr. Fletcher's flat, his little place. She climbed the long flights of stairs, knocked several times on the door and also rang the bell, without getting an answer. As she then came down again a woman appeared from a flat below and said:

"Was there something I could do to help you?"

"I was looking for Mr. Fletcher."

"Oh! Mr. Fletcher doesn't live here now."

"No?"

"He took a flat in London. Said he found the train journey every day very tiresome."

"You don't know the address?"

"I'm afraid not. He went off awfully suddenly. We all thought he looked ill. The stairs seemed to be too much for him. You'd hear him positively fighting for breath. In the way asthmatics do."

"Was he asthmatic?"

"Oh! pitifully. I thought he'd die once or twice. In fact I'm ashamed to say it but I watch the obituary columns every day—it's a dreadful thought, I know, but I wouldn't want to miss it."

Miss Stratton started to watch the obituary columns too. Almost a year later she read that Mr. Fletcher, who always read his newspaper upside down and could only express himself to her in such simple things as aconites, a bunch of primroses, a glass of sherry or a rose or two, had died.

Miss Stratton is now married to a man named Rawlinson, who has a wholesale business in paints, emulsions and materials of that sort. They live in a villa furnished down to the smallest, correctest detail by a firm of decorators; the garden too has been landscaped for them and has a professional, orderly, impeccable, shorn and bloodless air.

Rawlinson is a man of intensely scrupulous habits who gets up at half past six every morning in order to complete a holy ritual of shaving, clipping his moustache, oiling his hair, anointing himself with after-shave lotions, brushing his teeth and manicuring his neat shell-like nails in order to be at his desk punctually on the stroke of nine. Every day he lunches at his office. Every evening he goes home at nine o'clock to find the former Miss Stratton playing patience or knitting or reading or watching television, waiting for supper. When he is away from home, however far away, his office telephones him twice a day with the day's figures, orders and events in minutest detail. When he dines out he peruses, rather than reads, the menu with the same fine incisive attention to every single item, as if it were as sacred as holy writ.

His behaviour to the former Miss Stratton is equally scrupulous, impeccable, orderly and correct. He flatters himself that she has everything she could possibly wish for. There is nothing she lacks.

Sometimes, in the middle of this secure and well-ordered world, Miss Stratton thinks of Mr. Fletcher and such small things as his aconites, his primroses and his sherry; and sometimes, when alone or when Rawlinson isn't looking, she also reads her newspaper upside down.

It is only then that the world seems to her to be right way up and she can view it with a better understanding.

SOME OTHER SPRING

It was going to be rather something, he told himself, for the tenth time or so, to see the children again after nearly two years. They might well have changed out of all recognition; they might well be strangers.

It was partly for that reason he had left his car in the village and decided to walk the rest of the way, a quarter of a mile or so, across the fields. He would go in—no, sort of saunter in, quite casually, as if in fact the house were still his own—through the garden, by the back way. It seemed altogether too formal to use the front door. You couldn't very well knock and say "Hullo, good afternoon, excuse me, I've come to pay my visit to the children. I'm allowed to see them once a month, if you remember. You know, the court order, Yes I know I haven't—yes, it's been some time—I hope you got my letter. I did write to confirm."

The old Saunders place next door looked well, he thought, across the fields. The black and white front stood out in the August sun like a piece of iced cake against the black background of pines. He always envied the Saunders place, so marvellously well kept, so permanent, so immemorial somehow, so secure: all due, of course, to Elspeth, who looked after her father as efficiently as she looked after the garden, the house, the accounts, the cooking and everything else. She would have made someone an awfully good wife, Elspeth, he always thought: nice looks, charming, pleasant, affectionate, good taste, good clothes, good manners, good cook, good everything. He simply couldn't think why she had never made it. He supposed she might well have given up the thought of it now. But then, in a way, perhaps it was no loss: you had to have women like Elspeth, who ran their fathers' houses with efficiency, made miracles of gardens, pleased everybody, remembered birthdays, became miraculous godmothers and were always faultless friends. After all they couldn't all be wives.

The surrounding countryside looked pretty immemorial too, he thought. It was so long since he had seen it that he had forgotten how perfectly the low fold of meadows gave way to strips of cornland, the barley almost as white as the chalk on which it grew, and the glowing beauty of the dark beechwoods above and beyond.

If these old familiar things seemed to surprise him pleasantly the sight of his own house—it wasn't his own any more, but for some reason he couldn't get out of the habit of thinking it was—grated on him, it always had, with irritation. You could see even from a distance that it fairly sprouted shabbiness. Even the curtains of the window in the east gable hadn't been pulled back: that old, old bone of contention. Why on earth couldn't Carrie remember?

Naturally, of course, because she was Carrie. She was made like that. He could look at it dispassionately now. Untidiness, shabbiness, slopping about, come-easy, go-easy, dust and cobwebs: she loved it all; to her it was all, in a sense, romantic. A house in the country was merely a glorious ramshackle plaything for messing about with, whereas he himself had just as naturally wanted it to be ordered, civilised, a pattern.

For instance, the garden. He had been most passionately keen on the garden. He had gone to great expense in making, among other things, a rock-garden, with specially imported stone, and a lily pond. In no time the lily pond was full of rusty toys, old bricks, ice-cream cartons, ghastly little tricycles. The children dug sand castles among the rocks. They played absolute hell with his beautifully nurtured gentians.

Carry thought this natural, even funny. They must be allowed, she fiercely maintained, to be themselves, to give expression to this and that, to run free.

"But God, the wretched pool looks like a bomb-site. Look at the mess—look at the tin-cans—"

"Then let it look like a bomb-site. To them—"

"But damn it, hell, it isn't a bomb-site. It's a pool. A lily pool. I paid good hard-earned money to have the thing made and now look what the little horrors—"

"And how are they to know that? They don't know. They can't differentiate between a lily pond and a bomb-site. To them it's merely a place. They can't differentiate—"

"Oh! don't keep using words like differentiate."

"Oh! and why not?"

"Oh! it's sort of councilese—sort of—well, why don't you just say 'tell the difference'?—I don't know, it's sort of suburban—"

"Sort of, sort of—My God, it's no more suburban than that!"

By now he had reached the back boundary of the garden. He paused by the privet hedge. He seemed to see them still, the little perishers. He saw Nigel, the boy, actually riding a filthy tricycle through the lily pond, crushing lilies as they floated in full bloom, with Gilian, the girl, towed on behind in what seemed to be some sort of wretched fish-box on wheels. They were laughing uproariously, almost idiotically, and Carrie was laughing with them. No wonder he had hated and loved them; no wonder the end had come.

"You've got a sort of bead-frame mind, you have. Everything's got to be neat and in rows. Proper colours and added up. All nice and tidy and mathematical."

He was almost, at that moment, on the verge of turning back. It seemed the height of stupidity, suddenly, to rake it all up again. Could children change? He doubted it. Once there, the character could only manifest itself accordingly; like a plant, it was fixed: poisonous or not, fragrant or otherwise.

All of a sudden he was bothered by something about the hedge. It was somehow different. That end of the garden had always been a rampant wilderness, deep in nettles, a maze of bryony and elderberry everywhere. It was where the tin cans came from.

Now he was aware not merely of an air of change, but even of order. To his infinite astonishment the hedge had been smoothly clipped. The elderberry bushes that he remembered as being like untidy purple autumnal umbrellas had been laid low. The wicket gate, half way along it, had actually been painted, the slats alternately green and white.

With his hand on the latch of the gate he was halted by an oppressive thought. Had Carrie married again and not told him? Or had she now a boyfriend, for whom the new-painted garden gate was as essential a part of her attraction as the lipstick on her face? He suddenly felt, in any case, a dreadful stranger, an intruder, cold and out of it.

He supposed, now, that that was why she had invited him to tea: family gathering and so on. It would ease the situation: everyone on best behaviour. This, at least, was a relief. In such a situation he wouldn't have to play games, make pet mice out of handkerchiefs or pretend, as he jogged the children on his knee, that he was a raspberry jam factory.

He pushed open the gate and went into a garden that surprised him, like the hedge, with its air of orderliness. Gone were not only the elderberry bushes, but the tin cans. Shrubs, with an underplanting of silver foliage in many shapes, had supplanted them. The old brick wall that ran behind and beyond had been cleaned up and planted with a yellow *Mermaid* rose, still in full bloom, and a clematis that erupted over the crest of it in thick purple pennants, warm velvet in the August sun.

"And Good God, an *Abutilon Megopotanicum*. Incredible. What on earth's that doing here?" He stood staring at a shrub hung with many red and black and yellow bells, in shape not unlike a fuchsia, and felt a sharp strange pang of envy. Some new influence had been at work all right. How otherwise had she ever managed to plant that? It wasn't even hardy.

He started to finger the shrub's slender leaves, jealous now not only of the shrub but of Carrie. In a way it wasn't quite fair. He had always wanted to grow that particular *abutilon* but had never really dared to risk it. The three-coloured bells were so beautiful. They were like little pagodas. He fingered the leaves again. One might, he supposed, have a shot with cuttings?

"Are you trying to pinch bits from the garden?"

"Oh! no, I really wasn't doing that. Oh! no, I was just admiring."

He turned and saw his daughter, Gilian, standing on the edge of the path. He supposed she was seven now, or thereabouts. He couldn't accurately remember. She seemed awfully tall, anyway, he thought, and was wearing tartan trews, a red shirt-blouse and her blonde hair in a horse-tail.

"No, you really mustn't think I was stealing. Just admiring, that's all."

"That's what all the people said at the garden party. Oh! no, nobody was putting bits in their handkerchiefs. Just admiring, that's all. Did you want Mummy?"

"I'm your father."

For a moment he fully expected her to say something like "I might have known," but then, as the cold notion of being a stranger suddenly enveloped him again, he heard the familiar voice of Carrie, rather high-pitched as usual, saying as she came across the lawn:

"Ah! there you are. No wonder we couldn't see you—creeping in by the back way, eh?"

He refrained from commenting, although strongly and briefly tempted, on the word creeping, and merely said:

"Afraid I was caught in the act. Hullo."

"Well, after all, there is a front door bell."

He stood facing Carrie, not knowing what to say. He hadn't seen her, either, for nearly two years. She was very brown and rather leaner in the face, he thought. Her very light blonde hair was done in that chewed-off fashion that seemed to be so popular at the moment. He didn't like it. His daughter stood apart.

He felt he ought to refer, somehow, to the incident of the *abutilon*. He said he supposed that Gilian hadn't recognised him.

"Oh! nonsense. Of course she knew you. She's been hopping about expecting you all day."

"Yes? I must say the *abutilon* took me by surprise."

"The what?"

"The *abutilon*. The thing growing up the wall. I must say you've done wonders with the wall."

"Oh! that. That's not me, I'm afraid. That's Charles. He's responsible for all that."

Well, damn it, he thought. He felt she might have told him. He supposed, really, that he hadn't any real right to know of—well, any new set-up, liaison or whatever it was—but he was after all the father of the children.

Who was this Charles? Another gardener, it seemed. That struck him as pretty rich. He and Carrie had practically arrived at dagger point because of what she called his bead-frame mind, his meticulous passion for the straight line, proper colours and everything added up, and now here was this Charles and the garden as neat and ordered as a park.

He noticed that the children weren't dashing about it everywhere on those damned tricycles either. He looked hastily at Gilian, who in return gave him, shyly, a sidelong glance and a smile. She too, like the garden, was incredibly tidy, so utterly different from the sloppy, muddy little horror who had trailed about his lily pool that again he felt a stranger, cold, out of it all.

Then he remembered that, of course, he was a stranger. He didn't belong here. He heard Carrie ask if he wouldn't like to see the rest of the garden before tea and as they began to walk across the lawn, itself as smooth and even as a sheet of green baize, his eye caught in the middle distance a great orange crowd of tiger lilies, curled turbanned heads flaming against some artemesia-like cloud of grey.

He was at once stricken by a pang of jealousy. At the same time he had to admire the rightness of the combination, of the contrast between gold flower and grey leaf, fire and smoke. It was all most effective, if anything too damned effective.

"Oh! that's Charles again. Anything you see out of the ordinary, that's Charles."

He now supposed that Charles would, of course, be at tea. Conversation would have to be made with Charles: he would have to be polite. In irritation he wished he had never come. It was all a bit deceitful, not quite fair, not playing the game.

"I think you're awfully like your photograph."

He discovered that Gilian was walking very close to him. Her airy light horse-tail was almost transparent in the sun. He was aware of a presence very feminine and slightly strange too, not at all daughterly. Her sharp blue eyes, though shy, never left him.

"Oh! I take awful photographs. Which photograph was that?"

"The one where you're gathering wild strawberries. Up on the hills."

"Oh! yes."

"You've got your handkerchief knotted over your head because it was so hot. Don't you remember?"

Children had awful memories, he thought. They remembered the most ridiculous, impossible details.

"Oh! you remember that," Carrie said. "Even I remember that day."

"We gathered five pounds and afterwards we made jam and it didn't set very well." Gilian kept him in a sharp, prolonged sidelong glance, now partly in recollection, part in scrutiny. "You can't go up there now. They've ploughed it all up."

"Oh! yes I remember now." He didn't remember at all—or just, perhaps, very vaguely.

Glad to change the subject, he noted a new blaze of fire across the garden: a burning vermilion cluster of horns with small white honeycombs of dahlias below. Again the contrast was very striking, very right. He supposed it was a salvia of some sort?

"Oh! you must ask Charles. He knows all about names. I'm hopeless. You know, I think you and old Charles might have a great deal in common."

Old Charles, he noted with irritation and then saw that she was smiling at him. He noticed the particular quality of the smile with surprise. Formerly it too might have been an irritant. It was an old habit of hers to smile when acid, even bitter. Now there was no trace of acrimony.

"You must come and see my garden. I've got a piece all to myself."

"Oh! yes, you must see Gilian's garden. She's mad about her garden."

"When, now?"

"Oh! when she's ready. You're very honoured. Even I don't get asked."

"After tea, will you come?"

"Yes, of course."

Speaking of tea, Carrie said, she thought they might go into the house now. Where was Nigel? Would Gilian run and find him? He found himself recoiling coldly at the name Nigel. He had always hated that name. It had been a great source of conflict, that name, a great breeder of rows, but in the end he had given in.

"Oh! he'll come, won't he?" Gilian stood very close to him again, still holding him with that sharp, shy, sidelong glance. "He never comes if you go and fetch him."

"Oh! here's Elspeth anyway. Oh! there you are, Elspeth—nice and early, good."

Charles, he noted now to himself, didn't have all the monopoly of taste and the rightness of doing things. As Elspeth came across the lawn in a light cream linen suit piped at the edges with what seemed to be thinnest stalks of bright green reed she also seemed to have the quality of some well-placed flower. Her deep natural brown hair was burning and sombre in the sun.

"We all know about your dreadful memory, but don't go and say you don't remember Elspeth."

"Of course I remember Elspeth. Vividly. Is that the right thing to say, Elspeth?"

"Of course. Only there was a time when you used to kiss me too."

Elspeth held up her face to be kissed. He duly kissed it, on both cheeks, with polite affection. At the same time he remembered that he had kissed neither Carrie nor his daughter. It was perhaps remiss. On the other hand there was Charles.

"Oh! that's more like it." The eyes of Elspeth were like moist, gold-brown shells. "How are you? Let's have a look at you." She stood back to appraise him. Her smile, like the cheeks he had just kissed so lightly, was smooth and warm. "Pass with honours."

"Putting on a little weight, I thought," Carrie said.

"Oh! Carrie, nonsense. Not a gram."

"Have you put on weight? You have."

"Oh! why is everyone so obsessed with weight?" he said. "If you must know I've lost three ounces since yesterday. I've had my hair cut."

Elspeth laughed brightly at this, with rich amusement. Carrie seemed, however, not to think it funny and looked at him with what, in the past, he had sometimes called that old spoon look of hers. It was tarnished and unreflective.

"Well and what do you think of the garden? Don't you think we've livened it up?"

"We?"

"Oh! it's Charles and Elspeth who've done it all. You know how mad keen Elspeth always was. Charles and she talk the language. Just like you do."

The voice of Carrie was again an irritant. They were all walking across the lawn now, Gilian still close to him, still watching. The old white French rose, *Madame Alfred Carrière*, was flowering beautifully, for the second time, on the house wall, and for some reason he again thought of the *abutilon*.

"Oh! yes that was from a cutting of mine," Elspeth said.

"Everything's from Elspeth's cuttings. Elspeth brings them and Charles bungs them in."

He had no idea, for a few moments, what to say, and walked on in silence. Then something made him remember Gilian. Her eyes were still fixed on him and he said:

"What about your garden? Does Charles help in your garden too?"

"Oh! no. My garden's my own."

*   *   *

They would have tea, Carrie said, on the lawn, under the big cherry tree. She would put the kettle on; everything was ready on a tray.

It was close beyond the cherry tree where the lily pond had been. He looked for it now in vain. A bed of heathers, with dwarf conifers and clumps of blue-grey grass and a pocket or two of miniature scarlet roses had taken its place.

"Oh! yes I'm afraid the pool's gone for a Burton*. That was an early casualty. The aquatic things grew like mad and smothered the water-lilies and then the cherry leaves came down and in the end there just wasn't any

---

*R.A.F. slang of the Forties: "Going for a Burton" means being killed, or being "missing"— inspired by a wartime poster for Burton's Ales. An empty seat at the table: "Where's Joe?" Answer: "He's gone for a Burton!"

water. It was an awful mess. Charles couldn't have that. He filled it in."

Silently he mourned the pool. It had been rather a pet of his, the pool. Perhaps it was badly sited there, too near the tree, but all the same—

"Will you be long, Carrie? Can I help? If not, I'd rather like to show Roger that thing I snaffled from the old Abbey garden. The red thing. The one nobody's been able to name."

"As long as you don't drag it out too long. India or China?"

"China, I think. I know Roger likes China. He always did."

The eyes of Gilian watched him like those of a dog waiting to be tempted with a morsel of food, for the snap of a leash, for a run across the fields.

"I do want you to see this thing. Nobody has a notion what it is. I suppose you could send it to Kew and they'd know. How does the garden strike you?"

"It seems larger somehow."

"Oh! that's Charles. He's done a lot of clever cutting down, Charles. Opening up vistas and that sort of thing."

He suddenly felt the compulsive pull of two forces: a growing impatience with Charles and a submission to the deep brown warmth of Elspeth's voice, urging him to look now at a long serpentine valley of azaleas where once, he knew, nothing had grown but gooseberries. Of course the azaleas were over now, but in the spring—it had been marvellous in the spring.

"Did I hear a rumour that you were going to be married again?"

He knew it was a try-on; he knew there was no such rumour. He merely said:

"No, no. And you? What about you?"

"Oh! I still keep house for Father."

"Still? It isn't good for you."

"I suppose not."

She caught his arm, guiding him away from the azaleas. The new plan of the garden was all unfamiliar to him. It wasn't his any longer and he felt more than ever a stranger to it all, a cold intruder.

"Well, there it is. What do you make of it? I just snaffled a couple of cuttings and in no time Charles had it going."

He was coming to the point where, he thought, he could cheerfully have strangled Charles. The shrub he now saw before him, four or five feet high, flowering with a curious blood-red tassel, slightly flamboyant, was very beautiful. It was totally unfamiliar too but he said:

"It's that Obedient Plant thing, isn't it? You push the flowers round and they stay where you put them."

"Oh! I never thought of that."

"Try pushing the flowers round. Swivel them. They ought to stay where you put them. Like the hands of a clock."

He watched her fingers on the blood-red flowers. He saw her touch and twist and turn them, this way and that, and then saw that they were not like the hands of a clock. They didn't obey; they didn't stay where you put them.

"So it isn't that, after all."

"No, it can't be that. To me it always looks like a subtropical snapdragon. But of course it's not. No other thoughts?"

No, he said, he was afraid he had no other thoughts. It was something of a mystery. Of course she could, he suggested, always go back to the garden she had pinched it from and ask there.

She laughed, throwing her head back, and the sound was as warm and tawny as the tiger-lilies he had seen, not long since, burning across the garden.

"Supposing I took a flower and looked it up and dropped you a line?"

Oh! no, she said, she thought that would rather spoil it now. It would be better to let it stay as it was, something of a mystery. It might probably turn out to be some awfully ordinary thing, a rampant weed from Kenya or somewhere. One day you'd meet someone who would laugh in your face and say "What, that thing? We could never get rid of it."

Her alternate laughing and talking suddenly stopped. The garden, shut off at some distance from the house, became very quiet. A profound silence sang all about them. The warm brown eyes encompassed him and she said:

"Shouldn't ask this, I suppose. But why the long time coming back? Oh! it's difficult, I suppose."

"I wasn't exactly encouraged."

"Well, you're encouraged now."

She put her face to his, giving him no more than the shadow of a kiss on the side of it.

"Well, now tea I suppose."

"Well, yes, I suppose—"

She started to walk away. For a moment or two he felt left in air. Then he felt a powerful urge to take her by the shoulders and turn her back. After all he was free. There was nothing, not a thing, to hold him now.

"Well, come on. You heard what Carrie said. Don't drag it out too long."

He joined her without a word and together they went up through the new azalea walk, crimson here and there with a burning leaf or two, and so to the lawn and across to the house.

He became aware, half way across the lawn, of a waiting figure.

"Gilian's on the watch for you."

"So I see."

From the house Carrie appeared, carrying a silver teapot and plate of cream-cheese sandwiches. She smiled and said Oh! there they were and how perfectly they had timed it and her voice was dry.

"Milk or lemon, Roger?"

"Oh! lemon," Elspeth said. "He always did."

"I'll have lemon today too," Gilian said.

Set half in sun, half in shade, the table with its shining cups and china gave a twisted sort of sparkle.

"Well, did you solve the great mystery?"

No, he said, he was afraid he'd made a wrong guess.

"Obedient Plant, he thought," Elspeth said. "But it turned out not. It didn't obey."

Well, Carrie said, if it beat Charles it would beat anybody.

"What is an Obedient Plant?" Gilian said.

He started to explain about the Obedient Plant. A certain feeling of futility about the explanation suddenly made him impatient and he was on the point of stopping the whole thing when he saw the eyes of his daughter, large and transfixed, holding him as if mesmerised. Hastily he renewed the explanation, saying how the flowers could be turned this way and that, wherever you liked, and would stop where you left them.

"How clever. How did you find out about a thing like that?"

Oh! he supposed he'd swotted it up at some time, heard of it somehow.

"I think it's marvellous."

"I can't imagine," Carrie said, "where Nigel's got to. Gilian, go and look for him again."

"I looked. He said he wouldn't come. He's playing with water outside the dog-kennel."

"He's been truculent, that boy, all day. Apologies for your son—he's sometimes a bit like that."

Without a word he picked up his spoon and jabbed at the lemon in his China tea. Apologies: as if the truculence, the refusal to come to table, were all his fault. He was relieved, however, rather than offended. One of the things he had dreaded more than anything was to meet the boy. It imposed on him an obligation only equalled by the necessity, sooner or later, of meeting Charles.

"Oh! by the way," Elspeth said, "I brought a few seedlings of the other *abutilon* over. The mauve one, *vitifolium.* I put them in the greenhouse. You know it, Roger, don't you?"

"It's lovely."

"I really prefer it to the *megapotanicum.*"

"I think I do too."

"We had it once before but the last bad winter killed it. Now the new one has set seed."

"We had it here too and something killed it. Some truculent axe, I think."

At once the tea-table seemed to flame. An interval of what seemed the better part of a minute, but in reality only a few seconds, ignited and seared the air. He waited for yet a further whip of it to reach him from Carrie's tongue but she merely poured more hot water into the teapot and Elspeth said:

"I think they need over-wintering inside. They're that bit tender."

"I'll tell Charles."

The flame that had momentarily and dramatically flashed across the table by now was dead, leaving empty ashen air behind.

"I thought I heard the gate," Carrie suddenly said. "Go and see. It's perhaps the postman."

"It could be Charles," Elspeth said.

"Oh! no. He won't be here today."

Well that, he thought, was at least considerate. Thank God for that. At least the ordeal of meeting the universal Charles needn't bother him any more.

Gilian, he noticed, hadn't gone to the gate. He helped himself to a third cream-cheese sandwich. She took one too. As she did so he noticed, surprisingly for the first time, that she was wearing two circular badges on the lapel of her blouse: one scarlet and one gold.

"What are your badges for?"

"One's for good conduct and one's for the week's progress."

"But you're on holiday."

"Yes, but I'm just wearing them today."

He ought, he supposed, to talk about schools and progress and things like that. On the other hand—He went to drink more tea and found that his cup was empty.

"Let me fill you up. Was it right? Enough sugar?"

"Delicious. Just one lump."

Yes, schools. That was important.

"Do you like school?"

"You've touched on a sore subject," Carrie said. "No, she doesn't."

"Oh! no, that's not true. I do and I don't."

"Well, we were all like that. I remember—"

He stopped. He saw that not only was Gilian looking at him, eyes minutely watchful, but that Elspeth was watching too.

"Well, go on. I thought we were going to hear something terribly important—"

"No, no. Just that I—you know how school is."

There was a kind of light Madeira sponge cake, with jam filling, on the table. Would he care for some? No, he didn't think he would, really, he wasn't for sweet things all that much. Nor, it seemed, was Gilian.

"Strange, that," Elspeth said. "I notice all children are like that, nowadays. They're not much for sweet things. They all go for savouries. I've got a niece of three who gorges stuffed olives. I think I was twenty before I tried a stuffed olive and then I didn't like it."

"Oh! I hate stuffed olives. I hate savouries and fishy things and all that. I hate—"

"Now, now," Carrie said. "Don't let's have a hate day."

"Hate day?" he said.

"Oh! yes, we have hate days," Carrie said. "One day this week it was horses. The day after that, circuses, wasn't it? Yesterday it was Charles, of all people."

"Well, I do hate Charles."

"Now nobody on earth," Elspeth said, "could hate Charles. Charles is an absolute—"

"I hate him. He never lets me do anything. He's always mean and snappy and you don't have to touch things."

God, he thought, this was—He sipped slowly at his tea. A leaf from the cherry-tree, prematurely crimson, floated suddenly down in the windless air and settled lightly in the centre of the tea-table, making Elspeth say:

"Oh! leaves falling already. Don't say it's going to be an early autumn."

"I think that's the one thing that makes Charles really bad-tempered,"

Carrie said. "Leaves. Sweeping up. He hates them. They're so endless."

"Well, this year we've gone in for one of those patent sweeper-up gadgets. You must borrow it."

"Ah! that means you'll monopolize him. I think you've got even more leaves than we have."

"Well, we'll have to toss up for him again, that's all."

In mystification he sat mute. It struck him as being more than a bit liberal, two women tossing up for the husband of one of them, and again he felt out of it all, a cold intruder in a strange world. Was that the reason, perhaps, for the hatred? It was understandable. He was near enough to hating Charles himself.

"How much do these things cost?" Carrie said. "I might as well get one too. He hates borrowing things."

"Oh! no don't go to that expense. After all we share him. Let's share the gadget."

"All right, if you say so. By the way, since the days are drawing in, won't it soon be time we changed the timetable?—you have him in the mornings and me in the afternoons."

The mystification on his face evidently turned to astonishment, then stupefaction. He felt positively sullen. The intrusion on peculiar private affairs made him wish to God, once again, that he had never come. A certain warmth he had hitherto felt for Elspeth curled up and died inside himself like a dry worm. It wasn't any wonder there was hatred.

"Roger, you look terribly thoughtful."

Thoughtful? He started to say something about not being a particularly cynical man but of course if sharing Charles gave any satisfaction—then his sentence died too, cut dead by Elspeth and Carrie laughing.

"Roger, you're a scream—did you really think Carrie and I?—"

"In the *mornings* too!—God, I'm never any good in the mornings anyway."

"Oh! me, of course, I'm terrific. Can you see me?—all voluptuous in slacks and a wind-cheater, waiting for Charles in a wheel-barrow."

It was not, he thought, funny. He stared at his empty teacup, at the garden and then, quickly and sullenly, at Gilian. She in return hardly looked at him. There was no change in her face even when Carrie and Elspeth burst out laughing again, so loudly and high-spirited that it mocked hi. He felt like the victim of some bad, practical joke.

"Roger, what an idea—you didn't really think—"

"Well, perhaps we should try it some time," Elspeth said. She was still laughing, bright tawny eyes quite flashing in their amusement. "I never thought of it—hullo, where's Gilian hopped off to?"

The joke of Charles died out slowly, in repeated splutters, a damp but irrepressible firework. For him, too, the afternoon died. No, he wouldn't have more tea, thank you.

"I'm sorry you saw dear old Charles in such a bad light," Carrie said. Her voice now had that slight edge to it, fine with acidity. "I hope our poor old gardener is now acquitted without a stain on his character."

"It was a genuine mistake."

The aftermath of laughter was cold. He tried to think of an excuse for going very soon, without seeming to be too impossibly stiff, and was suddenly struck by the thought of the boy playing outside the dog-kennel.

"I suppose I ought to say hullo to Nigel before I go."

"Oh! you're not going yet? Go and find him yourself—he'd like that. There's plenty of time."

He got up from the table and walked across the lawn. Behind him he caught the echo of yet one more cackle of laughter, but when it died the afternoon was gripped in quietness.

The dog-kennel in the yard behind the kitchen was empty, graced by neither boy nor dog. He looked at it for a few moments, feeling empty too. He remembered the yard as a dumping ground for buckets, heaps of sand, bits of iron bedsteads lashed together in grotesque shapes of planes and cars, old bath tins labouring in sordid puddles or beached across the waste of unswept asphalt.

Now it was all carefully swept; there were even tubs of scarlet and pink geraniums set about it; the asphalt had been replaced by broad flags of paving stone.

He walked through the yard and out to the kitchen garden beyond. That too was neat and orderly: a barrack square filled with platoons of carrots and onions, beetroot and beans, enough potatoes to feed an army.

He went out of it by a wooden wicket gate at the far side. Beyond it, in a triangle of holly and briar and laurel, the garden ended, and it was almost a relief to see it end half in neglect, hidden away, in secret disorder.

In the centre of it sat Gilian.

"This is my garden. Charles won't let me have it any anywhere else."

"It's nice here. All on its own."

"Do you like it?"

An oblong plot of earth had been scraped out and lined with flints, half bricks and lumps of stone. He stared at it for some time, not speaking.

"I've got candytuft in there, but it hasn't come up yet. And Iceland poppies. They're really for next year."

"Are they carrots coming up there?"

"Carrots? No, that's supposed to be larkspur."

"It looks like carrots."

"Oh! no, I don't think so. I hope not. I sowed Chinese pinks too. That's what it said on the packet. Chinese. Do you think it's them coming up?"

"No, I think that's grass there."

She had only just made the garden, she said: only a week or two ago. It really hadn't got started yet. Everything seemed to be so slow coming up. Should they be so slow?

"It doesn't get an awful lot of light in here."

"No, I know. But it will later. In the winter. When the leaves fall.'

"Oh! yes. And in the spring. Plants respond to light as much as anything. You'll see an awful difference in the spring."

He stooped and pulled up a root of groundsel and threw it aside.

"Oh! must you pull that up? I thought it was a flower."

"Oh! I'm sorry," he said. "I didn't think you wanted it."

He would send her packets of seeds, he said, as if in compensation, and she said thank you, she would like that. She re-arranged a few stones along the edge of the plot and picked up a piece of broken glass or two and threw them away.

"You thought I was stealing bits from the garden," he said "Rather funny."

It disturbed him that she didn't say anything in answer. Perhaps it wasn't funny. He felt it time to go. Would she come too? He ought to go and say good-bye to her mother.

"No, I'll stay here. I've got quite a bit to do."

"Well, I'll say good-bye then."

He thought at first, foolishly, that he would shake hands with her. He actually extended his right hand and then dropped it to his side. Then she slightly lifted her face and he kissed it on both cheeks and it was almost, for a moment, as if he were saying good-bye to Elspeth instead.

"I must go now. Good-bye."

"Good-bye. You won't forget the seeds?"

"No, I won't forget the seeds. What seeds would you like?"

"Oh! I don't know. Not really. Anything."

"Well, you say and I'll send them."

"No, you choose. Anything you like. You choose."

"All right. I'll try to send some good things. Good-bye now."

"Good-bye."

For some reason it was the thought of Elspeth, not Gilian, that rode light and uppermost in his mind as he crossed the kitchen garden, then the yard, and came out to the lawn and flower beds beyond. He had been profoundly glad of Elspeth, without really realising it, all afternoon. Elspeth had helped enormously. Of course the misunderstanding about Charles was all perfectly ridiculous; genuine mistake though it was, all his fault. The idea of two women sharing—it was all preposterous but now he could, perhaps, seeing that it was all over, share the joke.

By the time he reached the lawn there was no one in sight. The tea-table was cleared. The lawn was empty. Then he saw the figure of Carrie, waiting on the steps of the house.

"I'm sorry. It was Gilian. I had to see the garden."

"You're very honoured. I told you. Did you see Nigel?"

"No, he wasn't there."

"I see."

"Oh! and has Elspeth gone? Oh! surely not. I wanted to say good-bye."

"She suddenly fled. She suddenly remembered she had some cream to pick up in the village. It was nearly half-past five."

He once again felt out of it all, cold, a stranger intruding.

"What did she have to rush for?"

"Oh! she's like that sometimes."

"I didn't say good-bye."

"She said to tell you good-bye. And if you ever had a thought about the name of that plant—"

"Oh! yes. Did you say honoured? Why?"

"Oh! even I haven't seen the garden yet."

He stared across the empty lawn, towards the tawny flame of tiger lilies with their attendant silver sprays, at the purple burning clematis on the wall. It was all splendidly kept, in beautiful order. There was hardly a leaf, a twig, a blade of grass out of place.

"What was the garden like?" Carrie said.

He paused before answering. He must go pretty soon. There was nothing to wait for.

"She has great plans for it," he said. He remembered suddenly her watching eyes, her long, waiting silences. "It should be marvellous in the—"

"In what?"

"Oh! in the spring."

Or if not in the spring, he thought, some other time: some other spring.

AND NO BIRDS SING

It wasn't only being alone; it was the way the house smelt dead.

She sat under a big sweet-chestnut tree, in the heart of the woodland, watching Mr. Thompson with grave brown eyes. Mr. Thompson was frying mushrooms over a hazel fire in an old half-circular billy-can. The peculiar aroma of hazel smoke and the tang of mushrooms was so strong on the October evening air that every now and then she licked her lips like someone in a hungry dream.

"Never had wild mushrooms before," she said. "Never knew you could get them wild."

"No?" Mr. Thompson said. He kept turning the mushrooms over with the point of an old bone-handled shut-knife. "And how old did you say you was?"

"Twelve."

"Don't they tell you nothing at school?"

"Not about mushrooms."

"The sort you git in shops eat like leather," Mr. Thompson said. He dropped another lump of butter into the mushrooms. The butter sizzled and he lifted the billy-can a few inches off the fire. "Don't taste of nothing at all."

"I only ever had them out of tins."

"Tins, eh?" Mr. Thompson said. "They git 'em up in tins now, do they?"

Mr. Thompson took the billy-can completely off the fire and peered down at the mushrooms. The girl sat holding an egg in each hand. Something about the neutral blankness of the eggs seemed to be reflected in her eyes and she hardly stirred as Mr. Thompson took the eggs away from her and broke them one by one into a battered coffee tin.

"Smells rich," she said.

Mr. Thompson beat the eggs with his knife. His face was rough and greyish from a two-day growth of beard. The battered brown hat that was pushed to the back of his head made his eyes appear to be protuberant, like a pair of big blue marbles, but at the same time docile, harmless and contented.

"It's quiet in the wood tonight," she said. "You don't even hear the birds."

"No, the birds are settling down. I heard an old pheasant a little while back though."

"Pheasant? Are they wild too?"

"Sort of," Mr. Thompson said. "Half an' half, this time o' year. Half-wild, half-tame. Till they git shot at a bit."

"Tame? You mean you could keep one in a cage? Like a budgie?"

"No," Mr. Thompson said. He laughed. "They ain't them sort o' birds."

She sat quiet, her eyes roving to and fro suddenly, half-wild, half-tame themselves. The birds, like the mushrooms, were another part of her many revelations. Their songs woke her in the early mornings, before the mists cleared, when she sometimes lay alone for a long time under Mr. Thompson's raincoat, staring up at the great roof of branches, wondering if Mr. Thompson had gone away and left her. This was the time of day when she remembered most clearly the way the house smelt: that dead smell, the smell of night before day washed it away.

But before very long Mr. Thompson was always back, bringing mushrooms, blackberries, wood-nuts, perhaps a bit of watercress, clean water for her to wash in and fresh branches for the fire. Once he brought a handful of wheat-ears and the sound of them being rubbed between the leathery palms of his hands was the sound that woke her.

"Mum works at the food factory," she said. "I told you that though, didn't I? She brings stuff home. I think she wins it—you know. That's how I know about the mushrooms that one time."

"Wins it?"

"Bones it. You know."

"Works too, does she? All day?"

"All day. She'd work all night too if they'd let her. Wants to get the fridge paid off. The telly took two years. She wants a spin dryer next. She's gone before eight in the morning and gets back about ten at night. Does a washing-up job at a hotel on the way back. That's what makes her bad tempered."

That too was why the house smelt dead. You didn't really live in it and it just smelt dead. It was a hole you crawled back to after work was over. Her father was away at half-past six in the morning and sometimes in the winter she didn't see him at all. With overtime he was knocking up big money. They were both knocking it up. Really big. All the time.

Mr. Thompson, giving the beaten eggs a screw of salt, poured them into the billy-can with the mushrooms and started to scramble them with his knife, holding the can at the very edge of the fire.

"Hand us that spoon, will you?" he said. "And you cut some bread with my knife. We'll be ready in a minute now."

She started to cut slices of bread from a loaf. The aroma of eggs scrambled in with mushrooms rose more richly than ever through the woodland air. Everything Mr. Thompson cooked was good. Everything that had happened with Mr. Thompson was good. Everything since she had first met him on her way home from school five days ago had been good. It was all a revelation.

"You can have the spoon back now. I'll eat mine with me knife."

The only utensils Mr. Thompson seemed to possess were the spoon, the knife, the billy-can, the coffee tin, a cup, an old blue plate and a kettle. Now he put half the scrambled eggs and mushrooms on the plate and the kettle on the fire.

"Eat up," Mr. Thompson said. "It gits cold quick out here."

She started shovelling eggs and mushrooms into her mouth with the spoon, cramming slices of bread in after them like wads of stuffing. Her own eyes were protuberant now: big with unconscious, happy greed. Small points of reflected firelight gave them excitement too, so that she might have been sitting there watching some complex sort of drama being played out on a screen.

While she was cramming in the food Mr. Thompson paused in his eating to wash out the old coffee tin with boiling water. Then he dropped a handful of tea and sugar and half a tin of condensed milk into the kettle and stirred it round several times with a hazel stick, finally letting it all boil up.

Even the smell of tea excited her. Like everything else it was good too. It was good and living. Lost and rapturous, she sat there eating madly, waiting for her cup to come.

"Been holding your cup out a good minute," Mr. Thompson said. "Don't you want it? Been thinking of something?"

She didn't say anything; she didn't tell Mr. Thompson how, for quite five minutes, she had been thinking again of the dead smell of home and how it seemed to strangle her: the living room with the telly, the fridge, the radio, the cooker and the washing machine all crammed in together, the table with

uncleared breakfast remains still on it when she got back from school, the
grey eye of the television set holding her a mute captive there in the dead
half-darkness while she waited for someone to come home.

She merely said instead: "I was thinking how you're always so friendly."

"Got nothing to be unfriendly about. Got nobody to quarrel with."

She gulped fast at her cup of tea, staring at him with big grave eyes over
the top of it. She was right about Mr. Thompson: he was always so quiet
and friendly—like the day she first ran into him, carrying his bundle of utensils, his raincoat and two loaves of bread. It was because he accidentally
dropped one of the loaves and she picked it up for him that they got talking
and finally walked on together. That was the first time she was struck by
the large, friendly eyes.

She had never really been aware of how far they walked that first afternoon; perhaps it wasn't all that far. But because Mr. Thompson walked
slowly, unprepossessed by time or distance, it seemed a long way. In an hour
they were in the woods and Mr. Thompson was saying:

"You'd better git back now, hadn't you?"

She remembered that moment very well. She knew for an awful certainty
that she wasn't going back. She remembered a shadow of sickness falling on
her as her thoughts went back to the living room and in a moment the strangle hold of it was round her neck.

She begged Mr. Thompson to let her stay a little longer and he said:

"Well, I'm going to boil myself a drop o' tea. You better have a cup
before you go."

After that, as she did now, she sat watching him over the top of the tea
cup. The shadows of late afternoon fell on his face, breaking it up into a
benign and trembling pattern, and she knew for the first time that she would
never be afraid of Mr. Thompson. There was something about that face that
gave you the same warm feeling of comfort and security as when you put
a glove on your hand.

Her father's face was never remotely like that. He worked a lathe in a
machine shop and when he got home at night it was as if you could feel the
lathe still whirling madly in the living room. You could feel a wild compres-
sor still driving through his blood: the telly's got to be paid for, the fridge
has got to be paid for, it's all got to be paid for—God, let me get out and
have a drink somewhere.

"You've only just got home," she said to him once. "You don't have to
go out again yet, do you?"

"Stop jawing. I'll mark you if you don't stop jawing. You got the telly to sit with, ain't you? Sit and watch the telly. I slave enough to get the telly, don't I?"

"Go and get yourself an ice-cream," her mother said. "Put that in your mouth. I'm tired."

After that first cup of tea with Mr. Thompson she was aware of feeling tired too: not exhaustively tired but rather as if she had been sitting for a long time in a too-warm room. The strong fresh air in the woods seemed to drug her and presently her eyes started to drift drowsily to and fro. When she woke she was lying under Mr. Thompson's raincoat and Mr. Thompson was sitting gazing at the fire.

He was gazing at the fire now, rubbing his two-day-old beard with thumb and forefinger. He reckoned it was time to get himself a shave, she heard him say.

This pleased her; the grave brown eyes started lighting up. She would be able to hold up the mirror for Mr. Thompson. It was only a cracked pocket mirror with some of the quick-silver worn off the back, but it pleased her to hold it for Mr. Thompson.

"Had enough tea?" he said. "I'll have to take the kettle down to the brook and fill it if I'm going to git a shave."

"I could drink another cup."

He poured the rest of the tea out for her and she said:

"There was something I was going to ask you."

"Yes?"

"Don't you ever go back home nowhere?"

"Puzzle me to," Mr. Thompson said. "I—"

"You mean you haven't got a house?"

"Had one once," he said. "A doodle-bug fell on it. My mother was in it. There was just a big pile of rubble when I got home."

"What did you do after that?"

"Started walking."

"Walking where?"

"Up and down the country."

"Nowhere particular?"

"Nowhere particular."

Sipping her tea, she asked him then if he never worked and Mr. Thompson said no, he never did. His mother had had a bit of money tucked away in the bank. It was his now and it did him for most things.

"Fancy never working," she said. The images of her parents danced frantically on the stage of her mind, like grotesque and desperate puppets on a treadmill.

"As long as nobody don't make me," Mr. Thompson said, "I don't see no reason to."

He laughed. He didn't often laugh and when he did so it was with a dry sort of cough, partly a chuckle. No, he didn't work and, funny thing, he didn't read no newspapers either. So that was another thing that never bothered him much: all that business about what was going on.

"I don't both people either," he said, "and most of the time people don't bother me."

"Was that why you let me come along with you?"

"People quite often come along with me," Mr. Thompson said. "Walk a mile or two with me and then go back. Company, I suppose."

"You like company? You ever get lonely?"

"I like company sometimes."

"I don't think I'd ever be lonely with you. I like it with you."

"Perhaps you would, after a time. You can very often be lonelier with people than without them, I say."

Throughout this conversation she was again aware of feeling a growing sense of security and comfort about her, like the drawing on of a glove, and she was almost disappointed when Mr. Thompson at last got to his feet, picked up the kettle again and said he was off to the brook to fetch water.

"I'll pack things up a bit," she said. "I'll wash up when you get back. Will you bring some watercress?"

"Might do," Mr. Thompson said, "if I see any."

Mr. Thompson struck off through the undergrowth of hazels. In a few open spaces thick bracken, turning fox brown already, grew higher than a man. A jay, like blue fire, flew suddenly over one of these spaces with a throaty screech, filling the wood with echoes that seemed to go zithering away far into the deep mass of branches.

Something about these noises disturbed Mr. Thompson; he stopped and stared about him. The presence of the girl had never really worried him very much; he had never laid a finger on her; she was just another companion on the way. She'd turn back all right when she wanted to—she'd get homesick or bored, or something else would make her go.

He waited, listening, but within half a minute the wood was deadly quiet again. The girl was right: there was hardly a bird to make a sound. She'd been quick, he thought, to sense the absence of the birds. There was a funny feeling about a wood when the birds weren't there.

The big wood ended in a line of yews and white-beam, at the bottom of a slope. A brook, six or eight feet wide, ran round its boundaries in a deep curve. There were a few deep pools in it and the night before last Mr. Thompson had had four fair-sized perch out of it and he and the girl had had them fried for supper. She had never tasted anything in all her life like that, she said. He remembered how she had sat sucking the perch bones as if every single one was a precious needle of sugar. That was the best fish she ever tasted, she said. You didn't get fish like that out of a fried fish shop. Up to then that was the only kind she'd ever had.

Stooping to fill the kettle from the brook Mr. Thompson was aware of a sudden uneasiness again. Thin white saucers of mist were forming and floating across the meadows beyond the wood and out of them Mr. Thompson could suddenly have sworn he heard another cry, followed by another, from a jay.

He was walking back up the slope before it came to him that what he had heard was the whining of a dog. He went back a few yards and stared across the meadows, listening. The sound of whining, this time of more than one dog, reached him again. It was quite a long way off yet and it had that eerie sound that hounds make when they're hungry.

Uneasy for the first time, he walked back through the wood to the girl. He found she had been busy collecting bracken and laying a pile of it out for herself as part of a fresh bed. She had made up the fire too and it was ready for the kettle.

He put the kettle on to boil. She was pleased to see him back, she said. She could wash up now and help him when he shaved.

Mr. Thompson rubbed his beard with the ball of his thumb and didn't say anything.

"You know what you said you might get down at the brook," she said. "Remember? Watercress."

Yes, Mr. Thompson remembered the watercress. Didn't see any, though, he said.

"Perhaps we'll get some tomorrow."

It was half in Mr. Thompson's mind to say that there wouldn't be any tomorrow, but he said nothing and merely pushed the kettle farther into the fire. He didn't like the water too hot for shaving and a few moments later

he washed out the coffee tin, filled it with a warm water and then started
to lather his face.

"Give me the mirror and I'll hold it for you," she said. "I like doing that."

He seemed, she thought, to take an extra long time to lather his face.
While she waited for him she took off her shoes and sat gravely watching
him. He seemed preoccupied and thoughtful and now and then he lifted his
head sharply, listening. While he was slowly lathering himself she washed
up the cup, billy-can, knife and plate. The lingering taste of mushrooms still
clung to her mouth and now and then she licked her lips slowly with her
tongue.

It was about six o'clock when Mr. Thompson began to shave. She squat-
ted in front of him, brown eyes grave again, and held the mirror so that he
could see. It would be dark in less than an hour from now and when it was
dark Mr. Thompson would make up the fire. It was the moment of the day
she longed most deeply for. She didn't dread the darkness—not like she did
at home. It was all so silent and shut away. That dead smell of the house
wasn't there and the big circle of outer darkness framed the central core of
crimson firelight, across which Mr. Thompson would presently gaze at her
and say "You'd better git your sleep now." The birds, except perhaps for
the last croak of a roosting pheasant, would all be silent by that time and
presently she would lie down on one side of the fire and go to sleep, with
Mr. Thompson dozing on the other.

In the morning the autumn singing of the birds would wake her and she
would experience once again the extraordinary sense of not belonging to
anyone or anywhere, as Mr. Thompson did, and of being free.

Suddenly Mr. Thompson gave a sharp impatient exclamation. She saw
that he had nicked the upper part of one cheek with his safety-razor, drawing blood. In a sharp turn of his head, as if attracted again by a sudden far-off
sound, he had forgotten to take the razor away. The half-shaven face, white
here and there with lather, stained for an inch or two with blood, looked
grotesquely ill at ease. She hadn't seen it look like that before.

"I'm sorry," she said. "I didn't hold the mirror straight, did I?"

"Wasn't that," Mr. Thompson said.

Mr. Thompson, drawing the razor hastily across his face, was sure beyond
doubt that he could hear the cry of dogs again.

"What's the matter?" she said.

"Hold the glass straight," he said and in his voice she detected the first and
only sign of sharpness. "I don't want to cut myself again."

The cry of dogs was nearer now; Mr. Thompson judged them to be somewhere out in the meadow. He suddenly jumped to his feet and rapidly wiped the remaining lather from his face with a rag of towelling.

"You go to go," he said.

Too astonished to speak for a moment, she saw him abruptly pour the rest of the kettle of water on the fire. The explosive impact of it tore out of her, painfully, a single amazed word:

"Go?"

"You got to go home," Mr. Thompson said. "Now. Quick. You got to do what I say."

"I'm never going back there—"

"You got to go now," he said. "Why'd you take your shoes off? Put 'em on. Quick."

He raised his hand. It was as if her father were threatening yet again to mark her and she was quick to duck. But Mr. Thompson's hand was raised simply to perform an extraordinary act—that of pushing his battered hat firmly down, for the first time, on the front of his head. It was exactly as if he wanted to hide underneath it and the shadow of the brim seemed almost to suffocate his face.

"Got your shoes on?"

She was struggling with the laces of her shoes. When they were tied she looked up at Mr. Thompson with bruised and frightened eyes.

"What are you sending me away for, Mr. Thompson? I never want to go back there—"

"You got to go," Mr. Thompson said. "Git hold of my hand. I'll take you to the end of the wood and then you git home. Quick."

"I won't go there."

"Listen to that," Mr. Thompson said. He was beginning to be half-frightened himself now; he could distinctly hear the dogs hungrily whining somewhere down by the stream. "You know what that is? Dogs—they're looking for you."

He started to run with her towards the upper edge of wood. It took them ten minutes to break clear to the boundary and already it was half dark beyond the trees.

"You go down here until you git to the railway bridge—"

"I'm not going. I'll never find my way—"

"Under the railway bridge," Mr. Thompson said, "and then after about

a mile there's a brick works. After that you turn right and you go straight
for the town."

She stood absolutely still, looking up at his face. She had nothing at all
to say. The grave brown eyes were darkened completely, all light beaten out
of them.

"You git back where you belong," Mr. Thompson said. "You be a good
girl now. They'll be waiting for you."

Soon she was running. She was running under the shadow of the railway
arch, past the chimney spire of the brick works and into the town. She was
running past the lights of grinning windows, into the night, back where she
belonged, to where the house was dead.

THE TRESPASSER

"Good gracious," Aunt Leonora suddenly yelled, "that damned cow's eating the lupins again!"

A moment later, gold spectacles prancing, she was rushing with revengeful haste through the open french doors of the sitting-room and into the garden, snatching up on her way out one of the many old ash-plants, gnarled as twisted parsnips, that she kept handy for the purpose of chastising trespassers, stray animals, tramps, idlers, salesmen and anyone else who might be standing about and up to no good in the process.

"Shoo, you beast! Get out of it! Cow, do you hear?"

I followed her immediately, searching the calm sunny borders of the June garden in vain for a single sign of any trespassing cow. I should have known that none ever came there, that they were as mythical as the marauding herds of deer that nightly threatened beetroot and bean-rows, bringing Aunt Leonora downstairs with beating sticks and flashing lanterns.

I saw instead a tubby, mild-looking man, with a white topknot of hair and a very scrubbed pink complexion, who looked not at all unlike a round fresh radish, standing with an air of absent surprise on the edge of the lawn, beyond which large colonies of lupin rose in gold and purple spires. A floppy black umbrella, on which he was pensively leaning for support, give him the estranged appearance of someone who had been unexpectedly dropped into the garden by parachute and did not know, in consequence, quite where he was.

Aunt Leonora, who was baggy and big-limbed and looked not at all unlike a rampaging cow herself, meanwhile rushed onward to enlighten him. It was still not clear to me whether, in her short-sighted way, she could distinguish between man and beast and I was half-horrified, a moment later, to see her brandishing the ash-plant with violent challenge in the direction of the tubby man, obviously in readiness to beat him furiously about the rump.

A providential turn of his body brought him face to face with her, just in time. Undismayed, she yelled an instant demand to know what had happened to that damned cow she had seen trampling all over the place a couple of minutes before?

"It's yours, I suppose, isn't it? It would be!"

A look of almost ethereal surprise enveloped the tubby man so completely that he stood there as if embalmed. The gravity of things was evidently still not clear to him and when his mouth finally opened it was merely to let fall a single hollow word.

"Cow?"

"Yes, cow. A damned great red and white one. Chewing the lupins. Trampling all over the place."

"I—"

"They're always at it. They're in here every day." It was a blatant lie, though I am sure she was unaware of telling it. "Trampling and gorging everywhere. Where's it gone to? One can't grow a thing without its being chewed up like a—like a—" Aunt Leonora made a questing search of the air for a suitable damning word—"like a field of tares!" she suddenly spat out. The word tares, delivered with a final hiss, had a positive fire in it and set the tubby man back another pace or two. "Who are you anyway? Take your cow home. You're trespassing."

After a glare of stunning power had struck the little man like a point of blank charge of shot he managed somehow to find an answer.

"I rather thought I was in my sister's garden," he started to say, "but—"

It was a most unfortunate remark to have made and Aunt Leonora at once seized upon it with peremptory scorn.

"That's a damn-fool thing to think," she said. "Sister? What sister? Whose sister?"

The tubby man, looking about him with deepening apprehension, almost despair, said he was terribly sorry but he could have sworn that this was *The Limes*. A flutter of repeated apologies ran from his lips in a muted scale, ending with the words "even the lupins looked the same—"

"Good God, man, *The Limes*. You mean you belong to Old Broody? Her? She's your sister?"

"Miss Elphinstone—yes, she's my sister."

Aunt Leonora let out the rudest of snorts and said Good God, she'd never known that Broody had men in the family and then, as if the withholding of this family secret from her was a sort of unneighbourly crime, glared at him with furious disbelief, plainly thinking him a liar. There was something ironical in the idea of her accusing someone else of not telling the truth and the little man stuttered as he said:

"Oh! yes. There are three brothers."

"Married?" She threw the awful word at him with typical point-blank candour, clearly determined that no second family secret should escape her.

"Oh! yes, we're all three married. In fact my eldest brother and I have each been married a second time."

"Caught twice, eh?" she said.

Unabashed, she bared her big friendly teeth and laughed into the tubby man's face with an expansive crackle and then a moment later further confused him by turning sharply to me and saying:

"This is my nephew. He just called to bring me some aubergine plants for the greenhouse. Raised them himself. I'm mad about aubergines. Like them stuffed. Do you garden?" Before the tubby man could attempt an answer she glared at me again, baring big teeth, and shook the stick. "You saw that damned cow, didn't you?" she said to me.

I started to say that I hadn't seen anything of the kind. Somewhere in the distant past a solitary wandering cow had so far trespassed as to reach its neck over the fence and take a few modest bites from a lilac bush. Since then Aunt Leonora's complex had developed from strength to strength and now rampaging cows were everywhere.

"I think it must have been this gentleman you saw," I said. "After all the light's very strong this morning—"

"What's it got to do with the light?" she said and suddenly hurled at me a dark accusation. "Your eyes wander," she said. "I could hardly mistake a man for a cow, could I?"

I kept silent; spectacles seemed to do little or nothing for her acute short-sightedness, and I refrained from reminding her that once, on a misty September evening, she had mistaken me for a wandering deer as I returned from a mushroom trip and had struck me a number of severe blows about the elbows before I could stop her. Deer were worse than cows; she was convinced that they actually jumped the fences; they could gorge a whole garden in a night.

"On a long visit?" she said, once again taking the tubby man by surprise with that fresh, alarming candour of hers, "or just here today and gone tomorrow?"

Startled again, he began to explain that he was here for a week and then, looking hastily at his watch, said that he thought he ought to be going. It was rather later than he thought; his sister was inclined to be particular about meal-times. He didn't want to upset her.

"Which one are you?" she said. "Charley? Now I come to think of it I think I've heard Old Broody talk of Charley."

"Oh! no, Charley's my elder brother. I'm Freddie."

"Oh! you're Freddie, are you?" she said, rather as if there were some awful mistake about his birthright, and then suddenly turned on him a smile of such masterful charm, her big teeth positively glowing, that I could have sworn his face reddened a little further. "Oh! yes, of course. I think I've heard Broody talk of you too."

"Well, I must go. I must bid you good-morning. It was awfully silly of me about—you know—and I—"

"We were just having a glass of sherry and a piece of saffron cake," Aunt Leonora said in the sweetest of voices. "Would you care to join us before you go?"

It was another blatant lie; we had been doing no such thing; she was merely putting it on for the trespasser.

"I honestly think I ought to go—"

"Oh! Broody and her lunch can wait. I suppose it's *risotto* anyway?"

"How do you know?" he said. "As a matter of fact it is *risotto*."

"Oh! I gave her the recipe years ago. She always has it on Thursdays. She's no imagination."

Back in the house I poured sherry into cut glasses at a side-board and turned once or twice to see the tubby Mr. Elphinstone's eyes blinking and winking sharply in their effort to re-focus themselves after the blinding outdoor light of noon. This gave him an air of fidgeting discomfort, or as if he were dying to ask a question that had been bothering him for some time. And presently the question came:

"It rather made me smile, you calling her Broody. What makes you call her that?"

Aunt Leonora, looking up from cutting saffron cake, which she was placing in slices on small pink china plates that made her almost masculine hands look far larger and clumsier than they really were, said:

"It's the way she walks. I say she always seems to have a clutch of eggs in her pants."

Mr. Elphinstone actually chuckled. You could see that he thought it rather apt. Still chuckling, he accepted a portion of cake from Aunt Leonora, but the chuckle died suddenly on his lips when she said with pungent vehemence:

"Your sister's an old flap-doodle. She's the sort of woman who you want to do things to. She seems to forget women are emancipated," she said, as if this had anything to do with it.

If Mr. Elphinstone had any thought of making a loyal and defensive pro-test about this accusative remark it was utterly useless: Aunt Leonora, in full cry again, gave him no time at all.

"You know what I mean?" she said. "You must have met women you wanted to do things to?"

A number of interpretations of this interesting theme sprang quickly to my mind and I sensed that they might be springing to Mr. Elphinstone's too. He sipped at his sherry swiftly and must have been wondering what sort of house he had trespassed into when Aunt Leonora, almost as if in an attempt to save him from further embarrassment said:

"I mean most of them should have been strangled at birth, shouldn't they? or sterilized or something?" The mere suggestion of these harsh and uncon-ventional measures made Mr. Elphinstone recoil. "I suppose your wives were different, weren't they?"

"Well—"

"Is your wife staying with Old Broody too? How do they get on?"

Mr. Elphinstone, who had been pensively gazing for some moments at a remarkable but useless collection of hunting horns, silver cups, animal claws and such trophies that Aunt Leonora always kept on or over the mantel-piece, now fixed his eyes on a large brass pestle-and-mortar and said that, as a matter of fact, his wife was not with him. She had passed away, he explained, some four or five years before.

With nothing more than a brusquely consolatory cough Aunt Leonora said she was very sorry to hear it and then turned to me and said "Give Mr. Elphinstone some more sherry," as if this would do something to help sus-tain him in his loss.

"What do you feel about the sherry?" she shot the question at him point-blank, as always, in a sort of bark. "Like it?"

"Oh! excellent. Excellent."

"It's absolutely awful," she said. "It's plain muck. Don't drink it. We'd have done better to have the red-currant wine. Get the red-currant wine," she said to me. "We don't want to poison Mr. Elphinstone, do we?"

I murmured that that would, perhaps, be rather drastic but I don't think she really heard.

"Bring the six-year-old," she called to me instead, as I went out to the kitchen. "That was a good year. I fortified it a bit that year—you can tell the difference."

When I came back with the bottle of wine—it was exactly the same brilliant colour as the ripe berries themselves—Mr. Elphinstone was just saying, as he gazed again at the hunting horns:

"I see that you hunt."

"You don't see anything of the sort," she said. "I loathe it." She glared at him sternly: her teeth were bared like an open trap. "Do you?"

"Oh! no, no, no."

"I love animals. I adore birds. A pair of fly-catchers arrived yesterday. They always arrive at this time, every year. Are you interested in birds?"

Mr. Elphinstone confessed that he wasn't, very, and she glared at him with increasing sternness again. Mr. Elphinstone, who must have felt that he couldn't seem to manage to say the right thing at all at any time, looked quite nervous, almost shaken, at these constant accusatory glares and I tried to take the edge off things by offering him a glass of wine. He accepted this with eagerness and an upward half-smile, the sort of smile that men often exchange when they feel that women are getting at them, and I half-winked in reply. At this he seemed, I thought, quite comforted.

"And don't wink," she said. "What there is to wink about I don't know." Another dark accusative glare followed: "It's always your eyes that give you away."

"I was merely saying cheers to Mr. Elphinstone," I said, "only in another way."

"Well, then say cheers," she said, "without the appendices.'

"Cheers," I said and Aunt Leonora said "Cheers" too, at the same time fixing Mr. Elphinstone with yet another severe glare through her flashing gold spectacles.

It couldn't possibly have occurred to Mr. Elphinstone at this time that these constant glares were the inevitable result of her chronic shortsightedness—she simply had to glare in order to see objects at all—or that the very brusqueness of her candour meant that she was very fond of men. Her drastic measures for the proposed extermination of her sex were not accidental; she had been figuratively killing off flap-doodles like Old Broody for years, just as she had been chasing and chastising imaginary hordes of cows and deer from her precious pastures of lupins.

Just as he must have begun to feel that the consistent barrage of glares was becoming too much to bear she suddenly smiled at him with utter sweetness, the sort of sweetness that only bony, toothy women of her kind can muster, and said:

"Well, what do you think of the wine?"

Mr. Elphinstone, who clearly wasn't going to be caught out on the subject of wine a second time, hesitated a moment before collecting his thoughts and then said:

"It's most refreshing."

"It's damn good!" she barked at him. "I'll tell you that. You won't get better."

"I will say it's unusual. It has a certain quality."

"No idea where I got the recipe for this from? No? The Black Forest." She took a great gulp of wine, rolling it ripely round her tongue. "I was on a walking tour there with a girl friend, years ago. We came to this place not far from Kreuznach, the spa you know, near the Rhine. Just a farmhouse, but we liked it so much we stayed there a month. Splendid place. We got sozzled on this stuff every day."

"Sozzled?"

The word sprang from the lips of the surprised Mr. Elphinstone before he could stop it. Sherry and the first half glass of red-currant wine had made his face pinker than ever, so that he looked more and more like a round, sparkling radish freshly washed.

"You don't need more than a couple of good big glasses," she said. "It's far more potent than any of your fancy hocks."

Two cuckoos, one chasing the other, both calling as they flew, went sailing over the garden a moment later and Aunt Leonora immediately jumped up and went over to the french windows on the chance of watching them. The midday light was glorious beyond her. The lupins, at their unsullied best, glowed like tremendous candles in the noonday sun.

"Just the day to drink this stuff," she told Mr. Elphinstone. "Good to be alive. You can taste the berries in it—it's got that cool sharpness."

I accepted this as a signal to fill up the glasses. She held out hers with alacrity but Mr. Elphinstone professed a certain wariness, confessing that he didn't really drink at lunchtime.

"Good God, man, drink up," she said. "You've nowhere to go, have you?"

Mr. Elphinstone was bound to say that he hadn't anywhere to go, particularly, and I took the opportunity of replenishing his glass to the top.

"A zizz in the garden, I suppose?" she challenged him. Zizz was a favourite word of hers.

"Zizz?"

"Forty winks," she said.

She was still at the french windows, big and dominant against the sun, and suddenly she put her head outside sniffing significantly.

"Wondering if I could smell the *risotto*."

This remark was nothing less than a piece of low corruption. I knew that it was uttered solely as a means of undermining Mr. Elphinstone's morale and I saw him start distinctly. But much worse was to follow:

"I've got cold salmon today," she said. As if the remark alone were not enough she gave another of those magnificently sweet, disarming smiles, her voice more airy than usual this time. "I suppose I ought to go and make the mayonnaise. Although the fresher it's made, I think, the better."

A confused Mr. Elphinstone took a long drink of wine and then stared for some moments into his glass, clearly torn between departure and a dream of mayonnaise.

"By the way," she said suddenly to me, "you promised to go and gather the strawberries for me and you never did. Are you going to be a lamb and run down and get them?"

This was another blatant lie. No word whatever had passed between us about strawberries; I had no idea there were strawberries; but suddenly, on an unexpected and curious tangent of memory, Mr. Elphinstone's question about Aunt Leonora's hunting sprang across my mind and I said involuntarily, aloud:

"By Heaven you do."

"You what?" she snapped. "What was that you said?"

"Nothing, aunt," I said. "I was just thinking aloud, that's all."

"Well then, don't," she said. "It's a bad habit." Yet another dark accusative glare followed: "It's even worse than thinking with your eyes."

After this I was determined, out of sheer obstinacy, not to hurry the strawberries and I deliberately poured Aunt Leonora, Mr. Elphinstone and myself another glass of wine. As she received hers she said:

"You'll find a dish in the kitchen. I think they'd look awfully nice in the green one—you'll see it, the one with the pattern of wine leaves."

I ignored this completely and stood sipping wine.

"Strawberries?" Mr. Elphinstone said. "You mean you actually have strawberries already? I say, that's very early isn't it?"

"I grew them under cloches," she said. "You get them three or four weeks early."

"How wonderful." Pinker than ever, Mr. Elphinstone looked at her for the first time with uninhibited if slightly unsteady admiration. A sort of rosy dew had settled on the lower lids of his eyes, like a sparkling distillation of the wine. "I think that's absolutely marvellous."

"Hadn't you better go?" she said to me. "It'll take some little time and I—"

"Just going," I said. "Enough for how many?"

"Oh! don't be ungenerous," she called to me as I went through to the kitchen. "I mean—there are plenty."

When I came back from the kitchen garden, twenty minutes later, bearing the dish of remarkably fat ripe strawberries, the sitting room was empty. But a peal of laughter of Aunt Leonora's from the kitchen, followed by a short chorus from Mr. Elphinstone, told me where to look.

In the kitchen Aunt Leonora was coaxing a basin of mayonnaise to its final smoothness and Mr. Elphinstone, now in his shirt sleeves and wearing a kitchen apron with a pattern of large red prawns all over it, was cutting up hard-boiled eggs into neat slices with a wire-cutter. Two glasses of red-currant wine stood on the kitchen table and between them, on a rosepat-terned dish, lay a very pleasant-looking portion of cold salmon, pink as Mr. Elphinstone himself, surrounded by sprigs of parsley and palest green circles of cucumber.

"Guess what?" Aunt Leonora said.

I guessed at once, and correctly.

"Mr. Elphinstone's going to stay to lunch," I said.

"Yes, I rang Broody," she said. "I asked her too but she felt she couldn't waste the *risotto.*"

This, I was sure, was yet another blatant and scandalous lie and I looked her squarely in the eye about it. In reply she deliberately made her spectacles twitch and turned away in shameless and divine ignorance to her mayon-naise, dipping one little finger into it and then slowly licking it in bemused appreciation.

"If you've finished the eggs," she told Mr. Elphinstone, "you could sugar the strawberries." And then to me: "Give Mr. Elphinestone some more red-currant. He's earned another swig."

It was a good idea, I thought, for all of us to have another swig, but when I came back from the sitting room Mr. Elphinstone had disappeared from the kitchen. I couldn't see him anywhere. Some moments later I observed a figure doing gymnastic exercises of a violent sort beyond the kitchen win-dow. It was Mr. Elphinstone, energetic as any athlete, wildly hurling a clothful of wet lettuce-leaves about his head like an Indian club, spraying drops of water everywhere.

He came back perspiring deeply, rosier, more radishy than ever.

"Good boy," she said sweetly. He beamed. He might actually have been a boy, praised suddenly for some good and sporting deed, and perhaps that was how she saw him, because a moment later she told me:

"We're going to eat in the garden. It's just the day. Then afterwards Mr. Elphinstone can lie in the hammock and have a zizz."

"I must be getting along," I said. "Is there something else I could do before I go? Will you want another bottle of wine?"

"What do we say?" she said. There was something devilishly and deliberately familiar about that "we" as she tossed it into the air. "Will we want another? I think we will, won't we?"

"Anything you say!" Mr. Elphinstone said, laughing with crackling merriment. Really rubicund now, he was tossing lettuce leaves into a glass dish with careless abandonment, rather as if they were useless lottery tickets. "Anything you say."

"I'll get another," I said.

"Magnificent stuff," Mr. Elphinstone said. "Absolute ambrosia."

"Don't forget the gooseberries and the eggs when you go," she called after me as I went into the cupboard under the kitchen to get the wine. "They're on the table just outside the french windows. I have heaps. Don't forget."

Having found the wine I couldn't resist asking, for the last time, if there was anything else I could do.

"What about the hammock?" I said.

"Oh! it's up. I used it yesterday. The night was so fine I didn't bother to take it down."

"What about cushions?"

"You're awfully dutiful today." This was really another dark accusation, deeply shot with suspicion. "Oh! Mr. Elphinstone will cope with the cushions, won't you, Mr. Elphinstone? After all he's the one who's going to have the zizz."

I took a last look from Aunt Leonora to Mr. Elphinstone. He seemed, I thought, to be having a sort of zizz already. His eyes, now rolling, now dancing, seemed to be like two excited valves bubbling pinkish water. He was actually chewing with rabbity pleasure on the crisp heart of a lettuce, as on a pale green cigar, and his forehead was so covered in perspiration that I fully expected to see it steam.

"Well, I'm on my way," I said. "Don't go over-eating the strawberries. Have a lovely zizz."

"Bless you, my boy!" Mr. Elphinstone called, the lettuce heart dropping suddenly out of his mouth. "Hope to see you many times again."

I said I hoped so too and went away in rumination across the lawn, past the gold and purple spires of lupins, the ancient Blenheim apple tree where Aunt Leonora's hammock hung in shade and finally out through the wicket gate in the hedge over which so many imaginary cows, not to say deer, so often seemed to rear their trespassing horns: quite forgetting, as I did so, to pick up the gooseberries and the eggs.

It was in fact three hours before I went back to pick them up. By that time, I reasoned, Mr. Elphinstone would long since have gone home to rejoin his sister: Aunt Leonora, if I were lucky, would be indoors, immersed in one of the numberless tasks the masterful energies of an emancipated woman so insatiably demanded, jamming gooseberries, preserving cherries, candying flowers, so that it might be possible for me to sneak in and out again without being mistaken, as Mr. Elphinstone had been, for some trespassing, marauding cow.

But greatly to my surprise the hammock was still swinging gently to and fro in the deep shade of the apple tree, with Mr. Elphinstone inside it, having his zizz. In the hot June silence Aunt Leonora was sitting beside him, a protective ash-plant at the ready, her large angular frame uncomfortably perched on a rather small red camp stool, rocking him gently to and fro like a child. The look of drowsy beatitude on her face gave her an air of such protective tenderness that she looked utterly remote from the woman who had so sternly chased him, a few hours before, as a trespasser.

I was silently escaping down an avenue of raspberry canes when a peremptory wagging of the ash-plant called me back. I was still several yards from the hammock when she recognized me and, in the sternest of low whispers, greeted me with yet another dark accusation.

"What are you prowling about at? Skulking like a tramp. I caught one stealing cabbages off the compost heap the other day."

"Mr. Elphinstone looks remarkably comfortable," I said.

"Don't disturb him," she whispered. "He's worn out. He insisted on helping wash up and then actually ran the sweeper over the sitting room." She showered on me the unexpected luxury of a toothy, angular smile. "He did love the strawberries. He had four helpings, and then finished up the cream with a boudoir biscuit." Mr. Elphinstone stirred suddenly—I could

have sworn with the buttonhole of one eyelid very slightly open—and gave
the most kittenish of snores before settling back into the luxurious depths
of his zizz. "He's had such a good long sleep. Don't you think he looks just
like a child?"

I didn't; I thought he looked just like a fat red radish, as in fact he still
does.

I suppose it was inevitable that Aunt Leonora should have married
Freddie Elphinstone. I suppose it is inevitable too that she always thinks of
herself as the masterful partner, tirelessly energetic in organization, up at six
in the morning, hardly ever at rest, battling ceaselessly with chickens, eggs,
the garden and its fruits, repelling idlers, cows and trespassers and still telling,
when it suits her purpose, those blatant innocent lies. I suppose too there
is a great deal to be said for women of her kind, who feel themselves to be
so strong that, out of a sort of powerful charity, they love to take the burden
of things off the shoulders of weaker creatures.

I suppose too there is much, perhaps even more, to be said for pink, tubby
little men like my Uncle Freddie, who always look like round fat radishes.
Uncle Freddie never gets up for breakfast; he takes it in bed, with *The Times*
and two other newspapers, at ten o'clock. At twelve he dresses, takes a walking stick, strolls two hundred yards to *The Duke of Marlborough*, drinks two
whiskies, chats about the weather and walks home for lunch at one o'clock.
At two o'clock Aunt Leonora insists on his having a zizz. Very occasionally,
when he wakes up, he plays golf or goes fishing, but not if it's too hot or
too windy or too wet or too cold. While he rests, Aunt Leonora, who
adores more than anything brisk, healthy exercise in the fresh air, bicycles
to the library, changes his books for him and hurries back so that he shan't
be unduly idle between tea, for which she always serves two kinds of bread-
and-butter, three of cake and scones and four of home-made jam, and sup-
pertime. After supper she busies herself with essential tasks like pickling eggs
or drying flowers for winter while Uncle Freddie drops into a doze from
which she finally wakes him with a glass of red-currant wine, mulled in winter, and a homemade ginger biscuit.

How nice it must be to be mistaken for a trespassing cow and thence to
achieve, with neither mastery nor struggle all your purposes—not the least
of which must be the long quiet zizz, under a shady apple tree, on warm
summer afternoons.

ABOUT H. E. BATES

H. E. Bates was born in 1905 at Rushden in Northamptonshire and was educated at Kettering Grammar School. He worked as a journalist and clerk on a local newspaper before publishing his first book, *The Two Sisters*, when he was twenty. In the next fifteen years he acquired a distinguished reputation for his stories about English country life. During the Second World War, he was a Squadron Leader in the R.A.F. and some of his stories about service life, *The Greatest People in the World* (1942), *How Sleep the Brave* (1943) and *The Face of England* (1953) were written under the pseudonym of 'Flying Officer X'. His subsequent novels of Burma, *The Purple Plain* and *The Jacaranda Tree*, and of India, *The Scarlet Sword*, stemmed directly or indirectly from his war experience in the Eastern theatre of war.

In 1958 his writing took a new direction with the appearance of *The Darling Buds of May*, the first of the popular Larkin family novels, which was followed by *A Breath of Fresh Air, When the Green Woods Laugh, Oh! To Be in England* (1963) and *A Little of What You Fancy*. His autobiography appeared in three volumes, *The Vanished World* (1969), *The Blossoming World* (1971) and *The World in Ripeness* (1972). His last works included the novel, *The Triple Echo* (1971) and a collection of short stories, *The Song of The Wren* (1972). Perhaps one of the most famous works of fiction is the best-selling novel *Fair Stood the Wind for France* (1944). H. E. Bates also wrote miscellaneous works on country life, several plays including *The Day of Glory* (1945), *The Modern Short Story* (1941) and a story for children, *The White Admiral* (1968). His works have been translated into sixteen languages and a posthumous collection of his stories, *The Yellow Meads of Asphodel*, appeared in 1976.

H. E. Bates was awarded the C.B.E. in 1973 and died in January 1974. He was married in 1931 and had four children.

Mikhail Bulgakov
The Life of Monsieur de Molière. Trans. by Mirra Ginsburg. A vivid portrait of the great French 17th-century satirist by one of the great Russian satirists of our own century. Cloth and NDPaperbook 601.

Joyce Cary
"Second Trilogy": *Prisoner of Grace. Except the Lord. Not Honour More.* "Even better than Cary's 'First Trilogy,' this is one of the great political novels of this century"— *San Francisco Examiner.* NDP606, 607 & 608. *A House of Children.* Reprint of the delightful autobiographic novel. NDP631.

Maurice Collis
The Land of the Great Image. ". . . a vivid and illuminating study written with the care and penetration that an artist as well as a historian must exercise to make the exotic past live and breathe for us."—Eudora Welty. NDP612

Ronald Firbank
Three More Novels. ". . . these novels are an inexhaustible source of pleasure."—*The Village Voice Literary Supplement.* NDP614

Romain Gary
The Life Before Us (Madame Rosa). Written under the pseudonym of Émile Ajar. Trans. by Ralph Manheim. "You won't forget Momo and Madame Rosa when you close the book. 'The Life Before Us' is a moving reading experience, if you don't mind a good cry."—*St. Louis Post-Dispatch.* NDP604. *Promise at Dawn.* A memoir "bursting with life . . . Gary's art has been to combine the comic and the tragic."— *The New Yorker.* NDP635.

Henry Green
Back. ". . . a rich, touching story, flecked all over by Mr. Green's intuition of the concealed originality of ordinary human beings."—V.S. Pritchett. NDP517

Siegfried Lenz
The German Lesson. Trans. by Ernst Kaiser and Eithne Wilkins. "A book of rare depth and brilliance . . ."—*The New York Times*. NDP618

Henri Michaux
A Barbarian in Asia. Trans. by Sylvia Beach. "It is superb in its swift illuminations and its wit . . ."—Alfred Kazin, *The New Yorker*. NDP622.

Kenneth Rexroth
Classics Revisited. Sixty brief, radiant essays on the books Rexroth called the "basic documents in the history of the imagination." NDP621

Raymond Quenau
The Blue Flowers. Trans. by Barbara Wright. ". . . an exuberant meditation on the novel, narrative conventions, and readers."—*The Washington Post*. NDP595

Robert Penn Warren
At Heaven's Gate. A novel of power and corruption in the deep south of the 1920's. NDP588